RECRUITER

RECRUITER
PARA-MILITARY RECRUITER™ BOOK 02

RENÉE JAGGÉR
MICHAEL ANDERLE

DISRUPTIVE IMAGINATION®

This book is a work of fiction. All of the characters, organizations, and events portrayed in this novel are either products of the author's imagination or are used fictitiously. Sometimes both.

Copyright © 2022 by LMBPN Publishing
Cover by Mihaela Voicu http://www.mihaelavoicu.com/
Cover copyright © LMBPN Publishing
A Michael Anderle Production

LMBPN Publishing supports the right to free expression and the value of copyright. The purpose of copyright is to encourage writers and artists to produce the creative works that enrich our culture.

The distribution of this book without permission is a theft of the author's intellectual property. If you would like permission to use material from the book (other than for review purposes), please contact support@lmbpn.com. Thank you for your support of the author's rights.

LMBPN Publishing
PMB 196, 2540 South Maryland Pkwy
Las Vegas, NV 89109

Version 1.00, December 2022
ebook ISBN: 979-8-88541-964-2
Print ISBN: 979-8-88541-965-9

THE RECRUITER TEAM

Thanks to the Beta Readers
Malyssa Brannon, Rachel Beckford, John Ashmore, Kelly O'Donnell, David Laughlin

Thanks to the JIT Readers

Wendy L Bonell
Dave Hicks
Christopher Gilliard
Dorothy Lloyd
Diane L. Smith
Zacc Pelter
Jan Hunnicutt
Paul Westman

Editor
The Skyfyre Editing Team

DEDICATION

*To Family, Friends and
Those Who Love
to Read.
May We All Enjoy Grace
to Live the Life We Are
Called.*

— *Michael*

CHAPTER ONE

Julie stared at Qbiit in shock for a moment before remembering how to speak. "What do you mean, you're on to me? On to *what?*"

"This helpless human act isn't going to wash with me," Qbiit growled. "You don't belong here."

Julie groaned internally. She was just getting used to the idea that she did belong here.

Ignore him. He's an ignorant, speciesist troglodyte, Hat assured her. *He thinks technology can replace magic. That should tell you everything you need to know about his supposed intelligence.*

Julie didn't want to make an enemy at the PMA, no matter how abrasive the troll was. "Hey, I was recruited by mistake, but can't we agree that I'm still here because I earned it?"

Qbiit's reply was interrupted by Taylor's arrival.

"Is everything all right here?" the elf prince asked in a neutral tone.

Qbiit's glare transformed into a sulky expression that wouldn't have looked out of place on a toddler who'd been told he couldn't have another cookie. "It's fine, Your Royal Highness."

Taylor shook his head as the troll turned on his heel and stalked to the main entrance. "What was all that about?"

Julie shrugged. "I guess he doesn't like the idea of a human working here."

Taylor's frown transformed into a smile. "Well, he's the only one who feels that way. You ready to get your ass handed to you before we get started on finding our next recruit?"

Julie's confidence returned and she flashed him a cocky grin. "Who said I'm the one who's getting my ass handed to me? I've got some moves, *Your Royal Highness*."

The impact knocked Julie breathless. Her back slammed into the mat, sending stars popping in front of her eyes. For a long second, she fought to suck in a breath that her lungs didn't want to take.

Above her, the Aether Elf chuckled. "Didn't see that one coming, did you?"

Julie managed a pathetic grunt instead of the admission, "I take back what I said in the parking lot," she tried to make.

Come on, snappy retort. Where are you when I need you?

"I think she's dead," a droll voice from the sidelines commented.

Finally, the breath rushed back into Julie's lungs. She sat up, coughing. "Taking it easy on the rookie today, are you?"

Taylor grinned at her as he held out a hand. "Okay, so that was a little sneaky, but your left was wide open. I couldn't resist. Let me show you how to keep from letting that happen again."

Julie gripped the elf's strong hand and allowed herself to be hauled to her feet. "I'm ready. Let's try that again."

Taylor raised an eyebrow. "Don't you want a break?"

"I'll take a break when I'm dead." Julie shot a glare at the attractive black fedora on the side of the springy floor mat, guarding her phone. "I'm not dead yet, Hat, but thanks for the assist."

Hat chuckled, his voice faintly British. "My pleasure, fair lady!"

She snorted and wiped her brow, then raised her hands in the guard that was starting to become familiar. "Like this?"

"Close." Taylor stepped back, his fists close to his face. "But you need to lift your left hand. Hold it closer to your cheek."

Julie did as she was told, balancing with one foot braced back. Around them, grunts of effort, barks of aggression and the thud of feet and bodies hitting the mats filled the gym.

Wearing gym clothes, mostly in matching red or blue, the paras in this gym all seemed to be much bigger and more toned than Julie felt.

Her gaze rested momentarily on the orc pounding his massive fists into a swinging punch bag in the back corner of the gym. Muscles rippled under his tattooed flesh and his lower jaw jutted out, his tusks protruding visibly as deep grunts of effort burst from his throat.

Julie worked to keep her focus on Taylor, even though the two sparring Weres on the mat beside them were shifting rapidly from wolf to human and back again. "Why can't the orb just download all the fighting skills I need to my brain?"

"It could." Taylor shrugged, his vest pulling tight over his broad shoulders. "But your body wouldn't know what to do with them. Keep your guard *up*!"

Taylor moved in a blur. Julie gasped, jumping back, but this time she threw her left fist up close to her face and dodged hard, swinging with her right.

Taylor slipped out of the way of her punch as though he was made of water, and it slid harmlessly past his neck. His elbow rammed into her rib, and she found herself knocked roundly on her ass again.

"Hey, that was much better!" Taylor stood over her, grinning. "I thought I was going to get you again with the same move, but this time at least I had to do something different."

Julie groaned as she rolled onto her knees. "Let me guess. Pain is just weakness leaving the body."

"What? That's crazy." Taylor shook his head, his black hair whipping. "Pain is pain. The whole point of learning to defend yourself is so you can avoid it."

Julie was barely on her feet before Taylor stepped forward again, swinging a punch. Julie repeated the move. Step back, fist up, punch. She missed again, but this time she felt her fist graze his cheek.

"Not bad!" Taylor raised a hand to his uninjured cheek. "You nearly got me, and you moved out of the way before I could hit you in the ribs."

Julie allowed herself a smirk. "Uh-uh, you won't catch me the same way twice, Mr. Woodskin."

"That's Your Royal Highness to you, human rabble."

"Oh yeah?" Julie pranced on her toes, her fists held high. "Come over here and say it to my face."

"Get him, Julie!" Hat shouted.

"Hey! Whose side are you on here?" Taylor threw up his hands.

Hat snickered. "Julie needs all the help she can get."

Taylor scoffed. "Not at the rate she's learning. Okay, are you ready to try something new?"

"Always." Julie shook out her hands and mopped at her forehead. "How come you're not sweating?"

"Elf magic." Taylor winked at her. "Ready for some gun defense?"

"Guns?" Julie quirked an eyebrow. "I was waiting for broadswords."

Taylor strode over to the edge of the mat and grabbed his water bottle. "We'll get to those."

Grateful for the break, Julie sat down beside Hat and fished her water bottle out from under him, sipping. "Thanks for doing this. I know it means you've got to be up an hour earlier every day to spar with me."

"Hey, I can't let my unmagical human partner get squashed by the next Yeti who happens to wander past." Taylor gave her arm a playful shove. "Besides, it's only a fifteen-minute walk to work for me. It's not like I have anything better to do with my time."

Julie cocked her head to one side. "When we met a few weeks ago, you seemed pretty much bent on avoiding having to do *anything* with your time."

Taylor's cheeks colored gray, the way they did when he was embarrassed. "Well, maybe I've changed since then."

"You don't say?" Julie raised an eyebrow.

Taylor shrugged, the humor in his voice gone. "Maybe the arrival of a particularly stubborn human made me stop to consider the fact that I might have something to offer other people in this life."

Julie looked away to hide her smile. *I always knew there was more to him than an airhead pretty-boy royal.*

Ooh, you think he's pretty, Hat teased telepathically.

Julie shoved her water bottle back underneath Hat. *Shut up, you.*

Is that any way to address a magical artifact several thousand years your senior? Hat retorted.

Julie got up. *Don't forget that I'm the one who rescued you from a lifetime of boredom in the Shrine of Previous Technology and Magic.* She turned to Taylor. "So, what were you saying about gun defense?"

Taylor smirked, grabbing a rubber practice weapon from a nearby shelf. "I was saying it's time to teach you some."

"It's going to have to wait, I'm afraid." Hat twitched to attention. "The captain wants to see you in his office."

"Oh, great." Julie sighed. "What did we do this time?"

Hat's brim folded in a shrug. "All I know is the message he sent to my system from his computer."

Taylor was gathering up his things. "And what did it say?"

"'MEADOWS! WOODSKIN! TO MY OFFICE, NOW!'" Hat recited.

Julie grimaced. "Well, that doesn't sound good."

"When does it ever with Kaplan?" Taylor headed for the men's locker room at a jog.

Scooping up Hat and her bag, Julie made for the women's locker room at a similar speed. It didn't do to keep Captain Kaplan waiting.

Ten minutes later, a slightly breathless Julie and Taylor stepped out of the elevator on the third floor. Even from across the smaller, individual offices that lined the communal office they could hear the captain's voice thundering from behind his closed door.

"Well, he's mad." Taylor sighed, tugging at the lapels of his well-cut navy coat.

"What else is new?" Julie straightened Hat, who was currently a smart black derby that neatly complemented her slacks and buttoned shirt.

"I don't see what he has to be mad about." Taylor checked his Rolex and frowned. "It's not like we're late or anything. Still ten to nine."

Julie sighed. "I guess we're about to find out."

Kaplan's loud voice echoed from inside his office as they traipsed across the huge room. They were still several yards away when they made out the words.

Kaplan's roar had an animal edge to it. "Nox is busting my balls out here to get this Yeti problem under control!"

"I suppose he means Julius," Julie muttered to Taylor.

Taylor whistled through his teeth. "Even Captain Kaplan has

to be careful of Julius Nox. He's a powerful and dangerous vampire."

Julie chuckled. "Oh, he's pretty cool. I like his flowers."

Taylor stared at her like she'd grown two heads. "You do know that Julius Nox is the king of all the vampires in the world, right?"

Julie shrugged. "Still has nice flowers. Exotic. He's crossbreeding frangipani and monster flower, did I tell you?"

"I don't know what any of that means." Taylor ran a hand through his still-damp hair.

"I'm surprised he's on Kaplan's case about the Yetis," Julie admitted. "He seemed pretty mad at Malcolm for getting mugged in the first place. Like it was more his fault than anyone else's."

"Julius Nox might be exasperated with his son, but Malcolm *is* his heir," Hat pointed out.

Kaplan's voice rose, silencing all three of them. "Just make sure to be seen to be doing *something*! If it takes dressing up in Yeti costumes and dousing yourselves with pheromones to lure the nuisances out into the open and make arrests, then you'd better damn well get sewing!"

This was followed by heavy breathing and the sound of fingers drumming on wood. Julie could only imagine what defense the hapless soul on the other end of the line was attempting to make.

"Is there really a Yeti problem?" Julie whispered to Taylor. "I mean, Malcolm was wandering the streets in the dead of night. Where I'm from, that's asking for trouble even without any paranormals involved."

"Oh, yes. It's becoming an issue." Taylor winced. "My security guards have gotten worse than ever. Yetis are showing up all over the state. Some of them are even allowing themselves to be seen by humans."

A faint nudging at the back of Julie's mind caught her attention. The magical training she'd received on her first day at the

OPMA had something helpful to add. She focused and allowed the words to trickle into her conscious mind.

Yetis are solitary creatures, preferring isolated environments such as mountaintops and valleys. They avoid each other in general, and humans at any cost. They are a shy and peaceful species that tends to avoid conflicts among other paranormals.

"So…mugging and gathering in gangs isn't normal Yeti behavior?" she asked aloud.

Taylor shook his head. "Not at all. I don't think I'd ever seen one until this year."

"It's strange," Hat interjected.

Julie spread her hands. "This is New York City. Not exactly an isolated environment. I could imagine them appearing upstate, but here? Why?"

"Something else is going on here." Hat tucked himself a little closer around Julie's ears. "There's got to be a larger influence at play."

"Don't be so paranoid, Hat." Taylor grimaced. "We already have enough to worry about with Yetis mugging other paras and letting humans glimpse them, if not record them."

"Well, the Bigfoot people are seriously going to like this." Julie snorted.

Hat sighed. "I'm just saying, there's more to this than meets the eye, and I've got a bad feeling about it."

There was the devastating crash of an unlucky telephone being smashed mercilessly into its cradle, and Kaplan's voice barked from inside his office. "Get your asses in here!"

Julie and Taylor exchanged a look of trepidation, then marched into the office as though ready to face the executioner's noose.

Behind Kaplan, an equestrian portrait showed him astride a rearing gray stallion with a tossing mane and wild eyes. Beneath it, a large window offered a view across the OPMA grounds, green lawns, and neatly trimmed shrubbery.

RECRUITER

The splendor of the grounds was eclipsed by the certain death burning in Kaplan's amber eyes. He sat behind his desk, his bushy eyebrows more awry than ever. His seven feet of pure muscle vibrated with rage as he rifled through several files scattered across the surface.

"Sit," he hissed.

They obediently took their seats in the overlarge armchairs facing the desk.

Kaplan's heavy breathing filled the room for a moment before he slammed the file shut and leaned forward with disconcerting suddenness.

"You two," he barked. "I need new recruits, and I need them yesterday."

Julie tried her best not to flinch, holding Kaplan's gaze as well as she could. "Respectfully, sir, why are you yelling at us? We've gotten you more recruits than most of your other teams in the past two weeks."

"Don't sass me, Meadows," Kaplan snarled. "You may have gotten Elspeth Feathertouch to join us two weeks ago, but she's only one Fae. We need more—a *lot* more—to handle this Yeti problem."

"Yes, but—" Julie cut off when Taylor applied his heel energetically to her shin, shutting her up. She looked into Kaplan's blazing eyes and decided that this was a wise choice in any case.

"No buts, Meadows." Kaplan folded his arms, biceps straining against his neat red coat. "I'm not interested in excuses. I'm interested in results. Since you two are my top recruiting team this month, you're the ones who need to get me more recruits, and soon."

Top recruiting team? Julie fought to keep her jaw from dropping. She'd known she and Taylor were doing well, but not *this* well.

That's right, Hat responded in her mind. *You two got a recruit in a single week! That's more than anyone else in the department can say.*

Julie sat back, a warm glow spreading through her chest.

Taylor had interlaced his fingers in his lap. "Sir, we've developed a list of possible recruits, and we're working our way through it. We haven't had any luck yet, but that will change soon."

"Well, work faster and find some luck." Kaplan waved a massive hand. "I don't care what you have to do to get the signings, as long as the recruits join of their own free will. That's all."

Oh, because I had so much free will when I joined, Julie scoffed privately.

Hey, you had a choice in the matter when you were offered an out at the end of your first week, Hat reminded her.

She stifled the urge to roll her eyes. *Well, yeah, Hat, but don't rain on my parade here. I'm trying to have a moment of indignation.*

"We could work overtime, sir." Taylor continued, unaware of Julie's inner conversation. "We could widen the net. Search farther away from New York City..."

It's not fair that shit rolls downhill. He should be pushing his worst teams to match us, Julie grumbled as Taylor babbled to Kaplan.

Hat made that little shrugging motion again. *The other teams only have the IRSA, not DUMB LE Dork, the greatest magical system that has ever existed.*

Julie stifled a grin. *Humble, too.*

You just ignore those IT trolls, okay? I'll get you your recruits, just like I got you the last one, Hat assured her.

Taylor was still trying to impress Kaplan with his plan of how to streamline the process. Julie leaned forward, interrupting. "Sir, you'll have your recruit within the next two weeks."

Taylor's head swung toward her, his eyes popping. Kaplan gave her a long, slow look, then relaxed back into his chair. "Oh, you will, will you?"

"Yes, we will." Julie crossed her arms. "As long as there's an incentive to go all out, of course."

Kaplan's lip curled, showing a flash of what seemed to be a

ridiculous amount of very white teeth. Julie could swear they were growing as she watched. Not for the first time, she wondered what the Were's other form could be. A deep rumble in the hollow of his chest filled the room, so low that she almost felt it across the floor rather than hearing it.

Beads of sweat were gathering at Taylor's brow when the growl stopped and Kaplan settled for a withering look instead of lunging across the desk and ripping her throat out, which she had partially expected.

"You're full of talk, Meadows, but actions speak louder than words." He jerked his chin toward her. "Get my recruit within two weeks and I'll give you a five thousand dollar bonus. Each."

Taylor's eyes widened even more.

Julie considered pushing it, but she was pretty sure she was lucky not to have been decapitated. "That sounds reasonable."

Kaplan snorted. "Why are you still in my office? Don't you have a recruit to find?"

Taylor flew to his feet. "Yes, sir. Thank you very much, sir." He disappeared before Julie could say another word, so she settled for giving Kaplan a salute that was just a little sarcastic and then hurried out of the door after her partner.

CHAPTER TWO

Taylor waited until they were just out of earshot of Kaplan's office before leaning close to Julie and hissing in her ear. "What was *that*?"

Julie chortled as she led the way to their office. She pushed open the door and walked into the cozy space with its cream-colored carpet and a Renaissance-style painting of a mermaid on the wall. "Which part? The making us look good to the boss part, or the securing you the means for financial independence part?"

"Oh, is *that* what it was?" Taylor flopped down into his office chair. "I could have sworn you were trying to get us both put into an early grave. I may be the spare-spare-spare-spare—you get the picture—spare heir, but I like the life I've built here."

Julie winked. "You'll find you like it a lot better without the royal accountant or whatever looking over your shoulder."

Taylor snorted. "Whatever. Come on, let's look for this recruit you promised Kaplan we would somehow produce in the next two weeks."

Julie laid down her pen and glanced at the time in the corner of her monitor. "Okay, it's three minutes past five. I don't know about you, but I'm *done*."

Taylor stretched his arms up above his head, blinking the dryness from his eyes.

"Me too." Hat sagged on Julie's head. "I haven't done that much searching in a long, long time."

"You did great, Hat." Julie pulled him off her head and stroked the crown the way he liked but would never admit. "We've got plenty of ideas to start with. We'll narrow down the search on Monday and go after our first recruit on Tuesday."

"Sounds good to me." Taylor got up and grabbed his jacket from where he'd hung it over his chair. "But right now, it's Friday at five, and I'm ready to be done."

"Same." Julie picked up her backpack from the floor and began to put away her things. "So, what are you gonna do with your five thousand dollars?"

"We haven't gotten the recruit yet." Taylor swung the strap of his bag over his shoulder and held the door for her.

Julie gave him a firm look as she went through to remind him that she could have done it herself. "Think positive, Your Royal Highness. We're gonna get that recruit and Kaplan's going to have no choice but to pay us out like he promised."

"I'd play along, but I still don't know." Taylor followed her over to the elevator. "What would *you* do with your five thousand?"

"I could really use my own washing machine." Julie smirked. "It's getting old, washing everything by hand."

"Ugh, yes. And you complain about it incessantly every Saturday," Hat chipped in.

"What's she like to live with, Hat?" Taylor raised an eyebrow. "I bet you don't get any rest with her constant wittiness."

"Quieter than you'd think. She reads a lot," Hat told him.

Julie swatted at his brim. "Shhh! That's a secret. We want

Taylor to think I'm always the confident social butterfly he sees at work."

"Oh, so you think I consider you a social butterfly?" Taylor muttered.

Hat jerked indignantly.

"What was that?" Julie asked.

Taylor held up his hands, laughing. "Nothing, nothing."

They left the elevator, crossed the lobby and headed into the parking garage. Julie carefully skirted around a three-headed goat chewing its cud contentedly in a pen beside the chariot it pulled. It belched an acid green vapor, then went on chewing.

"Where's your security today?" She fished her car keys out of her pocket.

"I'm driving myself today." Taylor gave her a grin and spun his car keys around his finger.

She raised her eyebrows. "Look at you, Mr. Independent."

Taylor waved her off with a hand. "See you tomorrow?"

"Tomorrow." Julie grinned. "It's going to be fun. You'll see."

They parted ways, and Julie strode across the indoor garage until she saw the familiar pewter shimmer of her car parked between a vast red truck and a stall containing an eight-legged horse.

As always, the sight of the muscle car Julie rented from her landlady made her heart squeeze a little. Even standing still, the car's lines whispered *speed*. The 1971 Mustang Mach 1 crouched against the asphalt as though ready to spring forward at any moment.

Julie reached out and gave the car an affectionate pat as she unlocked the doors. "Hey, Genevieve. Ready to go home?"

When she slipped inside and started the engine, Genevieve responded with a lusty bellow, eager to burn rubber. Julie backed out of the garage a little less carefully than she had a few weeks ago, before she was used to the fierce power of the Mustang.

Now, the surge of power each time she touched the accelerator was beginning to feel like a good friend.

A familiar beat came onto the radio as Julie drove out of the OPMA HQ gates, raising a hand to wave at the red-haired dwarf who worked as a gate guard. "Bye, Fred," she called.

Fred's beard split in a wide grin and he raised a thick-fingered hand in farewell.

Julie's attention wandered back to the radio. She turned it up and a peppy beat filled the car. Julie sang along, jiving behind the wheel.

The elegant part of Staten Island rolled past as she joined the thick stream of commuters making their way home. Cruising down Richmond Road, Julie reached forward and petted the dashboard lightly.

"I don't even mind the traffic, Genevieve," she murmured. "It's always fun with you."

Hat wriggled himself comfortably onto the passenger seat. "I would say it's rather more fun when there's traffic. It feels less like we might get killed at any moment."

Julie scoffed at him, leaning back in her seat. The bucket held her like an embrace. Genevieve was purring throatily, like she was alive and happy.

Bright May sunshine poured down onto the bustling streets, where tourists were hustling along the sidewalks and pausing to gaze up open-mouthed at buildings and generally being touristy. One of them snapped a pic of Genevieve. Julie resisted the urge to roll down the window, stick out her tongue and make the rock-and-roll sign.

Even her fellow commuters seemed chirpier than usual. The horns were mostly quiet and the faces Julie could see inside the cars weren't staring blankly at the road as usual. Occasionally, someone smiled back at her. Even the pedestrians in office clothes raised a hand to thank her when she stopped early at yellow lights, moving with a bit of pep in their step knowing that they were free until Monday morning rolled around again.

After a long, slow crawl across the Verrazzano-Narrows Bridge, Julie made her way to Bay Ridge and home. She stifled her yawns as she turned down the narrow street and pulled into the poky little garage with its persistent stagnant oil smell.

Still yawning, she tugged Hat firmly onto her head and rescued her backpack from the passenger seat before locking the door.

"Night, Genevieve." She gave the car's hood a gentle pat and checked the time. Just before seven. Lillie would still be awake.

Julie knocked twice on the back door before opening it. The cluttered living room was a familiar scene. Lillie's big fluffy cat stretched out on one arm of the sofa, and the television blared *Judge Judy.* Pookie's nails clicked on the old linoleum as she scampered to the door, her tail wagging.

"Hey, Lillie," Julie called as she bent to scratch behind the dog's ears.

The old woman on the sofa wore a floral housecoat and her white hair in curlers. She muted Judge Judy in the middle of chewing out a hapless would-be thief. "Hello, dear. Have a nice drive?"

"Yes, thank you. Traffic was heavy, but what's new?" Julie smiled. "Do you need anything? Did you have dinner?"

Lillie's eyes crinkled in pleasure at her concern. "I put a casserole in the oven, dear. Do you want some?"

Julie didn't smell anything cooking. She glanced through the clutter toward the open kitchen door. The oven's lights weren't on. "No thanks, Lillie. I was planning on making pizza. I've got a premade base in the freezer and a bunch of fresh toppings calling my name."

"If you're sure." Lillie adjusted her thick glasses. "You busy this weekend?"

"I'm going out with a friend this weekend, but I'll be home on

Sunday." Julie stifled a yawn. "We could go out for lunch, if you like?"

"That would be wonderful, dear." Lillie's grin lifted the fine creases that spread across her face, a map of remembered smiles. "Sleep tight now."

"You too."

Julie locked the door and clumped up the wooden stairs to her apartment. The apartment wasn't much bigger than her office at the Official Para-Military Agency's headquarters. Almost all of the wall space was occupied by thoroughly stocked floor-to-ceiling bookshelves, and a teetering stack of overflow books threatened to collapse on her nightstand.

"It's good to be home," Julie murmured, mostly to herself.

She pottered around the little room, turning on the lights and drawing the curtains on the window that looked out onto the street, then squeezed by her comfy armchair that was placed between the bed and the little table in the kitchenette.

"That's no way to handle a rare magical artifact like me!" Hat grumbled at being tossed onto the counter of the tiny kitchenette.

Julie laughed at his complaint as he landed softly beside the shiny new coffee machine perched at the end of the counter. "You're not exactly breakable," she told him as she switched on the lamp.

Hat grunted in approval. "I like your new lamp. It gives this place a warmer ambiance. It's less dumpster dive and more salvage chic."

"Hey, some of my best furniture was reclaimed from the curb." Julie chuckled as she touched the warm mustard yellow lampshade, which matched the cute little yellow cushion on her new armchair. "I can't argue the mismatched furniture is chaotic. These little touches bring everything together, right? I'm thinking I should look for yellow details on the new curtains I want to get this weekend."

"Sounds good to me." Hat shuffled across the crowded counter to his usual spot next to the microwave. "Are you ever going to replace the doorbell?"

Julie glanced at the little bell that hung from a string by the door and shook her head. "Nah. It's got a certain charm to it."

Hat snorted. "Suit yourself."

Julie opened the freezer and fished out the frozen pizza base. She unpeeled the wrapping. "I've got to admit, there are many things I like about the PMA..."

"Myself chief among them, I assume," Hat interjected.

"Sure. I always wanted a judgmental talking hat for a partner and friend." Julie had a flush of gratification when she opened the fridge on the fully stocked shelves. She grinned at Hat and grabbed a pack of shredded cheese. "The paycheck is another one of those things."

"I suppose it's one of the advantages." Hat's brim curled, as if returning her smile. "Speaking of which—"

Julie's phone buzzed in her pocket. She fished it out and grimaced at the caller ID. "Ugh, Mom."

"Ignore her," Hat suggested.

Julie shot him a look. "She's my *mother*. She'd send out a search party. I've got to take this."

"Suit yourself." Hat slouched on the counter, sulking.

Julie swiped at the screen and held the phone to her ear while she rummaged in the fridge for more toppings. "Hey, Mom."

She braced herself for Rosa's piercing voice, but her overenthusiastic trill was still like nails down the blackboard of her brain. "*Juliaaaaa*, honeyyyyyyyy!"

Julie gritted her teeth and started the coffee machine. She wasn't going to get through this conversation without a decent cup of joe.

"I was just calling to check in on my sweetest little cutie pie," Rosa cooed.

"Mom! Stop it. I'm an adult. Have been for a while now." Julie added some chopped mushrooms to her pizza.

Rosa laughed. "Aw, that's my little girl. Tell me, how was your week at work? How's your partner? Whatsisname. Tiger. Tyler."

"Taylor." Julie sighed. "He's good."

"That's lovely, honey. Are you impressing your boss? You know, a girl like you could score a few extra brownie points in many ways."

Julie recalled Kaplan's growing fangs. "Yeah, I think he's impressed enough."

Rosa made a noncommittal noise. "Listen up, honey. You know how I had to hustle hard to make ends meet after your father died to put you through high school. It was a very difficult time in my life, you know. Single motherhood isn't for sissies."

Julie poured her coffee and took a long, long sip. The deliciously hot, bitter liquid filled her stomach with warmth, and she glanced appreciatively at her coffee machine. It was so good to have real coffee for once. "So you keep telling me."

"Anyway, honey, I'm trying to share my experience. You've got to play to your strengths, and your strength happens to be the kind of body most celebs would die for. You understand?"

"Really, Mom? Are we going back to the whole pole conversation? Because I've told you, I'm not going to be a stripper."

"I'm not saying you should *strip* for your boss, honey. But maybe leaving one more button undone on your blouse... Well, it can't hurt."

"Mom!" Julie chugged some more coffee.

"Don't shoot it down, honey," Rosa scolded lightly. "Mr. Edwards at the restaurant was *much* kinder to me when I took my skirts up a couple of inches. It was my tips from working in his restaurant that kept you in clothing and supplies through high school, you know."

"I know, I know." Julie pinched the bridge of her nose. "But it's okay, Mom. I don't have to go to desperate measures. The job is paying great."

"Oh?" Rosa chirped. "So the job's going well?"

"It's going just fine." Julie sighed again. "You don't have to worry so much about me anymore. I don't have to worry about money."

Rosa didn't sound convinced. "As long as you keep up the good work."

Julie grimaced as she scattered shredded cheese over her pizza. "As long as I keep up the good work, yeah."

"That's good, honey. But don't get too relaxed, okay? You were pushing hard the first week. Don't let settling in become complacency now."

Julie groaned. What her mom didn't know was that she'd thought she was under threat of death by decapitation if she *didn't* perform in that first week. It had all been a farce, but it had felt very real at the time. "Hold on a sec, Mom. I have to put dinner in the oven."

Rosa was still babbling happily when Julie put the phone down. She flipped the oven open and slid the pizza inside. When she picked the phone up again, it sounded like she had been chattering on without interruption.

"You need to outperform every man in your department. Recruits *like* women. We're easier to talk to."

"They do, do they?" Julie sat down and stretched out her tired legs. "I mean, you would know, having done so much work in recruitment."

"Don't get snippy with me, young lady," Rosa chastised. "There's plenty to be said for life experience, and I've had more than enough of that. So, what dinner did you just put in the oven?"

Julie seized gratefully on the change of subject. "Oh, a really nice pizza. I bought these bases from the market and did my own toppings. They're—"

"*Pizza?*" Rosa screeched. "Honey, I'm assuming the base is wholewheat, right?"

Well, I guess the change of subject wasn't the thing after all. Julie rubbed the bridge of her nose. "Wholewheat pizza? Seriously, Mom?"

"You know that white flour is *terrible* for your digestion, Julia! When last did you have a bowel movement?"

Julie leaned back in her chair. "Did you really just ask me that?"

"Constipation is a real risk for you, honey. I hope you're taking plenty of aloe vera juice with every meal. *Especially* if you're making such unhealthy choices."

Julie glanced at the crate of plastic-wrapped aloe vera juice bottles sitting on the kitchen counter. A fine layer of dust covered the wrapping.

"Julia? Julia? Are you listening? Aloe vera juice is an excellent colon cleanser for you. Why, you can poop three times a day if you drink enough of it!"

"I'm sure *you* can, Mom." Julie gritted her teeth. "But you don't have to worry. Coffee is all the detox I need."

"Coffee? *Coffee?*" Rosa shrieked in her ear.

Julie held the phone away from her ear. "Yep. I've got a new coffee machine, so now I drink the real stuff. It's the elixir of life as far as I'm concerned."

"Sweetie, coffee is *so* three years ago!"

"Yeah, but it doesn't make me want to puke when I'm drinking it."

"Oh?" Mom perked up audibly. "So you *are* drinking it?"

Julie cleared her throat and changed the subject. "So, how's Ernesto?"

"He's fine, honey. A little under pressure at work as usual, but fine. Hey, I can give you more juice when you come to see us again. You're coming this weekend, aren't you?"

Julie's mouth opened and closed as she sought an answer. "I never said that, Mom."

"You said you were visiting *soon*," Rosa pestered. "Your 'soon' and my 'soon' are two very different things."

"I have plans this weekend, but don't worry. I'll visit soon," Julie offered weakly.

"You keep saying that. I hardly see you since you moved out." Rosa sighed. "We could go lay flowers on your father's grave again, if you wanted."

Julie swallowed, watching through the glass oven door as the melted cheese bubbled on the surface of the pizza. She remembered the tenderness in her mom's hug the last time she'd seen her.

"Sure. That sounds really great, Mom." Julie paused. "I'll give you a date this week, okay? I'm under a lot of pressure at work for the next two weeks."

"You'll knock 'em dead, sweetie. Can't wait to see you."

"Thanks, Mom. My pizza's nearly ready. I gotta go."

"Okay, honey. Love you."

The words came more easily than Julie had expected. "Love you, too."

The pizza still had a few minutes to go, so she opened her banking app and checked that all of her end-of-the-month debit orders had gone off properly. She blinked at the number on her bank balance for a second.

"That can't be right. Something must have been missed." She tapped on her balance and scrolled through her transaction record.

"What's the matter?" Hat asked, twitching on the counter. "You look worried."

Relief blossomed through her chest. "I was, but everything is okay. More than okay." She grinned. "All my bills are paid, I've got food in the fridge, and there's still money left. I can even pay Lillie my share of internet for the month."

"Of course you can. You have an important job and your pay reflects that." Hat snuggled back down into his place. "You've earned every dollar."

"Thanks, Hat." Julie turned off the oven, grabbed her mitts and took the pizza out. "It feels really good."

"I know money has worried you for a long time," Hat commented. "It must be a huge weight off to have some security."

"It's not just that." Julie tipped the pizza onto a plate and cut it carefully into eighths. "It's knowing that I can do my own thing now. I can be independent. Feels pretty great."

Hat laughed. "Funny little things, humans."

"What's that supposed to mean?" Julie picked up the plate without waiting for an answer. "I'll be back in a few minutes, okay?"

"Do you ever plan on eating dinner on your own again, Miss Strong-and-Independent Woman?" Hat inquired with amusement.

"I just worry that Lillie isn't looking after herself, that's all. She said she was cooking when we got home, but I didn't smell anything in the oven. See you later." She headed out of the door and down the creaky steps, then knocked on Lillie's door again and let herself in.

This time, Pookie stayed in her basket by the sofa and barely lifted her nose from her paws. The cat leaped up and trotted across the floor to Julie, arching his back against her legs and purring.

Lillie muted Judge Judy again and beamed at Julie. "You need something, dear?"

"I made pizza, and it's way too much for me to eat by myself." Julie held up the plate. "Have you had dinner yet?"

Lillie's cheeks flushed. "Oh, I was going to put some rice on the stove, you know."

Earlier, you said you had a casserole in the oven. Julie did her best to keep her concern off her face. "Well, now you don't have to."

She slid the plate onto the coffee table and plopped onto the couch next to Lillie. The cat jumped into her lap.

Lillie looked from the pizza to Julie. "You're already doing so much for me, dear. You should be out there enjoying your youth on a Friday night, not babysitting an old hellion like me."

Julie grinned. "Can't I eat dinner with my friend?"

Lillie opened her mouth to protest, but Julie picked up the remote from the coffee table. "What movie do you feel like?" she asked.

Lillie sighed. "All right, then. The least I can do is let you pick the movie, dear."

"Hmm." Julie raised an eyebrow, flipping through the channels and skipping past several classics and a '90s rom-com. "Oh, how about *6 Underground?*"

Lille took a slice of pizza. "Does it have any car chases in it?"

"Yep." Julie grinned. "It starts with a car chase."

Lillie cackled. "Let's do it."

The movie was due to start in five minutes, so Julie flicked to the correct channel and kept it on mute while the credits for the previous film rolled. She took a slice of pizza and bit into it. It really was good with the homemade toppings. "I think the car in this movie is an Alfa Romeo. Not a Mustang, but I guess it'll do."

Lillie's smile lit up her eyes behind her thick glasses. "Well, nothing beats Genevieve, but it'll work just fine. You know, I'm amazed I haven't gotten a single ticket in the mail yet, dear. Don't you know how to drive a 'Stang?"

Julie laughed. "Clearly not the way you know how, Lillie."

"Clearly not, dear." Lillie gave that wild laugh again. "We used to burn up the tarmac back in the day, me and my sister." Her voice trailed off, and her eyes wandered to the picture on the wall, the one showing twin sisters leaning on a bridge railing. They both looked so young and free.

Julie put her free hand on Lillie's shoulder. "Hey, maybe we should go out for a long drive in Genevieve sometime. A little road trip, maybe."

Lillie's lips twitched, her smile returning. "Why, that sounds wonderful, dear."

Julie gave the old lady's shoulder a gentle squeeze. "I need to clear the worst of my to-do list at work, but we'll go soon, okay?"

"Thank you, dear." Lillie nibbled the edge of her slice. "How is the new job going, anyway?"

"Oh, it's fine." Julie looked down at her feet, currently encased in comfortable flats. "I've got an important deadline in the next two weeks. We need to get a recruit by then."

"So strange that you've got to recruit people to work in insurance." Lillie laughed. "Times have changed, eh?"

"I guess so." The lie curdled uncomfortably in Julie's belly, but what else could she do? Telling Lillie about the paranormal world would do nothing except put her in danger.

That was what Taylor said, anyway. Julie wasn't going to take any chances. She thought of the night she'd scooped up a bleeding Malcolm Nox from the pavement after the Yeti mugging. The thought of anything similar happening to Lillie made her scoot a little closer to the old lady.

By the time the credits rolled, Julie was stifling yawns, and Lillie's head was nodding. The old lady shuffled to her feet. "I'm going up to bed, pet. You have yourself a lovely weekend, okay?"

"You too, Lillie." Julie got to her feet and scooped up the plate. "I'll let you know about our road trip."

"Sounds good to me." Lillie flashed a wicked grin. "I know all the best watering holes between here and the Hamptons."

Julie laughed. It was at times like these that she saw the firecracker Lillie must once have been—before her sister died. "I bet you do. You put me to shame. Night, Lillie."

Lillie patted her on the arm. "Goodnight, dear. Thank you for spending your evening with me."

Julie yawned all the way up the stairs to her apartment. Hat greeted her as she locked the door behind her.

"Have a nice dinner?" Hat asked.

Julie dumped the plate in the sink and ran the hot water. "Oh, yeah. We watched another actioner. I don't think Lillie can get enough of them." She started scrubbing this morning's coffee mugs once she was done with the plate.

"Hey! Watch out. You're splashing me," Hat grumbled.

Julie flicked water at him. "Quit your bitching. You're a magical artifact, as you keep reminding me. You can move. Or just magic these dishes clean."

Hat sniffed and shuffled out of the way. "I won't waste my powers on chores."

Julie reached for a dishtowel and her hand accidentally brushed against a large envelope of thick white paper that had been lying on the counter. It fell to the ground and an expensive and elaborate invitation slid out of it.

"Crap," Julie muttered. She dried her hands quickly and picked it up, scowling as she stuffed it back into the envelope.

"What are you going to do about that invitation, anyway?" Hat shuffled curiously nearer as Julie set the envelope back on the counter. "You need to RSVP soon."

"I'm not going to go and watch Malcolm throw his life away," Julie grumbled. "I don't understand why he's even dating that Cassidy bitch, never mind getting hand-fasted to her or whatever it is that you call it."

Hat cocked his brim. "Well, if you feel that strongly about it, aren't you going to do something?"

"I don't know what I can do," Julie admitted. "Who Malcolm marries is technically none of my business."

Hat chuckled. "I don't see how that's stopped you before."

"Yeah, well..." Julie sighed. "This is different. I mean, I doubt Malcolm would be having this ceremony if Julius didn't approve. If Julius approves, then I don't think there's much to do. You heard Taylor. I'm on his good side. I should probably try to stay there."

"Even if Malcolm's about to marry someone who will suck the life out of him, and not in the way you'd expect from a vampire?" Hat enquired archly.

Julie threw the dishtowel at him. "Hilarious."

CHAPTER THREE

Upbeat music blanketed the rooftop bar in sound, and everyone Julie saw was young and gorgeous and dressed in designer fashions. The rooftop terrace was giddily high up and verdant with plants and brightly colored umbrellas shading the little tables.

"You have to try the 230 mai tai." Taylor stretched out his legs luxuriously underneath the table. "It's delicious."

Julie glanced at the menu and whistled quietly. "It's fourteen dollars. For a cocktail."

Taylor waved a hand. "Oh, come on. You've hardly spent anything today."

Julie leaned back in her chair. A cool breeze ruffled her hair, reminding her that spring was not yet over. Her attention was captured by the heart-lifting view of the peaks of Manhattan enveloped by fading evening light that shimmered above the distant blur of the mainland. She'd never been anywhere like this before. Taylor had strutted in here like he owned the place, or at least frequented it.

Taylor noticed her staring and grinned. "You're not in Brooklyn anymore, Dorothy."

Julie laughed. "No shit."

"So don't act like it," he encouraged. "C'mon. Live a little."

"Not today." Julie put the menu down. "I'm still underage, remember?"

"I…did not remember. Silly human rules." Taylor shrugged. "Espressos it is, then."

Taylor beckoned to a well-dressed waitress and ordered two of the pricey little coffees. He watched the attractive woman with appreciation as she walked away.

Julie couldn't fathom why this irritated her. "Okay, but just because I'm about to spend a small fortune on an espresso, it doesn't mean you're going to turn me into you."

Taylor laughed. "What's that supposed to mean?"

"Just that I'm not one to spend several hundred dollars all at once like you just did."

"Hey!" Taylor protested, pouting at her. "I needed all of that stuff."

Julie raised an eyebrow. "Oh yeah? Like the lava lamp? The seventies called. They want it back."

"Lava lamps are timeless," Taylor countered in a faux-hurt voice. "Besides, it matches my other one."

"You spent a hundred fifty bucks on it!" she pointed out.

Taylor had the look of a man who didn't see the problem. "Hey, you did a little retail damage yourself, you know."

Julie's arched eyebrow dropped and she blushed. "Yeah, some curtains and nice bedlinens. You bought three T-shirts at the same store, one of which could pay my next month's rent."

"Rent?" Taylor cocked his head to one side. "Well, the 99% sure are interesting creatures."

Julie swatted him good-naturedly with a menu. She was happy with her bedlinens. They were the nicest she'd ever had, even if they weren't the Egyptian cotton ones whose price tag had made her eyes pop. She wasn't sure she'd ever have the kind of money to justify spending *that* on sheets.

Their coffee arrived as the sun sank behind the skyline. Every window in Manhattan seemed to catch the brilliance of the sunset until it felt like they were floating in light, an ocean of pink and gold. Julie hadn't ever seen a view like this before. She sipped the coffee, which was deliciously rich and bitter on her tongue, and couldn't think of anything to say for a long moment.

Taylor cleared his throat. "Hey, I'll get the check. I know we normally split it, but I kind of didn't think about the prices when I suggested we come here for food."

Julie shook her head emphatically. "No, thank you. Last time I was in a place this fancy, it didn't end so well."

"Oh?" Taylor glanced up from the menu.

"Yeah. It was the day before I got the draft notice from the PMA." She shook her head, laughing. "My mom nagged me into going on a date with this guy I met on a dating app."

"She did?" Taylor leaned forward, menu forgotten. "Does this guy have a name?"

"Sam." Julie chortled. "Sam the Jerk, in my head. He was a real ass."

Taylor was wide-eyed and enthralled. "What did he do?"

Julie grimaced at the memory. "Well, he took me to The Dancing Rose, on Coney Island."

"Ooh, fancy. I've taken a few girlfriends there myself."

Julie snorted. "Yeah, but I bet you didn't make it sound like you were going to pay for the meal and then decide to split the check at the last second. He saddled me with fifty dollars' worth of lobster thermidor while I was unemployed, and then turned around and asked me for a second date! He still texts me from time to time."

Taylor spluttered into his coffee, almost choking on his laughter. "He did not!"

"He did!" Julie shook her head, giggling. "I didn't even have the money left over for an Uber."

Taylor's jaw dropped. "Walk? From Coney Island to Bay Ridge?"

"The *edge* of Coney Island." Julie shrugged. "It was okay." She decided not to mention the seedy guys who'd nearly cornered her at the convenience store near Lillie's house.

"What an asshole." Taylor picked up the menu again. "You know I wouldn't do that."

Julie smiled. "Of course. I still think I'll pay for my own meal, thanks."

Taylor shook his head. "Ever independent. Ready to order?"

"Sure."

Taylor indulged himself in the miso glazed salmon, while Julie opted for the slightly more reasonable fried chicken sandwich. It was crunchy and glorious, even if it cost almost as much as the lobster on her date from hell. Fairy lights strung all around the terrace gave it a gorgeous ambiance.

"Are you happy about your bank account?" Julie mopped up a few last crumbs of chicken with her bread as a live band began to set up on the stage.

Taylor gave her table manners a horrified glance. "Oh, yes. Thanks for your help with that. I doubt I would have coped on my own."

Julie laughed. "Haven't you ever had your own forms to fill in before?"

Taylor turned faintly gray. "Well...no. We have people for that."

Julie dipped her head in a mock bow. "Oh, I do apologize, Your Royal Highness."

"Hey, I'm not complaining." Taylor grinned. "Like you said, it feels good to have my own money. My own account."

Julie laughed. "Even if you have to keep it a secret from your parents?"

Taylor's smile faded. "It's not exactly hard to keep secrets from my parents."

Julie wanted to ask him about them, but he held up a hand to the waiter and asked for the check before she could say anything.

The bar was getting crowded as the band tuned up and people flooded in, gathering expectantly around the stage.

They split the check and headed to the elevator. As they stepped out into the bustling street, Julie was surprised by how much warmer it was down here. The street was intoxicatingly filled with well-dressed pedestrians carrying shopping bags and laughing boozily into the night.

Bursts of music from the surrounding bars, hotels, and restaurants filled the air. Julie took a deep breath, unable to keep a smile off her face. This was exactly what she'd dreamed of when she'd graduated and announced to her mom that she was moving to the city to start her own life, even if it had turned out to be in Brooklyn instead of Manhattan.

"Thanks for today." She turned her smile on Taylor. "It was fun."

"Yeah, it was. Thanks again for your help with the bank stuff." Taylor glanced up and down the street. "So where's Genevieve?"

"She's in Parking 29 with Hat guarding her. He didn't feel like a long day's shopping."

Taylor held out his arm. "I'll walk you there."

"Seriously?" Julie laughed and waved him off. "I'm not some damsel in distress, you know. I can take care of myself."

He raised an eyebrow. "Your performance in the gym might suggest otherwise."

Julie scoffed. "Your standard-issue Manhattan mugger probably isn't a prince trained in combat since he could walk. Besides, I've got this baby." She reached into the pocket of her dark green trench coat and produced a small spray bottle.

"Air freshener?" Taylor enquired.

Julie reddened. "It's the only bottle I had, okay? Actually, it's pepper spray. Home-brewed and extra potent."

Taylor's lip twitched. "That's...impressive. Still, I'd feel better if I saw you safely to your car."

"Okay, Mr. Protective." Julie shrugged. "It's not like I'd mind the company, even though it's just two minutes' walk."

They set off down the sidewalk together. Above them, music pumped from the high windows of handsome Edwardian buildings with elegant wrought-iron bay windows that had been there since horses and carriages trotted these streets.

Taylor stuck close as Julie led the way, at ease surrounded by people and the crush of bicycles whizzing past on the bike lanes while traffic honked and crawled along the street. This was the home of her soul. She belonged here in the chaos.

Parking 29 was underground next to one of the pretty old buildings. The entrance was marked by a square doorway with glowing letters announcing ENTER.

"It's a bit of a walk to Genevieve's spot," Julie apologized as she led Taylor down the ramp and into the huge, dark space, lit at intervals by strip lights. "There wasn't a lot of space."

Taylor chuckled. "That's okay. I could use the exercise."

She poked him in the belly, her finger meeting rock-hard abs. "Sure could."

"Hey!" Taylor protested, his voice echoing off the concrete. "I'm not that—"

Julie stopped dead as her senses prickled a warning. "Shhh!"

"What?" Taylor continued. "I was just saying that—"

Julie grabbed his arm, squeezing it. "Dude, *shhh*! Do you feel that?"

Taylor shut his mouth, and shook his head, giving her a wide-eyed look.

The shimmering pewter of Genevieve stood out from the solid blacks and silvers of the surrounding cars two rows down from where they were standing.

"Feel what?" Taylor glanced around.

Julie shuddered, goosebumps crawling on her skin. "I don't know. Something doesn't feel…*right*." She looked around, but she couldn't see anyone else in this eerily abandoned part of the garage.

Taylor's nose twitched and he cleared his throat. "There's something funky smelling around here. Let's get to Hat. Maybe he can clear it up."

Julie nodded. "Good idea."

They started walking again, and Julie relaxed her grip on Taylor's arm. She noticed that one of the light strips nearby was out, casting a creepy shadow between the cars. Fumbling for Genevieve's keys, she kept her eyes on her car. "I think I should give you a ride back to your car, Taylor. Something's not—"

At that moment, a huge, hairy blur shot out of the shadows and slammed into Taylor. His yelp of surprise was cut short as the creature—the *Yeti*—bore him to the ground.

Julie froze with indecision as Taylor and the Yeti tumbled over each other, one a mass of hair, the other rumpled clothing. The Yeti closed its giant hands on his shoulders, slamming him into the asphalt as it straddled him.

Taylor broke its grasp with a swift movement of both forearms and landed a punch on its jaw. Drool flew from the yellowed tusks that jutted from its bottom lip.

"Hey! Leave him alone!" Julie grabbed the pepper spray as the Yeti shrieked in pain and clawed at Taylor's face. She hesitated before unleashing the spray. How would she spray the Yeti and not Taylor?

Taylor grabbed the Yeti's wrists and pried its blunt, dirty claws away from his face, as he bucked to break free. It roared, a guttural sound, and drove its tusks toward his face. Bringing his knees up as he flung its wrists sideways, Taylor forced the Yeti off balance and rolled out from under it.

He scrambled to get to his feet, but the Yeti grabbed his ankles and threw him to his hands and knees.

Julie yanked off one of her high heels and darted in as the Yeti pulled Taylor toward it, seizing his jeans hand over hand. "Let him go, you hairy asshole!" She smacked it on the head with her shoe to emphasize each word.

"Julie, no!" Taylor choked.

The Yeti released him with one hand to claw at her, allowing Taylor to get one leg free and kick it soundly in the jaw. It roared and turned its attention back to him.

Julie continued raining blows on its back. "Get your hands off him, you drain blockage-smelling monster!"

Taylor landed another kick in the Yeti's stomach. The hairy creature reared, giving him a second to roll out of its grip.

"Hey, you reject from a carpet cutoff sale!" Julie flung her shoe at its head. It bounced off and the Yeti whipped around, its yellow eyes landing on her. "Leave him alone!"

The Yeti lumbered toward her. Julie grabbed for her pepper spray.

"*No!*" Taylor yelled, tackling the Yeti around the waist. He looked very small and slender next to the huge creature, but it fell to its knees and struggled to get back up while it clawed to get his weight off its back.

"Julie, run!" Taylor yelled, wrapping an arm around the Yeti's thick neck.

"No freaking way!" Julie removed her other high heel and ran across the asphalt on her bare feet. "Get off him, you walking mangeball!" she shrieked as she slammed the shoe into the Yeti's face.

The Yeti struck out madly with one arm. Its grasping hand missed her, but its forearm thudded against her ribs with a force that threw her backward. She landed on her butt and skidded several feet before tumbling onto her back, knocked breathless.

"Run, Julie!" Taylor had hold of one of the Yeti's arms. He clung to it with determination, trying to twist it into a guard that had often reduced Julie to a squealing, tapping heap.

But the Yeti barely acknowledged he was there. It lunged to its feet and jerked its arm out of Taylor's grip, then reached over with its free hand and grabbed him by the back of his jacket and flung him against a nearby car with a sickening thud.

Taylor slid to the ground, stunned. His limbs stirred sluggishly.

"No!" Julie was on her feet before she could think, looking around for her pepper spray. She spotted it under a SUV several yards away.

The Yeti was lumbering toward Taylor, its huge hands balled into fists. Julie scrambled for the car on her hands and knees and reached under it. Her arm was just an inch too short. She stretched farther, hoping she wouldn't be too late.

A shadow swooped across the parking garage, accompanied by an eerie, piercing shriek as high as a bat's whistle. Julie's head snapped up as the vampire joined the fight.

Malcolm Nox moved faster than she thought possible, his arms outstretched toward the Yeti. A snarl transfixed his pleasant face, his eyes burning red and his fangs flashing in the fluorescent light.

Malcolm and the Yeti were circling each other. Malcolm moved with preternatural grace, and Julie noticed that his nails, which were elegantly manicured as they manipulated the buttons on a game controller the last time she'd seen them, had extended into the sharp curves of claws.

The Yeti whipped a meaty clawed hand at the vampire. Malcolm ducked the blow and landed a thunderous blow with a flat palm in the middle of its chest. The Yeti shot back and slammed into a pillar.

It wasn't enough to stop it. It charged Malcolm with a guttural roar, ignoring Taylor and Julie for the moment.

Julie ran to the elf, who was already getting to his feet. "Taylor, are you hurt?"

"I'm okay," Taylor told her, shaking his head to clear it. His hands curled into fists. He shook off her attempt to help him up and ran back into the fight.

The Yeti's full attention was on Malcolm. Taylor darted in with a roundhouse kick that landed squarely on the creature's ribs. The Yeti whipped around to face him, its tusks flashing as it let rip with a loose-lipped howl.

The vampire and the elf worked together to rain blows on the Yeti and wear it out. The Yeti spun, frustration driving its rage to boiling point.

Malcolm saw his chance. He swooped in and delivered a devastating uppercut to the Yeti's jaw. The blow landed with a force that lifted the Yeti clean off its feet, its head snapping back. It tumbled over like a felled oak and lay still, spread-eagled on the asphalt.

Julie fished her pepper spray out from under the car just in case and held it in front of her like a shield as she approached the Yeti and gave it a prod with her toe. "Is it dead?"

"No." Taylor bent to rest his hands on his knees, panting. "Just out cold."

Malcolm ran a forearm over his brow. His nails had returned to normal and his fangs had shrunk. "Good. The last thing I need is my father on my case about killing a para."

Taylor fumbled his phone from his pocket. "I'm calling it in."

Julie laid a hand on his arm. "Are you okay? You got rammed against that car pretty good."

Taylor looked up from his phone. "Never mind me. Are *you* okay? It sent you flying back there."

Julie snorted and slapped her ass. "I've got padding."

Taylor gave her a disbelieving look. "Is now really the time for your sense of humor?"

"Seriously, I'm fine." Julie turned her attention to Malcolm. She'd seen the nasty mess that the Yeti's tusks had made of his shoulder. "What about you?"

"Nothing I won't sleep off by tomorrow," Malcolm told her.

Taylor grinned. "I've been in worse fights. Still, thanks, man." He raised the phone to his ear. "I was in a hard spot there."

"Anytime." Malcolm held out a hand. "I've seen you at events before, but I don't think we've ever really spoken. Taylor Woodskin, right?"

Taylor nodded, accepting Malcolm's hand. "And you're the famous Malcolm Nox Julie's told me so much about."

Taylor stepped away, talking on the phone and Julie shrugged at Malcolm's raised eyebrow. "Why were you following us, anyway?"

Malcolm frowned. "Following *you*? I had no idea you were here until I saw that old car of yours parked here."

"Old car!" Julie spluttered. "Excuse me, Genevieve is a classic American muscle car!"

"Sorry." Malcolm spread his hands. "Just saying it as I see it."

"I see you have a lack of appreciation for automotive excellence," Julie snarked. "What were you doing here, then?"

"I was tracking *him*." Malcolm gestured at the slumbering Yeti. "I thought he was the one who mugged me."

"Oh." Julie took a reflexive step back when the Yeti twitched, raising her pepper spray.

Malcolm sighed, shaking his head. "I was hoping I'd found him, but this is a different Yeti."

Taylor ended his call and dropped his phone back into his pocket. "A team of agents are on their way."

"Should we tie him up?" Julie asked, prodding the Yeti's foot with her toe again. It really was a *big* foot. She guessed it was two or three times the size of Taylor's.

"It won't be any use. We'll just have to hope he stays sound asleep." Taylor glanced at Malcolm. "Which he probably will, thanks to that uppercut of yours. That was impressive."

Malcolm grinned. "Thanks."

"We'll just have to keep an eye out for any humans," Julie pointed out.

Julie was still flushed with adrenaline a few minutes later

when the clip-clop of approaching footsteps made all three of them jump. "Humans!"

Taylor gave her a pointed look. "Said she."

Julie scoffed and Malcolm held up a hand, grimacing. "No. Not humans. Smells like my dad."

CHAPTER FOUR

Taylor sucked a breath in through his teeth in sympathy, but when Julius Nox rounded the turn a few seconds later, he wasn't alone.

Julie recognized the tall vampire. He wore a black trench coat that billowed as he walked. His jet-black ponytail framed his sternly elegant, chiseled features. He looked like he'd stepped out of the eighteenth century with his hair bouncing on his shoulder. The frown lines around his red eyes were in full force as his gaze landed on Malcolm.

The elf walking a half-step behind Julius was also eerily familiar-looking. Julie's eyes darted to Taylor, then back to the other Aether Elf. It was difficult *not* to look at him. He was drop-dead gorgeous. He had Taylor's tawny complexion and tall, slender figure, and his hair and eyes were the same color. But where Taylor's hair fell softly over his forehead, this elf's hair was gelled and spiked, and his eyes were hard and piercing.

Julius opened his mouth to speak, but the Aether Elf talked over him. "Taylor, what the hell do you think you're doing?"

Taylor planted his hands on his hips. "Getting attacked in a parking garage, Shae. Thanks for your concern."

"Don't be snippy with me, little brother," Shae snapped.

Julie's mouth formed a round O of surprise. Even Julius was momentarily silenced, although judging by his glare, she guessed he was just surprised anyone would dare to talk over him.

"Sire—" Malcolm began.

"I don't want to hear it, son," Julius stated in a tight voice.

Malcolm squirmed under the weight of parental disapproval. "I was just—"

Julius' eyes raked the Yeti's still form. "I'm aware of what you were doing," he hissed. "We will discuss your reckless behavior when we get home."

Malcolm's shoulders slumped. "Yes, Sire."

Julius raised an imperious finger to point at the exit. "Go wait for me in the Bentley."

"Sire," Malcolm protested, glancing at Julie and Taylor.

"*Now*, Malcolm," Julius ordered.

The younger vampire sighed. Hanging his head like a grounded schoolboy, he stuffed his hands into the pockets of his coat and slouched in the direction Julius had pointed.

Julius turned to Julie and gave her a firm nod. "I'm pleased you are unhurt, Miss Meadows. I look forward to seeing you soon."

Julie had to swallow a giggle. "Thank you, Sire."

"Oh, yeah!" Malcolm paused and turned around, his grin returning. "I'm still waiting on that RSVP!"

"To the car, Malcolm," Julius snapped.

Shae bowed to Julius as the vampire turned to leave. "Thank you for the heads-up, Sire."

"Of course." Julius nodded coolly. "Family must care for family."

The words made him sound like a mafia boss, but Julie thought it was wise to keep this opinion to herself.

Shae rounded on Taylor again. "How could you do this,

Taylor? You've placed yourself at risk, and you've scared our parents!"

"Please, Shae." Taylor folded his arms. "You're fifth in line. You don't concern yourself that much with your safety, either."

"I know better than to drag the Woodskin name into scandal." Shae jabbed an accusing finger at his younger brother. "The political climate is stormy enough as it is. What do you think would happen if something happened to a Woodskin?"

Julie folded her arms. Shae might be a statue of masculine elegance, wrapped in a suit that probably cost more than half a year of her rent, but he lacked the warmth that his brother had.

"Quit pretending you care, Shae," Taylor spat. "I'm just living my life."

"You're *flaunting* it," Shae hissed, venom dripping from his tone. "You're putting yourself in danger."

"Hey!" Julie stepped forward. "Taylor can flaunt whatever he wants, thank you very much."

Shae's cold eyes pinned Julie with an icy glare and Taylor moved in front of her, as though to shield her. "Danger is part of my life. I work for the OPMA, you know."

"In *recruitment*. Where it's safe," Shae retorted. "Don't think I like being ordered to leave my date to check on you when I know that you can take care of yourself." His eyes flashed to Julie again. "It's the company you're keeping that has the family worried."

Julie felt a burst of heat behind her temples. "What's that supposed to mean?"

Shae shrugged. "No offense."

"I'm hearing that way too much lately." Julie gritted her teeth. "Offense *very much* taken."

Shae waved a dismissive hand. "Taylor is an heir to the Aether Throne. A distant heir, but if he was killed..." He glanced at the unconscious Yeti. "The political ramifications would still be immense."

Julie couldn't believe her ears. "You do realize the Yeti attacked *us*, right? It's not like we went looking for trouble."

"Julie," Taylor murmured.

She glanced at him. Was she making things worse?

"Trouble found you all the same." Shae shook his head. "Taylor, you've been summoned to appear before the Court."

Taylor's shoulders slumped, just like Malcolm's had done. "Okay," he murmured. Julie hated the flatness in his tone.

"Fine. Can you get yourself there without disgracing anyone?" Shae grumbled.

Taylor nodded. His older brother gave Julie a last glare, then turned on his heel and stalked out of the garage.

Taylor turned to Julie. "I'm sorry. You didn't deserve to be spoken to like that."

"*You're* sorry? What does that jumped-up asshat think he's doing, talking to *you* like that?" Julie exploded. "Sorry. I know he's your brother. But still!"

Taylor sighed. "Don't worry about it."

Julie got hold of her anger on his behalf. "What's this about appearing at court? You did nothing wrong."

"Not *at* court." A smile tugged at Taylor's lips. "Before the Court. I have to show my face to Mom and Dad."

"Oh." Julie's shoulders relaxed. "That doesn't seem so bad."

"I guess." Taylor ran a hand through his hair, which was still mussed from the fight. "I hear a car. Oh, it's the agents. Listen, Julie, I'm sorry but I've got to go. I can't ignore the summons without consequences."

Something about the way he said it sent a chill into Julie's stomach. "It's okay. I'll be fine."

"Thanks." Taylor managed a wan smile. "I'll see you at work Monday?"

She nodded. "Text me about how it went with your parents."

Taylor gave a one-shouldered shrug. "I will, and when I see you, I'd better find out what that RSVP is all about."

Julie grinned. "You bet."

A few moments after Taylor departed, a black SUV squealed to a halt beside Julie. It had an OPMA vehicle pass on the windshield. She felt abruptly silly, standing over the Yeti as though she'd vanquished it, and slipped her homemade pepper spray bottle back into her coat.

A hulking orc and a delicate, blonde Fae whose tight ponytail hung lower than her waist disembarked from the SUV. The orc strode over to the unconscious Yeti and rolled it onto its side before restraining it with handcuffs that looked like they were made from pure iron.

The Fae addressed Julie as her silent orc companion tossed the Yeti effortlessly over his shoulder and lugged him over to the SUV. "You must be Meadows."

"That's right. Taylor was just here." Julie gestured vaguely toward the exit. "He had to go—"

"We ran into Woodskin on his way out of the garage," the Fae interrupted. "Did any humans see this happen?"

"No." Julie bit her lip. "The Noxes were here."

"We're aware." The Fae took out a notebook and pen. "I'm going to need your full statement."

The Fae took Julie's statement while the orc bundled the Yeti into the rear compartment of the SUV with great effort. She kept interrupting to ask questions, and Julie was struggling to keep her cool by the time the two agents finally got back into their SUV and drove off.

Trudging toward Genevieve, Julie fished her phone from her pocket and sighed at the time. It was going to be a long, tiring drive home. She was already feeling stiffness from the fight creeping through her lower back and thighs.

The moment she opened the door, a purple beret leaped up from the passenger seat and attached itself to her face.

Julie! Hat cried in her mind. *Are you okay?*

A pang of guilt ran through Julie's gut. She hadn't paused to think about Hat other than to reassure herself that he was safe inside Genevieve.

I'm sorry. She peeled Hat off her face and placed him on her head before sliding into the driver's seat. *You saw everything, didn't you?*

Hat cuddled around her ears. *Yes. Are you hurt?*

No, we're all okay. Julie took a deep breath. *It was pretty scary, though.*

"I didn't see the start of the fight." Hat spoke aloud when Julie had safely closed the door. "What happened?"

"I don't even know. We were walking to Genevieve, and the next minute, the Yeti tackled Taylor." Julie started the car, relaxing at the reassuring sound of her three hundred and seventy-five horses. If any more Yetis appeared, she was pretty sure Genevieve could run them over.

"It's not right," Hat grumbled. "Yetis just don't do that."

Julie steered Genevieve out of the parking garage and aimed for Brooklyn. At least it was late enough that the traffic was flowing steadily. "Well, that's what happened."

"I know. It's just so hard to believe. Yetis will barely be driven to attack even in self-defense. A Yeti attacking someone out of the blue?" Hat snorted. "It's ridiculous. Absolutely preposterous."

Julie grinned and ran a hand over Hat's crown. "Hey, for a second there, you had me thinking you were worried about me."

"What? No. Rubbish." Hat sniffed. "I was confused about what happened, that's all."

"Yeah, yeah. Very believable, Hat."

Hat spent the rest of the drive home grumbling about how unnatural the Yeti's behavior had been. He was still ranting by the time Julie pulled Genevieve safely into the garage. It felt good to step out of the car and hear the *thunk* of the garage door rolling closed behind her.

Stories about Bigfoot or Sasquatch attacks are all bogus, Hat continued as Julie stumbled up the stairs.

"You know, Hat, the weirdest part of it all was that there didn't seem to be any reason for it to attack." Julie unlocked her door and stepped into her apartment. "I mean, when that other Yeti mugged Malcolm, at least there was a clear motive. Not every Yeti is going to be shy and secretive, right?"

Hat harrumphed in disagreement. "As far as I'm concerned, every Yeti *is* shy and secretive."

Julie pulled Hat off and put him on the counter. "Now who's perpetuating stereotypes?"

"You don't understand, Julie," Hat insisted. "These creatures have shyness in their very natures."

"Which makes it all the weirder that one of them went for Taylor out of the blue like that." Julie turned on the coffee machine. "Do you think it could be, like, a hit or something?"

"Why? Yetis don't get involved in politics, and Taylor isn't particularly important." Hat shuffled to the edge of the counter. "It would make more sense to go after Shae or one of his other older siblings."

"You're right." Julie opened the fridge and rummaged around for a snack. "It's just so...*wrong*. I'm glad Malcolm showed up when he did. I thought Taylor was going to get really hurt. Something's got to be done to stop anything like this happening again."

"The PMA needs to find out what is causing the Yetis to behave this way." Hat huffed. "If *I* was still their main system, things would be different."

"Maybe there's something we can do." Julie opened a yogurt and licked the lid. "But we're only recruiters, so I don't know." She chuckled at herself, sinking into a chair at the kitchen table. "I'm only human, so I don't even know what's going on half the time. What was the deal with Taylor being summoned to appear 'before the Court'? He said it was just seeing his parents, but he seemed…I don't know…defeated. Or scared."

"Every royal family is feeling the pressure of the political instability that's looming over the paranormal world," Hat explained. "Taylor might be a long way from the Aether Throne, but if war breaks out then it's not inconceivable that he might end up as the Aether King."

"War?" Julie stilled. "What do you mean, war? What's this political instability people keep referring to?"

Hat hunkered down. "I hope you're ready for a long story."

"Hit me with it." Julie spooned some more yogurt. "I'm totally wired. It's going to be a while before I can get myself to bed."

"All right." Hat cleared his nonexistent throat, presumably for Julie's benefit. "You know that the paranormal world is governed by the Eternity Throne?"

Julie paused with the spoon halfway to her mouth. "Yeah. Julius Nox explained it to me back when I was trying to figure out how to get recruits to join. It's held by the Lunar Fae, isn't it?"

"That's right." Hat chuckled. "You don't forget things, do you?"

"I try not to." Julie made a happy sound as she popped the spoonful of strawberry yogurt into her mouth.

"The Lunar Fae have controlled the Eternity Throne for the past three hundred and fifty years. There's always good and bad monarchs, of course, but Queen Esmerelda has provided structure and stability to the paranormal world."

"So it's an absolute monarchy?" Julie raised an eyebrow. "Seems a little old-fashioned."

"Not quite. Eleven councilor positions are held that have major influence over the reigning monarch. The final word is with the king or queen, but the councilors deal with a lot of the politics below them, and they do hold sway over the monarch."

"Like the Senate, kinda," Julie suggested.

"Something like that." Hat paused. "The councilors are hereditary roles and come from the seven ancient royal families who have controlled the Eternity Throne at one point or another for all history."

"Seven royal families," Julie mused. "Let me guess, the Aether Elves are among them?"

"That's right." Hat bobbed his crown in a nod.

Julie tossed her empty yogurt cup into the trash and took her spoon to the sink. "It all seems pretty set in stone to me. So why the instability?"

"Thing is, there's no viable Lunar Fae heir to the throne right now," Hat told her over the sound of running water.

Julie was getting the big picture. "Oh, yeah. The queen is three hundred years old or something, isn't she?"

"She's been on the throne for three hundred fifty years," Hat confirmed. "But she's been withdrawing from public life a little more each year for the last twenty years or so. If there's no Lunar Fae to take her place, then another family will be chosen."

Julie dropped the dishtowel in shock. "So Taylor might not be sixth in line to the Aether Throne. He might be sixth in line to the *Eternity* Throne."

"Exactly," Hat confirmed. "No one knows which family will be chosen."

"Wow. No pressure, right?" Julie put the spoon back in the drawer and hung the dishtowel on its hook. "Who is everyone's money on if that happens?"

Hat's tone became conspiratorial. "Popular opinion is that the Sylthana Elves will be the next family to rise to the throne. Your friends the Noxes are also in the running."

Julie grimaced. "Wait, so Malcolm Nox might be Eternity King, or whatever it's called? Is the para world ready for that disaster?"

Hat snickered. "I admit it's an amusing, albeit terrifying, thought."

Stifling a yawn as she kicked off her boots, Julie padded over to her closet and pulled out her comfiest pair of pajamas. "Well, the Yeti problem will have to wait till Monday. I think I need a long, hot shower and a good sleep."

CHAPTER FIVE

The numerous hot showers Julie had taken since Saturday night had done their job. She stepped into the gym feeling loose, limber, and ready for whatever Taylor was going to throw at her today.

She dropped her backpack beside their usual mat and placed Hat carefully down on the bag before sitting beside it to pull her shoes off. *I'm hoping for a little more encouragement and a little less snark today, okay?*

Ha! Hat scoffed. *I know which one I prefer.*

Julie tossed her head flippantly as she strode out onto the mat. *I know which one you're better at. I wonder where Taylor is?*

You know him. Hat chuckled. *He's probably been drowning his sorrows.*

She dropped her hands to her hips and glanced around the gym. On the mat next to hers, two dwarves swung rubber axes. The younger was practicing an overhand strike while the elder gave her feedback. Across the gym, a pair of magnificent stags circled each other on a larger mat, tossing their massive antlers as they feinted at one another. One charged unexpectedly, and their antlers locked with a thunderous crash.

Julie watched in awe for a moment as an orc practicing his deadlifts reached six hundred pounds and added more weights before pulling out her phone impatiently. It was 8:12 already. Taylor was often late, but never *this* late.

She bit her lip, remembering the hooded look in his eyes. She opened his chat and skimmed to the text she'd sent him yesterday.

How'd it go with the Court?

He'd read the message, but there was no response. She'd followed it up with a goat meme, hoping to cheer him up. He hadn't even opened that one yet.

Something's up. Julie returned to her bag and sat down beside Hat. *Taylor's never left me on read before. The Court... His parents won't actually* hurt *him, will they?*

Hat sighed. *Depends on your definition of "hurt."*

The minutes ticked by as slowly as syrup. Julie tried calling, but Taylor's phone went straight to voicemail. Worry began to claw at her.

Around half past eight, a familiar, petite figure strode into the gym. The Woodland Fae had her dark hair in a ponytail so long that it brushed against her shapely thighs as she walked to the row of elliptical machines. She put her bag down and plugged in her earphones, then stepped onto the machine and began to work out with brisk, confident movements.

Hey, Hat. Julie picked him up. *Is that* Ellie?

Hat wriggled in her hands. *It is!*

Julie grabbed her backpack and marched over to the elliptical machines with Hat dangling from her fingers. She waved to catch Elspeth Feathertouch's eye.

Ellie's eyes widened, and she pulled her earphones out without slowing down. "Julie, hey! It's so nice to see you!"

"Hi, Ellie!" Julie laughed. Ellie looked like an entirely different person from the nervous half-human, half-Fae she'd recruited at a modeling agency in Manhattan a couple of weeks ago. She was wearing almost no makeup. Her pointed features and warm skin tone were striking against the pale amber of her eyes. She was wearing olive green leggings and a matching tank top that showed off the taut muscles in her shoulders and arms.

"Are you here to work out?" Ellie asked.

"My sparring partner is a no-show today, but I might as well get in my cardio." Julie climbed onto the machine beside Ellie's and got to work. "So, how is boot camp treating you?"

"It's epic!" Ellie beamed. "I've never felt more at home than I do here. The orb is wild, by the way. It totally blew my mind with all kinds of intelligence and surveillance techniques and information about this world. I'm shipping out to Avalon in a couple of weeks. Can you imagine?"

Julie couldn't stop smiling. "That's amazing, Ellie. I'm so glad to hear you're fitting in here."

"I never realized how toxic that whole hive culture was back at the modeling agency. The people here are so real." Ellie kicked up her workout a notch, pushing the muscles rippling in her thighs and forearms. "I've only got a few more weeks of boot camp before I'll be unleashed on the world as Elspeth Feathertouch, agent of OPMA."

"I'm sure you've been putting your fencing skills to good use." Julie grimaced. "I'm still sorely lacking in that area."

"Fencing? It's nothing compared with learning to fight with a real broadsword." Ellie chuckled. "I'm living the nerd's dream life, right? But best of all, I feel like I'm not just *part* of this world that always felt so far away for me. I feel like I'm doing something *good* for it."

"I know what you mean." Julie nodded. "It feels like this work means something."

"So worthwhile, right?" Ellie took a sip from her water bottle without slowing down. "Hey, what's a recruiter doing sparring before work, anyway?"

Julie smirked. "I guess I always wanted to learn martial arts. What better way than getting your ass kicked by an Aether Elf for an hour every morning?"

They worked out in silence for several minutes. Julie was puffing by the end of it, but Ellie had barely broken a sweat. She straightened her ponytail as she stepped off the machine and glanced at her phone.

Julie mopped her face with a towel. "Well, boot camp sure seems to be working on you."

Ellie laughed. "I'm really enjoying it." She paused, her eyes searching Julie's. "Hey, I don't want to make this weird, but I want to thank you for recruiting me that day. My life has completely changed because of it. Joining OPMA is the most worthwhile thing I've ever done." She grimaced. "Did I make it weird?"

"A little." Julie laughed. "But thanks for saying that. With that attitude, you should be on a recruitment video."

"Probably." Ellie hooked her duffel bag over her shoulder. "See you around!"

Julie nibbled on her bottom lip as the young Fae strode away with her head up and her shoulders back, brimming with confidence. *Recruitment video*, she repeated to herself. *That's actually not a bad idea.*

Maybe you should talk to Kaplan about it, Hat suggested.

Julie jumped. She bent, picking up Hat and her backpack. *Are you spying on my thoughts?*

Just reading them. Hat squirmed in her hand, as though to get comfortable.

Julie headed for the showers. *Maybe I should talk to Kaplan about a recruitment video. But first, I've got to figure out what's going on with my AWOL partner.*

Hat obligingly became a fedora with a bold red ribbon after Julie had showered and slipped into her favorite pair of studded jeans and her leather jacket.

She frowned as she peered into the mirror and smoothed her pixie cut, which mostly seemed to smooth itself anyway. It was five minutes to nine. She checked her phone again. Unease curled in her gut like a snake.

Still nothing from Taylor, she told Hat, scooping him up from the bench and perching him on her still-damp hair. *I'm starting to get worried.*

He must be in the office, Hat suggested. *Maybe he was just too sore after the fight with the Yeti to do any sparring today.*

Julie remembered the way her partner had slammed against that car and the dreadful *thunk* of his skull hitting the metal. The snake in her belly writhed again.

She hurried to the main building and rode the elevator to the third floor. She scanned the rows of cubicles as she stepped out into the communal office. There was no sign of Taylor.

When she reached their office, his chair was conspicuously empty. Julie huffed, tossing Hat onto the desk. *Now I'm really worried.*

You need a distraction. Hat wriggled closer to the ancient computer. *I'm uploading a file to your computer with more intel on possible recruits. That should keep your mind off Taylor until he shows up.*

Grumbling to herself, Julie switched on the PC and waited impatiently while it growled and spluttered to life. She'd just started clicking through the file when the office door creaked.

Julie looked up, a rush of relief flowing through her at the sight of the Aether Elf walking in. "Taylor, I was starting to think you'd been locked up in a tower by your parents."

"I'm a prince, not a princess." Taylor's lips almost made it into a smile. He slinked to his chair and flopped down with a sigh. "Sorry I'm late."

Julie glanced at the time on her screen. 9:07. "It's okay."

She paused, waiting for more, but Taylor didn't volunteer anything as he turned on his computer. "So, are we going to talk to the Were-Fox today?"

Julie nodded. "It's worth a shot. She might not be one of the top three, but imagine Kaplan's face if we get him a recruit *today*."

There was no reaction from Taylor. He continued scrolling, the wheel on his mouse squeaking. Julie leaned forward and tapped the top of his monitor. "Hello? Are you having fun with Minesweeper?"

"Sorry." Taylor looked up at her, his eyes filled with an emotion she couldn't name. "I— Yes. He'll be impressed."

Julie cocked her head, concern replacing her annoyance. "Taylor, are you okay?"

"Yeah." The elf dropped his gaze back to his keyboard, but he didn't resume his scrolling.

"You know you can tell me, right?" Julie propped her chin on the top of the monitor to make him laugh. "We're friends. Friends vent to each other, and when venting isn't enough they show up with a couple of shovels and a body bag. Do I need to go buy a bodybag?"

Her attempt to cheer him up got only a faint smile out of Taylor. "Yeah. Thanks. It's just… Ugh." He rubbed his face with both hands. *"Politics."*

"Politics, like, family politics?" Julie asked. "Or politics, like, Eternity Throne politics?"

Taylor sighed. "In my world, there's not much difference."

Julie grimaced. "Did the summons not go well?"

"How could it? You heard what Shae said." Taylor shrugged, still not meeting her eyes. "My parents were pretty pissed with me."

Julie sat back in her chair, perplexed by the inner workings of the Aether Elf royal family. "I don't get it. You're not the one who attacked the Yeti."

"They don't see it that way. They said I disgraced the family name." Taylor shook his head. "'Brawling in parking garages is not princely behavior.'"

Julie waved her hands furiously. "What about, I don't know, defending the life of a lady, or whatever? Can't you try that angle?"

Taylor picked at a speck of dirt on his mouse pad. "It's no use trying *any* angle with my parents."

Julie thought of what Hat had said about the pressure on all of the royal families because Queen Esmerelda had no heir. "It's not fair. You didn't ask to be born into all of this drama. It's not right that all these expectations are piled onto you. You should have a right to decide what you do with your life. You're a grown-ass adult, for goodness sake. Your parents shouldn't be able to tell you not to walk through a parking garage like any normal person would."

"That's just the thing." Taylor had removed the speck and now pushed his mouse idly around the desk instead. "As far as my parents are concerned, I'm not allowed to be a normal person."

"You should be able to have your freedom," Julie insisted. "You're a person in your own right."

Taylor's lip curled into a grimace. "That's just the way it is, I guess. But thanks for being supportive about it. I'm sorry I missed sparring today. I should have texted you, but I've been avoiding my phone because Shae's been nagging me about shit."

"Want me to call him and give him a piece of my mind?" Julie held up both hands in an exaggerated karate pose.

Finally, Taylor laughed. "I don't think that's a good idea. Hey, what was Malcolm talking about when he said he was waiting on your RSVP?"

Julie grinned at him. "Oh, you didn't get an invitation, Your Royal Highness?"

Taylor laughed. "Not just anyone gets invited to a Nox family event, whatever that event might be. Are you going to tell me?"

Julie huffed. "It's a party to celebrate Malcolm's handfasting to the bitchiest vampire in the world."

Taylor's jaw dropped. He stared at her open-mouthed for a few seconds. "You got invited to Malcolm's *handfasting?*"

"Yeah, but you're missing the point, Taylor. She's *so* wrong for Malcolm, it's not even funny. She's—"

"Wait. Hold on a minute." Taylor held up a hand. "I'm still processing. I don't even think my parents were invited. The Noxes are famously exclusive."

Julie cupped her chin in both hands and batted her eyelashes. "Well, clearly I've charmed my way into their good graces with my wonderful personality and incredible looks."

"I don't believe it," Taylor stated. "You've been here all of two minutes and you're getting invited into vampire high society. Lucky you. I just hope you've been invited as a guest and not an entrée."

"Oh…" Julie sagged in her chair, blinking rapidly to dismiss the mental image of Malcolm's claws and fangs. "I hadn't considered that."

She caught Taylor's teasing grin and scowled at him, mad at herself for falling for it. Malcolm and Julius weren't feral, bloodsucking paranormals. They were people, and she liked them. She narrowed her eyes at Taylor. "Well, in that case, they must be pretty hungry because the invite allowed for a plus one. I'm sure they'd appreciate a juicy little morsel like you."

Taylor raised his eyebrows. "Oh, you think I'm juicy?"

Julie rolled her eyes. "Vain much? Maybe they'll go for you first and give me time to escape with my life."

Taylor snorted. "Okay, I'll come. But there's one thing you need to do."

"What? We need to bring swords?" Julie snarked.

"I know you know I was messing with you." Taylor looked her

up and down pointedly, one eyebrow quirked. "Listen, your fashion sense is great, but we're going to need to go on a shopping trip."

Julie grimaced. "Yeah...I literally have nothing to wear. The invite states it's black tie. There's a super cute little thrift store down the road from my apartment that has the nicest things. Mom's pretty good with needlework, so I'm going to pick out something, and—"

"No, no, no. *Darling.*" Taylor waved his hands, a look of horror that made Julie feel vindicated creasing his handsome face. "You don't understand. This isn't just any black tie. This is *Nox* black tie."

Julie shuddered at the thought of the month's-rent-shirts Taylor had bought on Saturday. "Yeah... We're gonna need a recruit before I can match your spending habits, bro."

Taylor sniggered. "That's what my trust fund credit card is for."

"No, no." Julie raised a finger. "Uh-uh. Thanks, but no thanks. I'm not comfortable with charity."

"It's not charity." Taylor's smile turned bitter. "It's me getting back at my parents for being speciesist about my human bestie."

"Awww!" Julie clasped both hands under her chin, raising her voice to a mocking pitch. "I'm your best fwend?"

"You're my only friend, dumbass." Taylor threw a crumpled sticky note at her head.

She caught it and threw it back. "Well, okay, then, if you're sure."

"I'm sure." Taylor tossed the note into the wastepaper basket.

"Charity I can't do. But I'm cool with revenge." Julie winced. "Honestly, I don't even know what to wear to a black tie event. I've never been to one before."

"Well, since my parents are so bent on reminding me that I'm a prince, allow me to conduct myself like one." Taylor raised his chin and squared his shoulders. "I've been to more black tie events than you've eaten hot dinners. I'll be your guide."

Hat spoke up. "Did I mention that I'm not limited to being a hat?" With a soft *poof!*, he transformed into a shimmering diamond tiara with seven ridiculously over-the-top points, each crowned with a gleaming sapphire.

"Okay, whoa there, cowboy." Julie giggled, prodding the highest point of the tiara. "I don't think we'll be needing *that*."

"Trust me. There's no such thing as being overdressed at a Nox event." Taylor's eyes gleamed. "I'm taking you shopping, and it's going to blow your mind."

Hat scoffed. "Fine, so you don't like the tiara." He turned back into a hat. "There are plenty of other options."

"Let me guess." Julie raised an eyebrow. "Cinderella isn't just a story, and I shall go to the ball, glass slippers and all?"

"Glass isn't practical, and Cinderella was overrated. Doves pecked her stepsisters' eyes out at her wedding ceremony." Hat snorted. "However, we could definitely work out something along the lines of one of the more famous designers."

"Oooh." Julie didn't think she could even name a designer, famous or otherwise, but the idea was appealing.

The office phone let out a blaring trill, making all of them jump. Julie grabbed it. "Uh... OPMA recruiters."

"Miss Meadows, you and His Royal Highness have been summoned to Captain Kaplan's office." The voice was trim and reminded Julie of Kaplan's near-invisible assistant, a Werecat who spent most of her time hiding behind a tiny desk outside his office.

"Okay. We're coming." Julie set down the phone and met Taylor's eyes. "You thought appearing before the Court was bad?"

Taylor groaned. "Let me guess. Kaplan wants to see us."

"Yep." Julie grabbed Hat. "Let's go face the music."

CHAPTER SIX

Julie was aware that every set of eyes turned toward her and Taylor as they passed through the busy communal space outside Kaplan's office. Everyone glanced up from their work, then quickly turned their attention back to their computer screens or papers.

Shit, shit, shit, Julie sang in her head. *Kaplan's going to kill us for fighting a Yeti.*

Probably, Hat agreed.

Not helpful, Hat.

The assistant peered at them, her pale green eyes with slit pupils partially obscured by the red hair that fell in neat bangs over her forehead. "The captain will see you now."

"Did she say, 'the captain will *eat* you now?'" Taylor hissed, holding the door for Julie.

Maybe she had. Julie swallowed the bulb of fear at the back of her throat as they stepped into Kaplan's office. The big man had his back to them and was staring out of the big window at the lawns of the OPMA grounds, where agents and soldiers were hurrying this way and that.

Julie longed to be out there in the balmy sunshine, not

trapped in here with a gigantic, angry person who could turn into something else. She didn't know what, but she was pretty sure it came with big teeth.

"Sit," Kaplan growled after a few moments.

Julie and Taylor sank into armchairs. Julie interlaced her fingers and squeezed.

"Sir," Taylor's voice was tremulous, "let me just say that—"

Kaplan's chair creaked as he turned it to face them. Taylor fell silent under the glare of those amber eyes burning underneath his thick, bushy eyebrows. The captain's face was unreadable.

He steepled his thick fingers in front of him and pinned them with a long, searching look. "Are either of you hurt?" he snarled.

This was not going according to the script in Julie's head. She blinked at him. "Um...excuse me, sir?"

"I asked if either of you were *harmed.*" The last word had the edge of a roar in it. "I understand you were attacked by a Yeti on Saturday night."

Wait... Julie had to stifle her grin. *Am I seeing* concern *on the captain's face?*

I think it's the closest he gets, Hat chuckled.

"No, sir." Taylor eyed the captain warily. "We're both okay."

"Good." Kaplan's huge shoulders visibly relaxed. He lowered one massive forearm to the desk and used his other hand to massage his hairy temples. "Now, brief me on what happened. *Exactly* what happened."

"Sir, the Yeti attacked Taylor out of nowhere. It wasn't his fault." Julie folded her arms. "He was defending us both."

"I'm not here to assign blame, Meadows." Kaplan lowered his hand, his voice calm. "I want to know what happened to you two, but your protectiveness of your partner is...noted."

Noted? Julie grumbled inwardly. *What's that supposed to mean?*

I'm a recruitment system, not a shrink, Hat snorted.

"We were in Parking 29, in Manhattan," Taylor told Kaplan.

"Both of us sensed a paranormal presence. We'd just been having dinner—"

Kaplan raised a massive, hairy brow and glanced from Julie to Taylor and back again. "You know we have a policy against fraternization, Woodskin."

"Not *that* kind of dinner," Julie interrupted.

"Hmm." Kaplan's frown returned. "Go on."

"We were walking to my car when a Yeti appeared out of nowhere," Julie told him. "It tackled Taylor and threw him to the ground."

Kaplan's eyes widened a fraction as he looked at Taylor. "Was it armed?"

Taylor shook his head. "No, sir. But its strength was weapons enough, if you know what I mean."

Kaplan's frown deepened. "I actually don't. I've never fought a Yeti. I didn't know they fought at all."

"It was pretty vicious. It didn't pull any punches." Julie winced at the memory. "It threw Taylor into a car."

"It certainly didn't feel like a mock fight," Taylor admitted. "It attacked Julie, too. I don't think I would have won that fight if Malcolm Nox hadn't showed up."

"What was Nox doing there in the first place?" Kaplan grumbled.

Julie ran a hand over the back of her neck. *I hope this isn't going to get Malcolm in trouble, but I've got to tell the truth here.* "Malcolm was tracking the Yeti. He thought it was the one who mugged him, but it wasn't."

"Malcolm was *tracking*..." Kaplan groaned. "Stupid boy."

"I'm glad he showed up, sir." Taylor bit his lip. "It was a hard fight, but he was the one who knocked the Yeti out before I called it in."

"There wasn't time to make any calls before that," Julie added.

Kaplan leaned back in his chair, rubbing his square jaw. "Did Nox attack the Yeti before it attacked you?"

Taylor glanced at Julie. "It didn't sound like it, sir. He was just following it."

"Yeah, that was what it sounded like," Julie confirmed. "I don't think Malcolm would anger a Yeti in the middle of the city like that."

"Malcolm Nox's stupidity sometimes knows no bounds." Kaplan sighed, then looked at Taylor. "You should know that after I received the call, I was the one to get in touch with your parents, Woodskin. Them and Julius Nox."

Taylor's face was very still. "Thank you, sir."

Kaplan nodded, looking a little guilty. "I know it doesn't seem like I was doing you any favors, but your parents told me Shae was close by. I didn't know if you needed more help."

Julie raised her eyebrows. *Was that an apology? From Captain Jack Kaplan?*

Today truly is a historic occasion, Hat commented dryly.

So everyone knows everyone else's business in the paranormal world, she mused. *It's...*

Invasive of everyone's privacy? Hat suggested.

I was going to say it's a lot like where I grew up in West Brighton. It may as well have been a small town for all the politics we had going on in our neighborhood. Julie stifled a grin. *Why didn't you tell me this, Hat? The Eternity Throne, the royal families... It's all very intimidating, but neighborhood politics I can deal with.*

"Meadows?" growled Kaplan.

Julie blinked, realizing she'd been lost in her conversation with hat. "Sir?"

"I said, you two had better restrict your activities to whatever it is you're planning to do to get me that recruit in the next two weeks." One of Kaplan's bushy brows crawled up his forehead like a caterpillar. "Is that clear?"

"Perfectly, sir." Taylor all but saluted.

"Actually, sir, we've been invited to the handfasting at the Nox mansion." Julie leaned back in her chair. "It would be a good networking opportunity, and I would prefer not to miss it." *Not to mention that I'm really looking forward to this whole black tie thing*, she added silently.

Hat snickered.

Kaplan's surprise registered only in a tiny flicker of his eyes. "Very well."

"Sir, if I may?" Taylor asked timidly.

"What is it, Woodskin?" Kaplan snapped.

Taylor, to his credit, didn't flinch. "Where is the Yeti who attacked us?"

Kaplan folded his huge arms. "He's being interrogated this morning. He's down in holding for now."

"Interrogated?" Julie leaned forward. "Can we watch?"

"Julie!" Taylor hissed.

"We *are* the victims." Julie spread her hands. "Sir, I would like to request if we can sit in on the interrogation. I want to know why he attacked us so senselessly."

Kaplan held her gaze for a few long moments, then nodded. "All right. But try not to get yourselves into more trouble than you already have, and don't forget that we have a deal with those recruits. Is that clear?"

"Abundantly, sir." Taylor got up, giving Julie a pointed look.

Kaplan grunted again and turned back to surveying the window. "Dismissed."

Taylor all but dragged Julie out of Kaplan's office. He paused when they reached the elevator, his finger hovering over the button marked -11. "Are you sure you want to sit in on the interrogation?"

Julie arched an eyebrow. "Do you think I would have braved asking Kaplan if I wasn't sure?"

"Well, when you put it that way." Taylor hit the button, and the elevator doors slid closed. "Why are you so interested, anyway?"

"Because the Yetis are acting totally unnaturally." Julie folded her arms. "It's weird."

"I'm telling you, something bigger is behind this," Hat added. "I'm certain of it. For once, I'm grateful for your curiosity, Julie."

Julie tweaked Hat's brim. "Yeah, well, maybe I just want you to quit nagging me about it all the time."

Taylor leaned against the wall and gave an exhausted sigh. "Don't you think this Yeti has already gotten us into enough trouble as it is?"

Julie searched him with a look. "If you want to go back to the office, go ahead. I can do this by myself."

"No, no." Taylor waved a hand. "Forget it."

The elevator juddered to an unexpected halt. The doors slid open and a gust of wailing wind rushed into the elevator. Julie looked outside and her stomach lurched as she looked straight down at a drop of hundreds of thousands of feet. The earth looked like a green blur far below smears of white cloud.

"What the—"

"Look out!" Taylor grabbed her arm, yanking her back.

With thundering wings, a mass of fur and feathers soared past the open elevator doors.

Hippogriff, Julie's training told her calmly. *One of the largest aerial predators in the paranormal world, apart from dragons. Known for speed, aggression, and incredible agility.*

"Aggression?" Julie yelped.

"Closecloseclose!" Taylor gasped the word over and over in a long string as he jabbed a finger at the button.

The hippogriff was wheeling and Julie caught a glimpse of talons, feathers, a sharp beak bigger than her face, and...*hooves?* It swooped toward them, a belling shriek echoing from its beak, talons outstretched—

The elevator doors closed, and the hippogriff rammed it,

clashing loudly against the metal. She heard its talons skitter on the doors for a moment before the elevator resumed its smooth descent.

"Let me guess." Julie turned to face a wide-eyed Taylor. "Confluence of magical dimensions again?"

Pathetic, sniffed Hat. *When I was in charge of HQ's systems, this never would have happened.*

Taylor grimaced. "It must have taken us to the aerial research station we have for researching declining numbers of hippogriffs."

"They can decline all they like if you ask me," Julie grumbled.

The next time the doors opened, it was on the right level. They stepped out into a wood-paneled hallway whose floor was tiled in a shade of pale cream that looked like it had been mopped almost into oblivion. A sign on the wall had arrows pointing in a multitude of directions. *Holding. Investigations. Traffic. Human Sightings and Mind Wiping.*

"Really?" Julie scoffed. "That's a whole department?"

"An important one, too." Taylor raised his hands. "Don't look at me like that. Can you imagine what would happen if humans found out about the paranormal world?"

"You've got a point." Julie followed him toward the barred door at the end of the hallway.

Taylor shook his head. "You watch too many cop shows."

"Is there such a thing as too many cop shows?" Julie retorted. "This gives me real police precinct vibes, is all."

"Well, you're not wrong," Taylor conceded. "Law enforcement is an important branch of the OPMA."

A looming vampire waited for them at the door, wearing a blue uniform and a grim expression. His hair was buzz-cut, and unlike the Noxes, he had a square jaw and fleshy cheekbones.

"Taylor Woodskin and Julie Meadows." Taylor flashed his badge, and Julie followed suit. "We're from recruiting."

The vampire folded his arms. "What do you want down here, then?"

"It's okay, Oswald. They're with us." The voice belonged to the bristling dwarf waddling toward them. He had wild yellow curls streaked liberally with gray, and wore a neatly tailored suit and a natty bowler.

"Kaplan sent them. They're here for the Yeti," the elf who strode along next to the dwarf added. An unlit cigarette butt hung from the corner of his mouth. He had a week's beard and the tips of his pointy ears protruded from underneath his shaggy red hair.

"Of course he did." Oswald sighed as he slid the door open and stepped aside for the dwarf and elf to access the containment unit.

The dwarf's cheery smile widened as he beckoned Julie and Taylor to follow. "Come on. We were just about to fetch him from the containment unit."

"He was in holding, but he was too violent to stay in there," the elf supplemented, following his partner. "He was trying his best to break out. We had to take him down to containment."

That's not Yeti behavior at all. Hat sighed. *When trapped, Yetis prefer to roll themselves into a ball, seeking camouflage or somewhere to hide.*

The agents led them to the elevator at the end of the corridor. *Could another para be behind this?* Julie asked Hat as she trailed behind Taylor and the two agents. *A Mind Eater, maybe?*

Oh, no. He'd be long dead by now if a Mind Eater was involved, Hat informed her.

"It's okay. You'll be safe." The elf grinned, shifting his cigarette butt from one side of his mouth to the other. "He's restrained."

The dwarf held out a hand once they were inside the elevator and heading for the sublevel below. "I'm Agent Palladius, by the way."

"Agent Leafeyes. I've heard all the jokes." The brown-eyed elf grinned.

They ceremoniously pumped both Julie and Taylor's hands, then stood side-by-side with the ease of an old married couple, their hands folded in the same way. Julie noticed that although Agent Leafeyes' hair was solidly chestnut brown, there were deep lines around his mouth and eyes. These two had been around the block.

"So you're the recruiter who fought that Yeti off, then?" Palladius asked.

Taylor grinned sheepishly. "Well, I had some help."

"Impressive. He's strong," Leafeyes told them.

Palladius whistled through his teeth. "Took three of us to take him down to containment. We'll have a pair of young guards help us to get him to the interrogation room."

Leafeyes chuckled. "Too old for that ourselves, these days."

"Do you think the Yeti is working for someone else?" Julie rubbed away chills on her arms. "Since he's acting so unlike his nature."

"Probably. Some evil megalomaniac, as usual." Palladius shrugged, as though evil megalomaniacs were as common as plumbing troubles.

"But don't worry. There's no perp we can't break." Leafeyes smirked. "Ten minutes in the box, and he'll sing like a canary."

Julie grinned at the cliché, intrigued to see how this homey pair were going to change once they were face-to-face with a criminal.

I'm telling you, that Yeti's no criminal. Something is forcing them to do these things, Hat insisted.

The elevator came to a halt. Julie was eager to see what the containment unit looked like. However, as the doors slid open, a blaring siren filled the air. Flashing red lights poured into the elevator, and an automated voice was shouting the same words over and over.

"*Warning! Containment breach! Warning! Containment breach!*"

"Get behind us," Palladius barked.

Leafeyes produced an improbably long sword from somewhere. Palladius was holding a stocky pistol down by his side, his trigger finger twitching beside the guard.

Taylor's hands curled into fists. "What's happening?"

Julie decided that this was not the time to make a stand and ducked behind Leafeyes.

Two orcs in blue uniforms came pounding toward them, wielding ugly, spiked maces. "Get those recruiters out of here!" one of them thundered. "They're in the stairwell!"

"They?" Leafeyes barked.

"Escaped prisoners," the second orc clarified. "Dwarves, a couple of Weres, and a Yeti!"

Julie's blood froze. "Yeti?"

"Get back in the elevator." Palladius told them, scanning the hallway and the cells.

Julie only had a vague impression of the cells thanks to the disorienting red lights, but she could see that they had barred doorways, several of which were wide open.

"You got it." Taylor hit the button. "Which floor?"

Leafeyes jerked his chin toward the ceiling. "Back up to your office. You'll be safer there."

"Wait! Shouldn't we help?" Julie stepped toward the closing doors.

Leafeyes sternly moved in front of her. "You're noncombatants. You can help by staying safe."

A terse silence ruled in the elevator as it headed back up. Julie's pulse pounded in her temples. Leafeyes and Palladius both stood with jaws clenched and weapons gripped, so she spoke to Hat in her mind instead.

Julie frowned. *How could this happen? Those orc guards were pretty big. I'm sure they'd be more than a match for a Yeti.*

Hat squirmed uneasily on her head. *Back in my time, there were far more guards. These days, OPMA relies on the automated magical system the IT trolls have developed for opening and closing the doors of the cells.*

Julie considered what little she'd seen of the containment unit. *The cell doors were open. They weren't broken, either. I didn't even see any scratches on the locks.*

My point exactly. Hat sighed. *There's something fishy about those trolls, Julie. They had no reason for throwing me out and replacing me with the IRSA and other systems. I don't trust them.*

Julie thought of Qtana, the sweet young IT troll who had stood up to Kaplan in her first week at the OPMA. *You really think the trolls would do this on purpose?*

I don't think. I suspect. There's a difference, Hat muttered.

I don't know. I can see them making some kind of stupid mistake leading to this, but letting prisoners loose? Julie shook her head minutely. *It seems crazy. I know you've got a grudge against them, but this seems like it's beyond them.*

Maybe, Hat conceded. *It might be more likely that whoever is behind the Yeti attacks orchestrated this escape.*

Julie shivered. *Really? I don't know. The Yeti wasn't the only escapee. Maybe someone's causing chaos to make the OPMA look bad.*

Not impossible. Hat sighed. *Especially with the political climate being what it is. Ambition is a powerful motive.*

Julie glanced at Taylor, not wanting to think about what it might do to him if his parents or siblings were behind something as cutthroat as this. Then again, who was to say that blood hadn't already been shed in pursuit of the Eternity Throne? Suddenly small town politics didn't seem to fit quite as well anymore.

The elevator came to a quiet stop and the doors slid open on the blessedly familiar sight of the recruitment floor.

"There you are." Palladius let out a breath. "You're safe now."

Julie stepped out of the elevator and turned back. "Are you sure there's nothing we can do?"

Leafeyes winked. "We'll be sure to call you if we need someone to beat up a Yeti in a parking garage."

Palladius hit the button for floor -11. "We've got to help the others. But we'll let you know as soon as we hear anything else."

He had to shout the last words as the doors slid shut.

CHAPTER SEVEN

"Well, that was terrifying." Julie turned to Taylor. "What are we supposed to do now?"

Taylor shrugged. "I don't know if there's anything we *can* do. The agents seemed to have it handled."

"You can do your jobs." Hat righted himself on Julie's head. "More recruits means more agents, which means better control over this whole situation."

"Good thinking, Hat." Taylor turned and headed for the office.

Julie plodded after him, her stomach knotting at the thought of the chaos going on belowground. "Hey, you know something?"

"What?" Taylor held the door to their office for her.

"Those two agents must be the only paranormals I've met who didn't comment on the fact that I'm human." Julie flopped into her chair as Taylor settled in at his desk. "They treated me like any other person."

Taylor paused his tapping at his keyboard. "I noticed that, too. It's refreshing."

Julie sighed. "I hope they're going to be okay."

"They're trained agents. I'm sure they're fine." Taylor's face was lit by the light from his monitor. "Okay, Hat, talk to me about these recruits. I know we did a lot of research on Friday, but let's run through it all again."

"I wish we could recruit a replacement for the IT trolls," Hat grumbled. "I'm sure they must be behind the escape."

"They're incompetent, not evil... I think." Taylor frowned at Hat. "Do you have any proof of that?"

There was a long silence. Hat sagged on Julie's head, sulking. "No."

Julie grinned. "Maybe we should investigate?"

"*No!*" Hat and Taylor chorused.

"Seriously. We're supposed to stay *out* of trouble, remember?" Taylor raised an eyebrow. "Now let's get back to doing what we do best."

"What, end up in the wrong place at the wrong time?" Julie quipped.

Taylor snorted. "You know what I mean."

"All right, fine." Hat hummed for a second, processing. "I found three good options. They'll come up on your screen now, Julie."

A second later, Julie's monitor flickered and an image of a pretty young woman with pointed features and a glossy red ponytail appeared on the screen.

"Marie Vos," Julie read. "A Were-Fox from Manhattan."

"She's unemployed and has been for a while." Taylor came over to her side of the desk and read over her shoulder. "She took martial arts classes while she was in high school."

"She seems okay." Julie bit her lip. "But she's not the big fish we're looking for, is she?"

Taylor stared at her. "Getting a recruit in the next two weeks isn't enough for you? We've got to find a 'big fish' now, too?"

Julie tossed her head. "Hey, I'm here to impress and exceed expectations."

Taylor groaned. "You're here to give me heart failure, that's what."

"Okay, okay. Focus, children," Hat chastised. "Let's look at the other two. Next one is coming up on the screen now."

Julie glanced at the picture of a blond dwarf, his bushy eyebrows knit close together in a frown. "Jason Isaksson. An accountant from Pittsburgh. He looks like he'd be a good agent... This is more like it."

"It could be hard to convince him." Taylor tapped on the annual income column on the screen. "He's got a cushy job as it is."

Julie grinned. "Eh, I'm pretty sure I can persuade him with my wit and charm."

Hat projected another file onto the monitor. "Here's the last one."

"Rural Montana?" Taylor snorted. "It'll take a couple of days to travel there, speak to this guy, and come back. I don't think it's worth it."

"I don't know." Julie leaned in to scrutinize the photo. "I've never seen a centaur in real life before." The person in the picture had the upper body of a swarthy man with high cheekbones and flowing brown hair that poured over his neck and shoulders. The bottom of his plaid shirt met with the body of a powerful bay horse.

"Kick-ass warriors," Hat supplied before Julie's orb training had a chance. "They often have strong moral values and an overwhelming sense of justice."

"Cironius Achilleos. Sounds freaking epic." Julie scrolled down her screen. "He's a horse rancher?"

"A lot of centaurs are. Those who still live out in the human world, anyway." Taylor hesitated. "He'd be a high-value recruit."

"Great!" Julie slapped the desk. "So let's go get him!"

"I still think Marie Vos is a safer bet." Taylor ran a hand through his hair. "Our goal is to get a recruit, *any* recruit. Not the most high-value recruit. I don't know about you, but I'm eager to get that off our plates."

Julie noticed the dark rings under his eyes. "I know you're stressed out, but think about this. With the situation being what it is right now, which agent would you rather bring into the OPMA? A young Were-Fox, or an experienced centaur?"

Taylor sighed. "I hear you, but still."

Hat hopped from Julie's head to the desk and shuffled around to face Taylor. "You're acting like it isn't an option to go for both."

"Both?" Julie grinned. "That'll blow Kaplan's socks off."

Taylor rubbed his chin. "Well, it'll take a couple of days to get permissions and file for our travel allowance. There are a bunch of regulations we have to follow and paperwork to file. We could do that now, and then visit the Were-Fox after lunch."

"Brilliant." Hat chuckled. "I don't think I've ever been to Montana before."

"Neither have I. The farthest I've ever been from home was a trip to Washington, DC with my school one time." Julie smiled. "Mom worked so hard and I waited tables to afford it. It was pretty special."

Taylor stared at her in shock. "Really?"

Julie shrugged. "Hey, not all of us grew up with a trust fund."

"Sorry. I didn't mean it that way." Taylor returned to his desk and sank into his chair. "My mother only buys her clothes in Paris. I used to hate going with her. She's, well… I guess I shouldn't speak ill of my queen."

My queen. Suddenly aloe vera juice didn't seem so bad.

"Okay, Hat." Julie tapped his crown. "Pull up the paperwork and we'll print it and get started."

Hat burst out laughing. Taylor joined in, cackling with amusement. "Oh, the innocence!"

Julie folded her arms and scowled at them both. "What?"

"We can't just print the paperwork." Taylor got up from his chair. "We have to go down to the admin department for that."

"The admin department!" Hat wailed, with a ghostly woo-woo noise.

"Wait, is it run by the undead or something?" Julie would have clutched at her pearls if she'd had pearls to clutch at. "Because I draw the line at zombies."

"Don't be ridiculous. There's no such thing as zombies." The elf prince sniffed. "But you might just turn into one by the time you're done waiting. Come on. Let's get this over with."

The elevator took them—uneventfully, this time—to the first sublevel. Taylor led Julie down a long, grim hallway, then made a left into a cramped waiting room that smelled of ink and old tea. Julie immediately felt that suffocating weight of bureaucracy descend on her shoulders, like it had done the day that she'd gone to the DMV with her mom for her license.

Rows of uncomfortable plastic chairs were crammed close together, lining three walls of the small, hot room. The other side of the room ended in a wood and glass divider. Pale individuals in brown uniforms sat behind the hatches that were placed at regular intervals in the glass, typing busily on clunky old computers. Their hatches were each labeled with a number, all of them invariably faded and peeling.

"Well, this is nice," Julie whispered.

Taylor shuddered. "This place gives me the heebie-jeebies."

"Absolutely useless," Hat sniffed. "I could whip this place right back into shape if I was given command here."

"We know, we know," Taylor muttered.

They trudged across the floor to the hatch labeled "Reception." The chairs they passed were all occupied by paranormals slumped with attitudes of annoyance, boredom, and despair. Their uniforms were from every department in the OPMA.

There were agents in blue, scientists in white lab coats, officers in red, even a couple of other recruiters in olive green.

The whole space was lit by a handful of bare bulbs that hung from the ceiling. One of them wasn't working, casting deep shadows around the room.

A slender Fae sat sandwiched between an orc and a hulking Were whose placid eyes and vast build suggested something vaguely bovine. The Were had his shoulders hunched, shrinking in on himself, but the orc sat with her knees spread wide apart and chewed gum noisily. The Fae seemed to be wishing that he was dead.

Julie peered through the grimy glass at the reception desk. The elf on the other side was broad, portly, and wore a pastel pink twinset and pearls. Her ears jutted out severely on either side of an unbelievably tight bun.

"What do you want?" she growled in a hoarse voice.

Taylor gulped. Julie smiled warmly. "Hi! How are you today?"

Her peppy manner had the opposite of the intended effect on the elf. Her lips drooped ominously. "What do you *want*?"

Julie swallowed. "Um, we need to fill out our paperwork for out-of-state travel. Please."

The elf's eyes were fixed on Taylor. "How about you, *Your Highness*?" Acid dripped from her words.

"Me too," Taylor stammered. "Uh, please. If you don't mind."

The elf leveled a long glare at them both. Someone in the waiting room coughed. If the term "done with your shit" could be mined, this elf's glare would be the motherlode.

"Take a ticket." The elf gestured to a roll of printed tickets on the desk in front of Taylor. "Wait your turn like everyone else."

"But the forms are right there," Taylor pointed out.

The elf's glare intensified and Taylor fell silent.

"Okay," Julie whispered, tearing off a ticket. "Okay."

They backed away, and the elf's furious eyes followed them as they cast around the room for open seats. There were two empty chairs in the mustiest, darkest corner of the room. A preposterously fat dwarf was half-sprawled on one of them, his rheumy eyes staring listlessly at an existence made pointless by the length of time he'd been waiting.

"I'll sit next to him," Taylor whispered.

Julie grinned. "Chivalry isn't dead, after all."

They squeezed themselves into the chairs, Taylor squashed up against Julie, the dwarf making no effort whatsoever to accommodate them. Julie glanced at her ticket. Number 125.

Hatch number two opened slightly to reveal the weary face of a thin young vampire. "Seventy-six," she called.

The skinny Fae leaped to his feet and practically ran across the room.

"Seventy-six?" Julie groaned. "This is going to take a really, *really* long time."

It ended up taking two hours that trickled by like a couple of centuries. Julie scrolled her social media. Taylor played a helicopter game on his phone. Hat resorted to asking them riddles.

Okay, here's a good one. What has four legs in the morning, two at noon, and three in the evening? He hunkered down on Julie's head in anticipation of her answer.

Julie's back ached from the uncomfortable chair. "Taylor, your elbow's in my ribs."

"Sorry." Taylor shifted slightly, eliciting a low growl from the dwarf beside them.

Well? Hat prompted.

Too easy. Julie scoffed inwardly. *A man. A baby crawls on his hands and feet, a young man walks on two feet, and an old man walks with a cane.*

Hat cursed.

Julie smiled. *You're going to have to try harder than a sphinx riddle if you want to catch me.*

The farthest hatch from the door slid open and a bored voice mumbled, "One hundred and twenty-five."

"Finally!" Julie leaped to her feet, clutching her ticket.

Taylor stayed close behind her as she hurried to the hatch. The young vampire behind it looked sallow in her brown uniform. She yawned when they reached her. "What do you need?"

Taylor leaned eagerly on the scarred wood. "Paperwork for out-of-state travel, please."

"Sure." The vampire produced a huge stack of forms from underneath the desk. Julie expected her to take a couple of them off the top and hand them over. However, she opened the hatch as wide as it would go and stuffed the entire pack of forms through it.

Taylor grabbed them before she changed her mind, crumpling a few of the sheets.

Julie beamed. "Thank you!"

The vampire shrugged and looked at her list. "One hundred twenty-six!"

Julie and Taylor hurried to the door, but not before the scary receptionist elf barked, "Your Royal Highness!"

Taylor cringed, then more or less tiptoed back to her desk. "Yes?"

The elf leveled that glare at them again. "Ensure you fill out those forms with total accuracy." She leaned forward, hissing the words. "In *triplicate*."

Taylor gulped. "Yes, ma'am."

They fled the stifling department and got into the blissful cool of the elevator. Hitting the button for the third floor felt like liberation.

Julie waited until the doors were safely closed before speaking. "What was that lady's problem, anyway?"

Taylor grimaced. "I, uh, guess I haven't always been the best at following procedures and filling out paperwork."

Julie took the stack of papers from him and looked down at

the heavy forms. "Well, it's not too late to make a good impression."

"Trust me." Taylor shook his head in sorrow. "It's far too late for some of us."

"Don't be ridiculous." Julie gave him a poke with her elbow. "Wow, it's past one already. Let's go get lunch while we fill that stack out."

"Lunch?" Taylor clutched his stomach. "I thought we'd never eat again."

"Drama queen," Julie chuckled.

Julie and Taylor weren't the only people who'd had a busy morning. The dining hall was still packed as they helped themselves to clam chowder with thick wedges of bread still steaming from the oven.

Julie glanced at the other tables as they left the buffet table and took their seats at the end of one of the three long tables that ran the length of the big room. Many of the paranormals in the room were wearing blue. Agents. Some looked ragged and exhausted. They picked at their chowder, worry lines worn deep into their foreheads.

Julie dipped her bread into her chowder. "I wonder if they caught those escapees yet."

Taylor frowned at her manners and took a genteel nibble on the edge of his. "Me too. I have a feeling they haven't, judging by how defeated these agents look."

Julie spotted Leafeyes and Palladius sitting together at the other end of their table. The elf's cigarette was lit and he sucked at it hungrily while Palladius stared into space.

"They look like shit," Julie remarked. "I'm going over there."

Taylor's eyes widened. "Julie—"

She ignored Taylor's protest, grabbed Hat, and marched over

to where the two agents were sitting. Leafeyes stared right through her, but Palladius spotted her immediately and mustered a smile that barely parted his tangled yellow beard. "Hello, Meadows."

"Hey, guys." Julie cleared her throat. "Looks like you've had a rough morning."

"You could say that again." Leafeyes blinked out of his stupor. "The prisoners got away."

"It's not common knowledge yet. Kaplan's doing a press conference this afternoon." Palladius shook his head. "Terrible thing."

"We can tell you, though." Leafeyes rubbed his temples. "Seeing how you were one of the victims."

"I'm sorry." Julie paused. "Where would they have gone?"

Leafeyes' mouth turned down at the corners. "They got hold of the scientists' access to Switzerland."

Palladius sighed. "They're long gone. Into the Alps and away."

Julie recalled the elevator button marked "Switzerland." She'd accidentally ended up there on her first day at the OPMA. "I'm sorry to hear that."

Leafeyes drew deep on his cigarette. The smoke vanished in a faint shimmer of magic as he exhaled. "Now we don't have any answers."

Palladius waved away the magical residue that hung around Leafeyes. "Not to mention a bunch of dangerous detainees on the loose."

Leafeyes raised his eyebrows at his partner. "So you better take care of yourself, okay?" he told Julie.

"Yeah. Try to stay out of trouble." Palladius patted her on the arm in a fatherly manner.

"I'll do my best." Julie smiled. "Good luck, guys."

"Thank you," the two agents chorused.

It was so strange to talk to paranormals who didn't judge her humanity. Julie wanted to pull up a chair and enjoy a conversation with them, but they looked exhausted so she touched Hat's brim to them and returned to sit with Taylor.

Taylor splashed in his chowder with his spoon, his brow furrowed as she told him everything she'd heard. "It's a problem. I'm glad we're heading for Montana for a few days. Hopefully we'll be well out of the Yetis' reach."

"Why? Because Montana is so much farther from Switzerland than New York is?" Julie snarked.

Taylor rolled his eyes at her. "Montana doesn't have a magic portal to Switzerland."

"Touché." Julie took a bite of the excellent, creamy clam chowder. "We'd better get started on this paperwork, or we're not going anywhere."

She flipped open the first form, fished a pen out of her pocket, and started to scribble answers to the list of questions. "Reason for travel," she mumbled, jotting down *Recruiting*.

It took an inordinately long time to write down all of her personal information, and Julie's chowder had gone cold by the time she got to the end of the page.

"Okay, next page." She flipped it open. "Do we have a case number?"

"Yeah, I've got it here somewhere." Taylor pulled out his phone and thumbed through his notes, then read it aloud.

Julie wrote it down. "Look at you, Mr. Prepared."

Taylor yawned, scribbling away. "Not really. I just hate paperwork, so streamlining the process is in my best interests."

Julie answered a few questions about immunizations. "What do they think I'm going to catch in Montana? Yellow fever?" Her dietary restrictions. "Is this trip catered?"

Taylor chuckled along as Julie snarked her way through the inquisition. She turned the page again and the next question brought her up short.

"What kind of questions are these?" she asked Taylor.

Taylor shrugged without looking up from his forms. "Oh, just the usual."

"What do you mean, 'the usual?'" Julie held up the form and tapped the question. "What on earth is *usual* about asking someone to name their top five favorite national landmarks in order?"

"That's just what they asked." Taylor held up his hands. "Don't shoot the messenger."

"And this! 'What is your approximate tolerance for alcohol?'" Julie laughed. "Is this a joke?"

"You'll like this one." Taylor held up his form. "'Approximately how many bowel movements do you require per day?'"

"Sounds like my mom." Julie snorted. "They'll want my bra size next."

"Oh, yeah." Taylor looked back at his form. "That's on page eighteen."

"What?" Julie flipped through the paperwork. "You've got to be kidding! Oh, you are."

When their paperwork was finally done, Julie and Taylor celebrated with decadent chocolate brownies for dessert. Julie took two to reward herself for working out with Ellie this morning, even though that felt like a million years ago.

The dining hall was almost empty as they wandered back to their table. The tired-looking agents had left, and except for a few paranormals in various uniforms dotted here and there, they were alone. A knot of IT trolls were huddled at the end of the farthest table in the corner. Julie recognized the IT manager, Qbiit leaning over the table and talking rapidly and slamming his hand on the table at intervals.

"Qbiit seems pretty mad," Julie commented, pronouncing the name "Cubert" in the troll style.

"I'll bet he does. It was his team who caused the snafu in containment," Hat grouched.

Julie eyed the trolls as she bit into her brownie, making a sound of appreciation when its richness filled her mouth. She wrinkled her nose in distaste as Qbiit continued. "Is he always such an asshole?"

Qtana was sitting opposite Qbiit, her head hanging as he tore a verbal strip off her. Even her blonde ponytail looked sad and limp and she was blinking rapidly behind her thick glasses, a pink tint to her green skin.

Taylor followed her gaze. "Ugh, yeah. He's got a reputation for having a foul temper."

"Poor Qtana." Julie shook her head. "Remember how she stuck up for me that day that we recruited Ellie?"

Taylor nodded. "I do. She's always been nice to me, too."

"Incompetent troll," Hat opined.

Julie patted his crown lightly. "Oh, come on, Hat. I'm not saying she's brilliant, but I don't think she deserves to get chewed out by Qbiit like that."

Hat sniffed. "She called me senile. Can you believe that? *Senile!*"

Brownies finished, they stopped by the office to drop off the completed paperwork. Julie picked up her backpack and fished around in it for Genevieve's keys. "Do you have an address for Marie Vos?"

"Sure do." Taylor waved his phone, grinning widely. "C'mon! Let's go."

"What's got you all excited?" Julie laughed, following him out of the office.

Taylor's eyes sparkled. "You'll see."

I'm glad he seems to be in a better mood. Julie stepped into the elevator.

Hat snorted. *About time he got over himself.*

Hat! Come on. Give Taylor a break. He's had a hard time, Julie chided.

Hat twitched on her head. *So have you, and you haven't been sulking like an ogre with a headache, have you?*

"Hey, are you two talking about me?" Taylor eyeballed Hat.

Julie winked at him. "Just a little gossip."

Taylor practically bounded across the lobby to the parking lot where Genevieve was waiting. In a few seconds, the big V8 engine was purring happily, and they headed out of the parking lot and into the city to find their next recruit.

CHAPTER EIGHT

"Okay, I don't get it." Julie stopped. "Why are you so excited about going to see a hobo Were-Fox?"

In front of them, just visible through the almost perfectly round hole that allowed a footpath through underneath the 110th Street Bridge, the brilliantly green lawns of Central Park rose and fell, half-hidden among stands of trees. It was a gorgeous day, and bright picnic blankets were spread everywhere. A serious woman, all Botox and gym clothes, jogged past them, headed into the park. An overwhelmed teenage dog walker panted as she was half-dragged past them by her pack of canine charges.

Taylor tugged at her arm. "Come on! It's this way."

Julie jogged to catch up to him as he strode along the concrete pathway, heading for the bridge. "You're acting weird, Taylor. *What* is this way?"

She hadn't been to Central Park often. Reading was more her speed, and besides, it was miles away from her home in Bay Ridge. She found it a little incongruous to see city buildings rising in the distance while greenness stretched out in front of her.

Taylor grinned. "Marie Vos' home."

Julie groaned. "You've been super cryptic ever since we left HQ. I thought maybe she lived in one of those swanky apartments next to the park." She checked her phone again. The GPS appeared to have dropped the little red balloon in the middle of the park at random.

"Just a little farther. Then you'll see *everything*," Taylor promised.

Julie sighed, tugging at Hat. *Help me out here.*

I don't think so. Hat chuckled. *I think you're going to enjoy this surprise.*

What surprise? Julie threw up her hands as Taylor marched purposefully along the path, avoiding a nanny pushing a screaming baby in a stroller. *There's nothing here.*

The bridge was built of old, rustic stone, its texture dappled by the surrounding trees. The stone was finely cut gneiss, Julie remembered from a history book. The grass here was a little overgrown, and a McDonalds cup lay abandoned by the edge of the path leading through the almost perfectly round gap underneath the bridge.

Julie picked up the cup and tossed it into the nearest garbage can as Taylor led her back onto the path. "This is starting to feel like a wild goose chase, my dude."

"Come on." Taylor was practically bouncing in place. He gripped Julie's arm and towed her forward. "You'll see it now."

As they stepped under the bridge, Julie shivered as a sudden tingling rushed over body, like sparks sliding along her skin.

"What the—" She bit the sentence off short as her vision swam and the world tipped queasily under her feet. With a yelp of panic, she grabbed Taylor's arm tightly.

"It's okay! It's okay. We're almost through!" Taylor tugged her forward one more step, and Julie's vision and her sense of balance abruptly returned to normal.

However, there was nothing normal about the scene in front

of her. Julie couldn't help her reaction. She gasped, raising both hands to her mouth.

The park had vanished, replaced by a huge old plaza that was cobbled with stones of all different colors. Some of them sparkled like gems. Five narrow and winding streets led onto the plaza itself, and it was lined with boutique stores and bistros. Banners and flags hung from every surface in brilliant colors from yellow, purple, azure, to deepest crimson and silver. The music that drifted through the plaza out of nowhere was fine and piping, as though moonlight had been turned to melody.

Everywhere Julie looked, the plaza was crowded with paranormals.

Werewolves the size of small ponies loped across the plaza side-by-side. The rest avoided running into them while chatting and hurrying this way and that. Fae with shopping bags over their elbows, a curvaceous elf pushing a cart of fresh vegetables with three little elves clinging to her skirts, a dwarf in a well-cut suit swinging his briefcase as he walked. Julie drank it all in with a sense of wonder.

Through the open door across from where they were standing, she spied a pretty Fae with gossamer wings folded carefully against her back cutting the hair of a heavyset dwarf into a mohawk. Conversation bubbled from the outdoor tables of a restaurant on their left. In the play area beside the tables there was a little castle with a slide on one side. A small boy was repeatedly slithering down it and then turning into a gecko to run back up to the top while his mother sipped her coffee and watched.

Julie's attention was snatched by the sound of hoofbeats. She could only stare as a massive unicorn with rippling muscles under his coat and his horn glinting like diamond in the sunlight trotted into a store, lifting his shimmering hooves delicately over the threshold.

Taylor laughed aloud at her awed silence. "I told you that you'd like it."

"What *is* this place?" Julie asked in a near-whisper.

Instead of answering, Taylor grabbed her arm and pulled her aside as the sound of gigantic, leathery wings filled the plaza.

Julie's heart almost beat out of her chest when a huge, reptilian head with smoke curling from its nostrils appeared from the portal, followed by the rest of what was undeniably a dragon. The massive beast was covered in scales that shimmered in purple, blue, and gold.

The dragon's shadow fell over them as it skimmed above their heads. It flapped a wingspan several times the length of Genevieve and flew in a curving swoop around the plaza. The crowd parted nonchalantly as the dragon folded its wings and plunged toward the cobbles, its attention fixed on Julie.

She stepped back, her heart hammering as the dragon scrutinized her. It blew a plume of smoke that burned her nose, and for a second she was transfixed by its gigantic amber eye before the wind of the dragon's passing buffeted her. Before she realized she was holding her breath, the dragon had launched itself into the sky, rapidly gaining height and vanishing over the pointed rooftops.

Julie became aware that her mouth was hanging open and that she was staring like a complete idiot. When she turned back to Taylor, she couldn't manage a single sound. Her mouth opened and shut a few times like a goldfish.

Taylor's cheeks were bright pink as he laughed. "Looks like you caught the interest of one of the Lords of the Deep."

"Wh-what was that all about?" she stammered.

Taylor shrugged. "Maybe he never saw a human before? I don't know if a human has ever even been here. Truth be told, I was a little worried you wouldn't be able to get in. But it looks like the same mutation that allows you to see us also allows you to go beyond the Veil."

"What is this place?" Julie couldn't help turning slowly, feasting her eyes on the details all around her.

Taylor took her arm and gently guided her out of the way as a carriage shaped like a pumpkin, drawn by six white horses, clattered past. "You've gone beyond the Veil, Julie. You're in the paranormal world."

Julie blinked. "A whole new world?"

"Yes." Taylor grinned. "This is one of my favorite villages. Our Were-Fox lives here."

Julie swallowed, her heart rate beginning to return to normal as Taylor led her to the sidewalk and they headed toward one of the streets branching off from the plaza. "Does this paranormal world have a name?"

Taylor nodded to an elf who bowed to him as she passed. "Avalon, and this is Avalon Town."

Julie's snarkiness returned. "Ooh, original."

Taylor snorted. "It didn't take you long to get over your awe and wonder."

Julie shrugged, noting that the passing elf wasn't the only one keeping a respectful distance. Maybe Taylor underestimated his importance in the paranormal world. "I'm just saying. The name's not very original."

"It is, actually," Taylor told her, oblivious to the attention his presence was garnering. "The original Avalon, I mean."

Julie's jaw dropped again. "Wait, are you saying this is *King Arthur's* Avalon?"

Taylor grinned. "Exactly. This is the village in Avalon that the Lady of the Lake comes from. My grandma used to have tea with Nimue sometimes. Nice lady. Shy."

Something wasn't adding up for Julie. "But shouldn't Avalon be in Britain?"

Taylor waved a hand. "There are portals to Avalon all over the world. This one was placed in Central Park when humans first settled here. I learned about why in history when I was a kid, but honestly I don't remember. I just know it's one of my favorite parts of the paranormal world. The shopping here in the Village is *amazing*."

Julie glanced at the spot in the sky where she'd last seen the dragon, but it was long gone. Another thrill of adrenaline—and something she couldn't identify—ran through her veins at the thought of it. She probed her subconscious for information from the orb.

Dragon: royal family known as Lords of the Deep. After extensive persecution during medieval times, the Eternity Throne passed an edict prohibiting dragons from revealing themselves to humans.

Prohibiting? Julie scoffed inwardly. *I'm not sure anything could stop a dragon from doing whatever it wanted.*

Don't underestimate the power of the Eternity Throne. Hat chuckled. *Enjoying yourself, are you?*

I'd be lying if I said no. Julie stopped to stare through a shop window. There were all sorts of tanks and cages inside. The pen nearest the window contained a diminutive bird with red plumage. Its crest smoked slightly as it cocked its head at her.

"A firebird." Taylor paused next to her. "They live wild in the grounds of the compound where I live. Nuisances, really. One of them set fire to my laundry one time."

"It's pretty cute." Julie reluctantly stepped away from the window. "Are there any good bookstores here?"

"More than you can imagine." Taylor laughed. "But first let's look for that Were-Fox. What's her address again, Hat?"

"She's on Second Street. Number twelve." Hat wriggled on Julie's head. "It's nice to be able to talk aloud in public."

No one in the bustling crowd gave the talking hat a second glance. Julie struggled to peel her gaze away from a group of pixies no bigger than her closed fist, who were perched on teeny chairs on a pedestal outside a nearby coffee shop.

"Don't stare." Taylor pointed at one of the streets leading off the plaza. "Second Street is this way."

"How am I supposed to not stare?" Julie fell into step beside him. "This place is beyond amazing."

The street led them away from the busy market square vibe of the plaza and into the tall buildings that rose on either side. The upper stories looked like apartments, and there were storefronts at the street level, some with sidewalk tables. That was where the resemblance between buildings ended.

On Julie's left, a beautiful old sandstone building rose imperiously above the street. There were shuttered windows with daisies blooming in window boxes up above. At street level, boozy laughter emanated from the narrow wooden door that was propped open with a rock. The hand painted wooden sign hanging from chains over the door read *YE FLOATING FAIRY*.

On Julie's right, the building was a shimmering wall of metal and glass. She could see through the glass into what looked like an elegant boardroom with abstract art on the walls and minimalist modern furniture. Elves in suits were watching a Fae give a presentation on a huge touchscreen.

"All these buildings crammed in together should look like fairy puke, but it's kind of cozy," Julie commented.

Taylor laughed. "If you want to see fairy puke, come visit during a solstice festival. Everyone tears it up to celebrate the turning of the season. It gets wild."

"Things have changed since the last time I was in Avalon," Hat mused.

Julie touched his brim. "This place must have been familiar to you if you were part of the Sword in the Stone myth. Or legend, I suppose, since it's all real."

"Familiar?" Hat laughed. "I was here when Excalibur was forged."

Julie scoffed. "Not to brag, or anything."

"It's not bragging if it's true." Hat squirmed on Julie's head to get a better view of an ancient stone tower sprouting from the sidewalk beside them. "*That* is Merlin's old home. It used to be rather dark and dingy. That was when this was in the middle of nowhere, of course, before this area was built-up."

Julie's neck was beginning to ache from looking left and right. Taylor had to push her sideways to save her from crashing into a streetlight.

"Slow down," he cautioned with a laugh. "You don't have to look at *every* detail right now. Avalon's not going anywhere."

Julie craned her neck to gape at the large, printed sign over the door of the shop across the street. "I've never seen anything like this."

PEST CONTROL EXPERTS!
We will rid your home and garden of:
- Gnomes
- Tokoloshe
- Leprechauns
- Imps
- Curses
- Invisibility spells
- Unwanted charms
- Unexpected guests

"That last one sounds pretty handy, regardless of which world you live in," Julie commented.

"Right? This way." Taylor turned right, leading her across the road and down a tiny, winding street lined with cottages, each more endearing than the next.

Toadstools—real ones—sprouted in many of the gardens. Firebirds fed from enormous pink flowers that Julie couldn't begin to name, their little beaks dripping with nectar. She paused to touch the soft blue petals of a creeper that spilled out onto the cobbled street. The flower jerked back and turned to face her, teeth snarling in its yellow center.

"Shit!" Julie jumped back.

"Oh, yes. Biting daisies are carnivorous." The flower growled at Taylor when he shooed it back. "Down! Bad daisy!"

"I bet Julius Nox would love this." Julie shoved her hands into her pockets, lesson learned.

Taylor snorted. "Oh, no. They're a common weed. A real pain, actually. Their bites itch like mad."

The next cottage had a brass number twelve on the front door, surrounded by hanging baskets full of flowers. Julie made sure not to touch any of them. She rang the bell hanging from a chain beside the door and waited.

The door swung open, revealing a woman whose ponytail was neatly pointed and white at the tips. This was unmistakably Marie Vos. She blinked at them out of huge golden eyes. "Sara's inside. I'll get her for you."

"Are you Marie Vos?" Taylor asked.

Marie smiled, revealing pointy little teeth. "That's me. Aren't you here to see my sister?"

Julie held up her OPMA ID. "Actually, we'd like to talk to you."

"Me?" Marie's eyes widened and her cheeks reddened. "Look, about that wolfsbane, I didn't know it was wolfsbane when I bought it. I thought it was just...well...you know."

"Oh, we're not agents." Julie filed wolfsbane away in the ask Taylor about it later box. "We're recruiters. We would like to offer you an opportunity to join the Para-Military Agency."

Marie raised a hand to her mouth, the end of her ponytail swishing from side to side. "What? Really?"

"We need new recruits to support the cause of the Eternity Throne." Taylor held up her file. "Can we come in? Then we'll be able to tell you more about it."

"Actually..." Marie sighed, her ponytail sagging. "This would be a pretty great opportunity, but I can't leave Avalon right now. I'm living with my sister and she's expecting octuplets."

Julie did some brisk mental math. *Eight babies?*

She is a Were-Fox, you know, Hat reminded her.

"She needs my help right now, and for a few weeks after the

kits are born." Marie bit her lip. "But afterward, I'd love to find out if there's a place for me at OPMA. Do you have a card?"

"I do." Julie fished one out of her pocket and held it out. "You can call me any time when things change for you."

"Thanks. I'm sure I will." Marie flashed that pointy-toothed smile again. "I'd better go. Sara's craving peanut butter and mint cookies and I can't bake fast enough for her."

She closed the door, and Julie turned away, grimacing. "Ew. Peanut butter and mint?"

"I've heard that the larger the litter, the worse the cravings." Taylor sighed. "So much for blowing Kaplan's socks off."

"We still have two weeks. I'll come up with something," Julie promised.

CHAPTER NINE

Taylor checked his watch. "It's nearly five back on the other side. We might as well spend some time shopping, if you want."

"What do you mean, on the other side?" Julie frowned. "Did we cross time zones?"

"Something like that." Taylor laughed and showed her his watch, which had a whole bunch of little faces contained within its large main face. The main face showed the time as ten past three. He tapped one of the smaller faces, which showed three minutes to five. "Time runs differently in Avalon."

"O-*kay*." Julie followed him out of the garden and back down the street, heading toward the plaza. "Hat, please explain?"

"Linear time is a human concept," Hat began. "You know the stories about humans visiting 'fairyland—'"

"*Hat!*" Taylor hissed, glancing around to see if anyone had heard.

"What?" Hat snapped. "I know it's derogatory and inaccurate, but it's the frame of reference she has."

Julie cleared her throat. "I know what you mean. There are plenty of myths about people going...*beyond the Veil*, then coming back decades later without having aged a day. Or coming back days later looking much older."

"That's because humans lack the genetic component that makes it seem like paranormals live longer," Hat explained.

"So it's not that elves are immortal, or, technically, age more slowly than you do." Taylor idly flicked one of the biting daisies. It snapped at him, barely missing his finger. "Our internal clocks just reset regularly."

Julie chewed the inside of her cheek for a few seconds. "Like sea urchins?"

Taylor blinked. "I was expecting bafflement. Sea urchins?"

"You know." Julie gestured. "Small spiky things that live in the sea."

"I know what a sea urchin is." Taylor frowned. "I just don't get what it has to do with elven ageing?"

"Sea urchins regenerate," Julie informed him. "They can regrow limbs, they reproduce for their entire lives, they basically never stop growing, and they exhibit only negligible senescence. Much like a certain elf I know."

Taylor stared at her. "Girl, you're the one who's supposed to be confused here, not me."

Julie tossed her head. "I prefer *woman*."

Taylor shook his head in confusion. "I don't understand a word you just said."

"Sea urchins don't age," Julie translated. "They regrow dying cells and their internal clock resets regularly."

"Okay, whatever you say." Taylor laughed. "You seem to have a handle on this."

They turned back onto the busier street, and Julie inspected Merlin's tower with interest as they passed. It had a sign on it: *Keep Out. No entrance to the public*. A greenish glow emanated from the window high above, which Julie found deeply satisfying.

"What about vampires?" Julie asked. "You said earlier that vamps aren't considered adults until they reach fifty."

"I'm not sure how it works," Taylor admitted. "Something to do with blood that keeps them young."

"The only immortal—or almost immortal—paranormals are dragons." Hat turned on her head to stare up at the tower as they passed. "They're the most magical of us all, and they don't age."

"How about orcs?" Julie straightened Hat slightly when his squirming started to tug at her hair. "Or dwarves? They don't seem to avoid ageing, from what I've seen."

"Near as I can tell, their method is a combination of stubbornness and spite." Taylor snorted. "Especially in the orcs' case."

"This is *much* more complicated than this simple elf would have you believe," Hat muttered.

"Hey, I heard that!" Taylor protested.

"Good for you," Hat retorted.

"Okay, okay." Julie chuckled, holding up both hands. "Cool it, you two. I'm about at my limit for complexity for one day, thanks. Especially if we're going shopping. I assume for whatever we're wearing to the handfasting?"

Taylor's grin broadened. "You assume correctly. The store I'm thinking of is going to blow your mind."

Julie gestured all around her, flailing a little. "Dude! You don't think all this has *already* blown my mind?"

Taylor chuckled. "Oh, I think it can take a little more blowing yet."

Julie didn't voice the fact that she doubted anything could surpass what she'd already seen.

Taylor wasn't wrong. Julie's mind was even more blown by the boutique he took her to. The store's facade was all glass, allowing passersby to look inside. Soft, flattering lighting emanated mysteriously from the walls. Gentle, flutey notes and piano riffs floated out of the open doors, accompanied by a glorious smell. It was fresh and yet spicy at the same time, like a cross between eucalyptus and cinnamon.

That was nothing compared to the designs hanging on the mannequins in the display window. Julie realized that her mouth was open and she was staring, but she couldn't stop. Some of the dresses were made of fabrics she could name. Shimmery tulle, delicate lace, strong and shiny mikado. But the majority of the clothing on display defied explanation. There was a blue material that rippled and flowed over the mannequin's curves like real water. Another mannequin wore a scarf that resembled a captive fluffy cloud.

"If you're going to stare, at least shut your mouth," Hat whispered.

Julie obeyed and followed Taylor into the store on numb feet, reading the sign in a modern, understated script over the door: *Iris*. The simplicity of the name told her that it was supposed to say it all.

Once inside the store, Julie glanced at the dressing rooms near the back. They had satin curtains and little catwalks surrounded by mirrors and lit from underneath. A nearby dress caught her attention next. It was hunter green and studded with gold and blue butterflies whose wings opened and shut gently in the air conditioning.

"What do you think?" Taylor asked.

Julie stared at him, then back at the dress. Nothing here had a price tag on it. She guessed that if one cared about price tags, one didn't belong here. "It's a good job I'm helping you get back at your family. Otherwise I'd have to take that second job on the pole after all to afford shopping here."

Taylor raised his eyebrows. "Pole?"

Julie half groaned, half laughed. "It's a running joke between me and my mom. She tried to get me to sign up as a stripper before I got the job at OPMA."

"Oh, um..." Taylor's eyes flickered as he fought the involuntary urge to stare at her body, then he focused somewhere just above her head. "Ah, I—"

"Excuse me, madam," a sharp voice interjected. "May I help you?"

Julie turned to her left. The elf who had approached them was impeccably dressed in a burgundy suit and had gemstones glimmering at her throat. The nametag on her chest read *Mikayla*, and in smaller letters underneath it, *Sales*.

Julie winced. Judging by the look on the elf's face, which said that she would like to toss Julie out on her ass, she had overheard the stripper comment.

Raising her chin, Mikayla stared haughtily at Julie, waiting for an answer.

Julie forced a smile. "I'm looking for a dress. For a handfasting."

"I see." Mikayla's eyes traveled up and down Julie's body, the corners of her mouth turning down. "I'm afraid I'm not sure we have anything to suit your kind."

"What's that supposed to mean?" Julie snapped. *"Your kind?"*

"Well, madam, we generally do not serve..." Mikayla paused, then almost whispered the word. *"Humans."*

"Now look here," Taylor spluttered.

"Tayyyyy!" a melodic voice squealed, and another elf emerged from the mannequins. She charged across the shop floor, bumped Mikayla bodily out of the way, and threw her arms around Taylor.

Julie stared. This new elf's torrent of wavy brunette hair reached well below the end of her figure-hugging mini dress, which was made of what appeared to be the night sky. She would have thought that the silky black material was covered in glimmering diamonds if not for the way they twinkled like real stars. Her simple black heels were both elegant and understated, and she wore a single diamond pendant on her necklace and matching stones in each ear.

When she finally let go of Taylor and stepped back, still gripping his hands, her smile was wide and guileless.

"Who's this, Taylor?" Julie asked, trying not to feel intimidated by the elf's beauty and her apparent closeness to her partner. "Your girlfriend?"

The elf laughed musically. "I was just going to ask him the same thing about you." She let go of Taylor's hands and gave him a playful bump with her hip. "She's quite the catch, Tay."

Taylor groaned. "Don't listen to her, Julie. This is my best friend from childhood, Iris."

"Iris?" Julie blinked in surprise. "As in, the Iris from the sign over the door?"

"That's right. I'm the owner and designer." Iris beamed, holding out her arms. "*You're* the famous Julie? It's great to meet you! Tay's told me so much about you! Come over here and give me a hug. You deserve it for getting this idiot out of his shell."

Julie laughed, embracing the elf briefly. She smelled glorious: sweet, exotic, and sexy. "Your place is amazing. I can't believe I'm even allowed in here."

Iris scoffed. "Don't mind Mikayla. She's a snob, but I have customers who love her for some reason." Squealing, the elf interlaced both hands under her chin. "I just can't wait to dress a human! You *did* bring her here so that I could dress her, right, Tay?"

Taylor grinned wickedly, spreading his hands. "She's all yours."

"Merlin's cotton socks!" Iris twirled, eliciting a silky rustle from her dress. "This is, like, the best day of my *life*. Come on, Julie." She grabbed Julie's arm. "To the dressing room!"

Julie found herself being borne helplessly through the store on a tide of excitement. Skipping the catwalks and silk curtains, Iris led her and Taylor into a private dressing room in the back.

"Isn't this where you meet with exclusive clients?" Taylor whispered, glancing around the room.

Iris beamed. "Only the best for my bestie, of course."

This dressing room was just as grand as the rest of the store. The floor of the carpeted sitting area was thick and soft under Julie's feet as she walked to the plush sofa that had a low table in front of it. One corner was curtained off, and the other half of the room had a marble floor and mirrored walls with a circular plinth in the middle like the one Julie had seen in *Say Yes to the Dress*.

"Have a seat, both of you." Iris towed Julie over to the sofa and plumped the cushions before letting her sit down. "You can eat paranormal food, right?"

"Uh, yeah." Julie sank onto the sofa beside Taylor, overwhelmed by the opulence. The sofa was comfier than any bed she'd ever slept in.

"Wonderful!" Iris bustled out of the room, reappearing a few seconds later with a tray of tiny, exquisite nibbles. She set them down on the table and added an ice bucket containing a bottle of champagne.

"These are so pretty," Julie breathed, looking over the diminutive cakes and savory bites.

"Wait till you see my dresses!" Iris trilled. She perched on a chair opposite them. "So, what exactly are you looking for?"

Julie couldn't resist taking one of the cakes. "Well, I'm going to the Nox handfasting, and it's black tie."

"Wait, *Malcolm* Nox's handfasting? That's amazing!" Iris gushed. "It's the social event of the year. That means we can go all out without worrying about you being overdressed."

Julie had expected her to say something about how strange it was for a human to be invited, but the elf's smile only widened. "Nox events are incredible. You're going to have such a great time! *And* you're going to look absolutely gorgeous."

"Thanks." Julie couldn't help joining in with her giggle.

Iris popped the champagne expertly and poured it into two long flutes. "So, what colors do you like best? Specific cuts? Styles?"

"I like purple and black," Julie hedged. "But honestly, I have no idea about the rest of it. I borrowed my prom dress from my aunt. It's all new to me."

"Paranormal black tie isn't quite the same thing as human black tie, either," Taylor chipped in, taking one of the flutes. "And a handfasting ceremony has its own twist on the dress code."

"Human dress codes are complicated enough," Julie admitted. "I'm feeling a little lost."

"That's why I brought you here." Taylor nodded at Iris. "She's the best. She'll have exactly what you need."

"I certainly will!" Iris clasped her hands. "This is *so* great. I'm so excited to finally meet you, Julie. Dressing you is going to be my privilege!"

"Hey, what about me?" Taylor teased.

Iris scoffed, tossing her hair. "I've dressed you since you were a kid. You're boring."

Taylor laughed. "Hey, no fair!"

Iris left the room again. This time she returned with a long rolling rack of gowns that made Julie gasp all over again. Some of them stirred quietly in a magical breeze. One had a waterfall instead of a hem. The steady sound of rushing water filled the room, although the carpet underneath the dress didn't look like it was getting wet.

Iris wheeled the rack behind the silk curtain and held it open. "Let's try a few things and see what you like. Ready?"

"Ready." Julie put down her flute and handed Hat to Taylor, who leaned back on the sofa with a wide grin and crossed his legs.

Iris closed the curtain behind her, and Julie felt a momentary pang of terror as the elf lifted a long column dress from the rack.

There was no way she was going to be able to get into that on her own. Iris held the dress up with an expectant smile on her face. Was she supposed to *strip*, right here, in front of this drop-dead-stunning elf?

Julie took a deep breath and told herself that Iris had seen a whole variety of bodies in this dressing room, then slipped out of her shirt and jeans.

"Here you are. Arms up," Iris instructed.

Julie did as she was told, and the elf slid the dress over her head with a practiced movement. Iris was matter-of-fact and businesslike. She fussed around the skirt, smoothing it out and straightening it. A breath of relief rushed out of Julie. It was okay.

"There!" Iris stepped back, beaming at her. "Let's see what you think."

She pulled the curtains aside, and Julie stepped out in front of the mirrors. Taylor wolf whistled.

"Tay, cut it out!" Iris giggled. "Here—let me help you up."

Julie stuck out her tongue at Taylor and stepped onto the plinth, then turned this way and that in front of the mirrors, awed. The silky lavender fabric hugged her body like it had been made exactly to her measurements. When she raised her arms to admire the way the sleeves flowed against her skin, the scent of fresh lavender filled her senses.

"Whoa," she murmured. "That's pretty cool."

"All of my dresses are magically fragranced." Iris smiled at her in the mirror. "Do you like it?"

"It's *incredible*. I've never seen anything like it." Julie looked over at Taylor. "What do you think?"

Taylor did a chef's kiss. "Your ass is on point in this one."

"Ignore the vulgar peasant," Iris scoffed. "Okay, so we'll jot this down as a maybe."

Julie wasn't sure what Iris meant by *maybe*. She'd never worn anything so perfect in her life, but Iris seemed bent on her trying on some other dresses so she allowed herself to be towed back into the curtained area, stripped of the lavender dress, and gently stuffed into a fluid black A-line with a V neck and long, wide sleeves that tapered to points hanging almost as low as the hem of the floor-length gown.

"It's *so* pretty," Julie gushed, touching the velvety fabric reverently.

"Wait a moment. It's not quite ready." Iris waved a hand over the skirt, and with a soft hiss, yellow flames appeared and cascaded down to the hem.

Julie yelped and snatched her fingers back.

Iris laughed. "It's okay. It's magical fire. It won't hurt you."

The fire crackled around Julie's ankles as she stepped onto the plinth. Taylor barely gave the fire a second glance. "I liked the other one better," he offered.

"As if anyone asked you!" Iris laughed. "What do you think, Julie?"

The flames rippled in Julie's reflection. She smiled. "I think it suits me."

"So do I." Iris grinned, leaning a little closer. "It brings out your inner badass."

"That it does!" Hat called.

Julie giggled and ran her hands over the beautiful, soft fabric. "I usually shop at consignment sales and thrift stores. I've found some great things there in my budget, but this is an amazing experience. You're so talented, even without the magical effects."

Taylor grinned. "Today you're getting the royal treatment."

"Aw, you should have been born into royalty so you could have this treatment every day!" Iris winked at her in the mirror. "I've got one more for you to try. I think this one's going to be the winner."

The black dress hugged her curves so perfectly that Julie expected to struggle her way out of it after Iris had extinguished the magical flames. However, it slid off as easily as a sweatshirt.

"You must have a lot of elves or models in my size," Julie commented.

"Oh, no. The adjustments are all magically done as soon as you put on the dresses. They relax again so that the dresses are easy to take off." Iris beamed. "A little charm I invented myself. Like it?"

"I love it." Julie watched as Iris selected another dress.

This one was sapphire blue, with lace and ruffles and a huge poofy ballgown skirt. Julie hesitated as Iris held it up for her. "I'm not sure," she admitted. "It might be a bit much."

"Hey, don't decline a dress just because you hate it on the hanger." Iris held it out. "It can't hurt to try it on, right?"

"Nothing is too much for a Nox event," Taylor reminded her.

Julie shrugged. "Okay."

She held up her arms as Iris slid the dress over her head, and felt the fabric cinch itself magically around her body. When she stepped out from behind the curtains, the first thing she saw was Taylor's face. He'd been on his phone, probably playing a game, but when she stepped out, his eyes all but popped out.

"Whoa," he murmured. "Who are you, and what have you done with Julie?"

"Now *there's* a princess worth slaying dragons for," Hat whispered.

"Sexist," Julie countered, suppressing a smile. She *did* feel like a princess in this dress, but she'd never admit it.

She stepped onto the plinth and looked in the mirror, and her heart fluttered in her chest. The lace detailing on the bodice glittered with embellishments and blood-red roses. Julie touched the petals. They were velvety and real. The gown hugged her figure perfectly, then curved out in a ballgown skirt that seemed to make her two inches taller. The layers of petticoats made a rich, rustling sound when she moved, and she couldn't help gripping it gently with both hands and turning this way and that.

"See that?" Iris pointed at Julie, her eyes shining. "That's how you know a girl's found her perfect dress. When she does that."

Julie giggled without meaning to. "I *love* it. Can I take this one?" She looked at Taylor, who was nodding enthusiastically without saying a word.

"Shut your mouth before a fly goes into it," Iris chided with a chuckle.

Taylor shut his mouth and nodded enthusiastically. "Only the best for your bestie, right, Iris?"

"Only the best," Iris confirmed.

Julie almost wished she didn't have to take off the dress, but it felt good to slip back into her jeans and jacket. Iris hung the dress over her arm and winked at her. "I'll get this wrapped for you."

Julie hugged the elf. "Thank you so much. I had a great time trying them all on."

Iris laughed. "Anytime. You were a dream to dress, by the way. Everything looks fabulous on you."

Iris left the room with the dress over her arm, and Julie stepped out into the sitting area as Taylor knocked back the last of his champagne. "Ready to go?" He scooped up Hat and held him out to her.

"Yeah, thanks." Julie took Hat and popped him back onto her head. "Hey, Taylor, thanks for this. This was amazing."

"I'm glad you liked it." Taylor grinned mischievously. "Thank you, too. I think I'm about to make a suitably large hole in the trust fund."

They stepped out of the dressing room and headed for the shop floor, passing a doorway leading to what Julie assumed was another private dressing room. The door was slightly ajar, and a familiar voice floated through it.

"A *human*! An actual *human*! At *my* handfasting!" it wailed. "Can you *believe* the insult?"

Julie froze. Taylor's eyes darted to hers, widening.

"I can't believe Julius invited her," the voice went on. "A *human*! What are we going to invite next, stray dogs?"

Julie felt her cheeks flush with heat. She gripped Taylor's arm. "Come on," she whispered. "Let's just go."

"No, wait," he hissed. "Is that her? Cassidy? Malcolm's betrothed?"

Julie grimaced. "Yes."

"So she's talking about you," Taylor growled.

A few other feminine vampire voices chorused their agreement.

"I mean, since when has a human ever been invited to a Nox family event?" one of them protested. "It's utter madness. Julius has only ever met her once, you said?"

"Once!" Cassidy fumed. "Malcolm's met her two or three times. That's all. It's not as if they're friends at all."

"Never mind the part where you saved his life!" Taylor snarled.

"It's ruining the whole experience for me," Cassidy moaned. "I mean, look at this! I'm supposed to be enjoying shopping for my handfasting dress, not thinking about the *human* who's going to be there!"

"Well, I certainly thought that the Nox family was above inviting rabble to such an exclusive event," another vampire huffed. "What is the world coming to?"

"I don't know. I thought I was marrying into a classy family." Cassidy sniffed. "Seems like maybe I was mistaken, if they so closely associated with humans."

"Okay, that's it." Taylor bunched his hands into fists and stepped forward.

"Taylor, no." Julie grabbed his arm and dragged him away from the door. "Let's just go."

The shop floor's sights, scents and music seemed a little less magical as they walked up to the counter. Taylor's cheeks were colored with rage. "Don't pay any attention to them, Julie," he growled. "They don't know what they're talking about."

"It's high time the paranormal world lost some of its prejudices." Hat hunkered down close on Julie's head, squeezing her in a hug. "I'm sorry you had to hear that."

"It's okay, guys. Seriously." Julie tried to laugh off the sting of the vampires' mean girl attitudes. "I mean, it's not the first time."

"She's wrong, and stupid, and ugly on the inside, where it counts," Taylor told her.

"And very, very wrong," Hat added.

Iris met them at the counter with a garment bag that rustled wonderfully. "Here you are!" She draped the bag on the counter. "All yours." Her smile faded a little when she looked at Julie's face. "Hey, what's wrong? Don't you like it?"

"Oh, no. I *love* the dress." Julie forced her smile back in place. "It's just—"

A clatter of heels on the polished floor made them all look up. Cassidy and a horde of glamorous vampires swept across the store. All of them wore long veils, but that didn't hide the way Cassidy's red eyes drilled into Julie even from a distance.

"I'm trying on dresses at a few different stores too, Iris," she called without taking her eyes off Julie. "I'll let you know what I decide."

"That's fine. Thank you for coming." Iris' tone was clipped. "I look forward to hearing from you."

"Oh, you might not." Cassidy tossed back her head, still glaring at Julie. "It's sad to see Iris Fashions getting so rundown. You should consider not letting just any old riff-raff in here. It's bringing down the value of your business."

With that, Vampzilla and her flying monkeys swept out of the store. Julie felt hot, angry tears prickle behind her eyes. She turned to Iris. "Iris, I'm so sorry. I didn't mean to cost you her business."

"You didn't. Don't you give them another moment's thought,

Julie." Iris reached over the counter and squeezed her shoulder. "I could recommend a trash heap where Cassidy and her friends would fit in just fine."

Julie blinked back the sudden sting in her eyes. "But she said, about your business—"

Iris waved off her concern. "Don't you worry about the business. I can do just fine without the likes of her. Between you and me, if I could get away with lacing their dresses with holy water, I would."

"Yeah." Taylor leaned an elbow on Julie's shoulder. "If a sprinkling of garlic powder finds its way into their bags, I'd gladly take the blame. I know you said she wasn't nice, Julie, but..." He blew out a breath. "I feel sorry for Malcolm."

Julie's smile came more easily. "Thanks, guys. Thanks for everything, both of you."

"Any time, Julie." Iris beamed. "Hey, we should grab a coffee sometime."

"That would be great." Julie hesitated. "I don't suppose you could text me from here?"

"It's Avalon, darling, not the nineteenth century. What's your number?" Iris laughed and produced the latest iPhone from her pocket and typed Julie's number into it. "Great. I'll text you."

"I look forward to it." Julie waved as they headed for the door. "See you."

"So?" Taylor asked as he took the bag and slung it over his shoulder. "How did you like your first trip to Avalon?"

"It was really great, actually." Julie straightened Hat, deciding not to let Cassidy pour water over the magical experience. "You guys hit it out of the park with this surprise."

"Thank you," Hat purred.

"We saw some amazing things, I almost got eaten by a daisy, I got the loveliest ballgown ever, and I made a new friend." Julie savored the warmth she felt. "A good day. I'm particularly pleased about that last one, though. My social life needs a necromancer to revive it at this point."

Taylor spluttered, pressing a hand to his chest. "What am I, chopped liver?"

Julie bumped him with her shoulder, laughing. "Pretty much."

They crossed the bustling plaza, and before heading underneath the bridge, Julie took a look back at Avalon. The paranormal world was even bigger than she'd thought, and she'd barely scratched the surface.

CHAPTER TEN

Hat was in his purple beret form today. He hopped from Genevieve's passenger seat onto the dashboard and positioned himself to catch the sun. "I'm glad to be a little more cheerful than yesterday. Being a gray beanie got old."

Julie laughed at him, signaling as she changed lanes and turned toward the Verrazzano-Narrows Bridge. "It was cold for May, okay? My ears needed you."

"At least I could be on sleep mode for most of it." Hat wriggled around to face the windshield. "I don't know if we've ever had a more boring workday than yesterday."

"I was ready for a boring day after our visit to Avalon on Monday." Julie couldn't help grinning wildly at the memory. "It was so much fun, but exhausting."

Hat scoffed. "Yet you still had enough energy yesterday to spend a couple of hours running errands for Lillie."

"Hey, Lillie needed me." Julie slowed down as Genevieve joined the gridlocked traffic on the bridge. "I'm starting to worry about her. Did you notice I had to remind her three times to put the cream in the fridge?"

Hat made a sound of concern. "I did."

"I can't remember her being that forgetful when I first moved in." Julie glanced at her reflection in the rearview mirror and straightened a stray hair on her forehead. "Maybe going for that road trip we planned will help her." She patted Genevieve's wheel. "Lillie loves you, big girl."

The traffic had just started to flow more normally after leaving the bridge when Julie's phone binged once, then twice.

"Ooh, I hope it's Iris." She glanced at Hat. "Can you check?"

"Do I look like a text reader to you?" Hat scoffed.

"I was just asking." Her phone buzzed, and its Bach ringtone filled the car. Merging with flowing traffic, Julie didn't look down, letting it ring to voicemail.

Bing, bing! Two more texts.

"Someone really wants to talk to you," Hat remarked.

"Yeah, well, I'm driving. They'll have to wait." Julie patted Genevieve's dashboard. "She's not the kind of girl who settles for only half of my attention."

Bach resounded stridently from Julie's phone again. Wincing at the tinny sound from the phone's speaker, Julie reached over and muted it without taking her eyes off the bustling road. She still heard it buzz several more times before she drove up the street leading to OPMA HQ.

She rolled to a halt several hundred feet from the gates. A row of vehicles waited in front of her. SUVs, cars, a carriage drawn by a pair of winged horses that shimmered with the illusion spell cast over them, and Sleipnir. He whinnied when he saw Julie, causing his rider to struggle with him for several moments.

"What's all this?" Julie muttered. "There's never a queue to get into HQ."

Since they were at a standstill, she picked up her phone and thumbed quickly through the new texts. They were all from Taylor.

Something weird at HQ. There's a queue at the gates. IDK what's happening.

Something's going down.

You have (1) missed call from Taylor.

Increased security. Lots of questions!! Call me.

Julie, call me!

You have (2) missed calls from Taylor.

?????

The final text was a bunch of random emojis.

Julie rolled her eyes. "What's he freaking out about?"

Hat's voice was unexpectedly grim. "Something's not right."

Julie put her phone aside as the queue crept forward. Slowly, she followed the various vehicles up to the gates and eventually turned in and stopped by the guardhouse.

Fred Orloffson, the blue-uniformed dwarf who was the gate guard during the day, was looking even less friendly than normal. His face was a wrinkled frown over the rich red beard that cascaded over his short body.

Julie rolled down the window manually, with some effort. "Hey, Fred!" She flashed her ID card.

"Sit still." Fred pulled out a wand. An actual wand, with a big glowing magic jewel in the end. "This won't take long."

Julie stared at the wand in confusion. "What's going on, Fred?"

"Sit still," Fred repeated. He walked around Genevieve, waving the wand up and down the car like a metal detector. When he reached the driver's door again, he stepped back. "Please step out of the car."

"Okay, sure. What's up with all this?" Julie stepped out, swiping Hat from the dashboard and jamming him over her head. "Normally you just look at my vehicle pass and I drive in."

Fred gave her a long look, and for a second Julie thought she saw tears in his eyes. Then he held up the wand. "Spread your arms and legs."

"Don't be getting frisky on me, now." Julie spread her feet and held her arms up, and Fred waved the wand up and down her body. It didn't do anything.

Fred nodded and set down the wand, then picked up a clipboard. "Name and species," he grunted.

Julie looked at him incredulously. "Fred, come on. You see me drive in here every day."

Fred pressed his lips together. "*Name* and *species*, if you please."

Julie searched his face, but it was as unreadable as a brick wall. She relented. "Julie Meadows. Human."

He scribbled it down. "What is the purpose of your trip to this building?"

"Uh, I work here?" Julie told him. "You know this, man."

"In what department?" Fred persisted.

"Recruitment." Julie tapped the ID badge she'd clipped to the front of her jacket, which matched the beret. "Says so right here."

"What type and level of magic powers do you possess?" Fred didn't look up from his clipboard.

Julie rolled her eyes in annoyance. "Dude. *None*. I'm human, remember?"

"Do you have in your possession any magical artifacts, including, but not limited to: staves, wands, rings of power, invisibility cloaks, cloaks of levitation, amulets, powerful gemstones, magic mirrors, grimoires, or enchanted objects?" Fred droned.

"Can't you just tell me what's happening?" Julie pulled Hat off and held him in front of her.

Fred didn't look up. "Please answer the question, Miss Meadows."

Julie sighed. "Okay, sure. I do have a magical artifact. DUMB LE Dork, the old system."

Fred barely glanced at Hat as he scribbled on his clipboard again. "Are you carrying any weapons, including, but not limited to: swords, bows, arrows, clubs, a sling, firearms, cannons, death curses, potions, axes, trebuchets, tridents, bolts of lightning, or hammers?"

"None of those," Julie answered. "Unfortunately. They all sound pretty epic."

"Very well." Fred stepped back. "Anything else to declare?"

Julie held up a hand.

Julie, tell me you're not going to do the whole "All this" routine, Hat groaned.

Okay, fine. Maybe this isn't the time. Julie let her hand fall back to her side. "No, Fred. Not a thing."

Fred peered at Genevieve. "Is your conveyance magical or nonmagical?"

"I guess it depends on who you ask." She reached back and ran a hand along Genevieve's roof. "But she's nonmagical."

Fred raised bushy eyebrows. "Are you sure about that?"

"Pretty sure, yeah." Julie patted the door. "But you're magical in your own way, aren't you, Genny?"

Fred stared at her.

Julie swallowed. "A joke. I was joking."

He stared at her for another long moment, then stepped back and gestured vaguely at the building behind him. "All right. You may proceed."

It was a quarter to nine by the time Julie finally jogged into the gym, panting, only to find that Taylor was outside waiting for her.

His hands were shoved into the pockets of his suit, and his

forehead was deeply furrowed. "Julie! I'm glad you got through security okay."

"What on Earth is going on?" Julie straightened Hat. Guards in blue uniform were everywhere, watching them with wary eyes.

"Let's get to our office." Taylor shivered. "Nobody's in the gym. I think it's best we miss our training session for today."

Julie followed him toward the main building. "But what's happening?"

Nothing good, Hat muttered. *The whole department is on red alert. There's been a breach.*

"A breach?" Julie echoed.

"Yes." Taylor's mouth flattened into a thin line.

There were four guards at the entrance hall door. They checked Julie and Taylor's IDs before allowing them inside.

Julie swallowed despite her dry mouth as they entered the hall. It was swarming with soldiers in blue, white-coated scientists, and an abundance of trolls with the blue "IT" in a circle on the backs of their lab coats. The elevator was closed, danger tape crisscrossing the doors, and glowing symbols had been drawn on the doorway all around it.

"A protective spell." Taylor led Julie to a side door. "We'll have to take the stairs."

The stairwell was bustling with paras, mostly scientists examining the walls like they expected something creepy to crawl out of them.

Julie stuck close to Taylor as they climbed the stairs. "Okay, I'm freaking out now. Can you tell me what's going on?"

Taylor's shoulders slumped. "There isn't any easy way to say this. A group of Yetis broke through from Switzerland in the night. They killed a bunch of scientists, and two agents."

Julie's heart thudded painfully against her ribs when he dropped his gaze to the floor. "Anyone we know?"

"I'm sorry, Julie." Taylor put a hand on her shoulder. "They killed Leafeyes and Palladius."

The world tilted under Julie's feet. *So you better take care of yourself, okay? Yeah. Try to stay out of trouble.* The last words that the two agents had spoken to her echoed through her mind.

"They were so good to me," she whispered.

"I know. I'm sorry." Taylor tugged at her sleeve. "Come on. Let's get out of the way. They're investigating here."

Julie plodded after him, a nasty hollow in the pit of her stomach.

Are you okay? Hat murmured.

I barely knew them. Julie wiped away tears before Taylor could see them. *But this...* She tried not to think about her dad, and how suddenly he'd been wrenched away from her.

The door at the end of the stairs was open, and Captain Kaplan was down on one knee beside it, examining the doorframe. Or...*sniffing* the doorframe? Julie blinked. He was definitely sniffing.

Taylor cleared his throat to get Kaplan's attention. "Good morning, Captain."

The captain looked up, his huge brows knitting, and rose to his feet. "Woodskin! Meadows! Have you brought me that recruit yet?"

"It's been two days, sir," Julie stated in a numb voice. "We're good, but we're not *that* good."

Kaplan narrowed his eyes. "I need action from you, Meadows, not attitude. We're down two agents and we can't afford the losses."

Julie swallowed, looking away.

Taylor stepped forward. "Sir, we've spoken to one potential recruit already and we'll be flying out to see another as soon as our paperwork is approved."

"Consider it approved," Kaplan ground out. "Now get your asses on a plane."

Getting out of HQ had been almost as difficult as getting in, but once Fred had searched Genevieve for stolen artifacts and Julie had left the campus, the traffic had thinned. She gunned the engine as soon as they reached the freeway, and Genevieve ate up the miles with the insatiable roar of three hundred and seventy-five horses.

When she got home and hit the button on her remote to open the garage door, a tiny, scruffy shape shot out from under the half-open door and bolted down the street.

"*Shit!*" Julie leaped out of Genevieve, leaving the engine running. "Pookie! Pookie, get back here!"

The little dog scampered along the sidewalk, narrowly dodging a guy on a bicycle. Julie's heart hammered in her mouth.

Keep your voice calm, Hat instructed, *or you'll only frighten her more.*

Helpful! Julie spat inwardly. "Pookie! Here, girl! Come here!"

Pookie stopped and turned to look back at her over the scruffy hair around her eyes. Julie crouched and held out a hand. "C'mon, Pookie. Come here to Auntie Julie. That's a good girl."

An engine rumbled at the end of the street, and a beat-up sedan pulled out and thundered toward them. The little dog looked tiny in the face of the approaching car.

"Pookie, please. Come on. Come here," Julie called.

Pookie turned around and ambled to Julie. With a gasp of relief, Julie swept the dog into her arms just as the sedan drove past, narrowly missing the back of Genevieve.

"Good girl. Good little girl." Julie's arms were shaking as she scrambled back into Genevieve. She balanced Pookie on her lap and drove into the garage.

Hey, deep breaths, Hat soothed. *It's okay. You're unusually riled up. I didn't know you were so attached to Lillie's dog.*

It's not just the dog, Hat. Julie made sure the garage was completely closed before getting out of Genevieve, Pookie tucked under her arm. *Lillie would be completely devastated if something happened to her pets. I don't know how much more devastation she can handle.*

Lillie's back door was wide open. Julie had a nasty pang in the pit of her stomach as she hurried up to it, but when she stepped inside, the old lady was on the couch, watching *Judge Judy* and petting the fluffy cat, which lay on her lap.

"Hey, Lillie," Julie shouted over the sound of a young man nervously trying to defend himself under Judge Judy's irate gaze.

Lille jumped, muting the TV. "Julie! You're home early. Are you okay?"

"Everything's fine." Julie shut the back door and put Pookie down on the floor. "Pookie ran out when I opened the garage door. I'm sorry about that. I didn't know you kept the back door open during the day."

"Oh, I never do, dear." Lillie shook her head. "I don't like the draft that blows in under the garage door. But Pookie wouldn't run out. She's a good girl."

The dog jumped onto the sofa, and Lillie petted her. "You're a good girl, aren't you?"

Julie didn't know what to say. She glanced into the kitchen and noticed that Pookie's water bowl was dry. She went inside to fill it and took a surreptitious peep inside the fridge. She'd made sure it was well-stocked yesterday, but she still made a mental note to call the burger place down the road and have them deliver something tonight, just in case.

No wonder the dog ran out, if she didn't have water, Hat mused.

Lillie's never forgotten to fill Pookie's water before. Julie sighed, setting the bowl down on the floor. *I hope she'll be okay while I'm gone.*

Lillie squinted at her as she came back into the living room. "So, why are you home so early, dear?"

Julie perched on the armrest of the sofa. "I'm afraid I have to go away for the night, Lillie. I've got a work emergency and I have to fly out to Montana this afternoon."

"An emergency?" Lillie raised an eyebrow. "What kind of emergency do you insurance people have?"

Julie hesitated.

"Oh, ignore me, dear. I'm a silly old bat." Lillie waved a hand. "Will you be all right?"

"I'll be fine." Julie reached over and squeezed Lillie's arm. "I'm a bit worried about you."

"Don't you worry, dear." Lillie cackled, patting a large wooden box that had been pushed underneath the sofa. "I've still got my permit for the shotgun, and I might not be able to see much of a target, but that's exactly what a shotgun is for, isn't it?"

"Lillie!" Julie gasped.

"A woman's gotta defend herself, honey. You should get yourself a little something, too. My sister always kept a Colt in Genevieve's glovebox. Maybe it's still there." Lillie sighed, seeming to shrink a few inches. "I don't remember."

Julie had cleaned out the glovebox recently. She was relieved she hadn't found any random old guns in it. "I'll call every night, okay? I'm sorry. I need to hurry."

"Go, dear, go." Lillie flapped a hand.

Julie hurried up the stairs to her apartment. She tossed Hat onto the counter and grabbed a duffel bag from under her bed. "Okay, okay. Packing for Montana... What's the weather going to be like?"

"Tomorrow's forecast is a high of sixty-five with a low of thirty." Hat hopped from the counter to her kitchen table to the comfy chair beside her bed. "Pack comfortable clothes for the flights, too. They're going to be long."

"Thanks." Julie opened her closet and grabbed a few things. "What should I take for the flight?" She remembered her flight to DC. "Airline snacks are so overpriced."

Hat chuckled. "You've got a travel allowance, remember? You have layovers, so you can get meals at the airports."

"So, no snacks. Got it." Julie considered her closet for a moment, then chose a couple of smart outfits plus a pair of sweatpants. "I guess I'll need my earphones."

Hat straightened with pride. "Not necessarily. I'll be putting a magical privacy bubble around you two so that you can discuss paranormal stuff without the humans hearing."

"Sounds good," Julie told him. She grabbed her Chromebook and stuffed it in, then reached for her pepper spray. "Oh, and this."

"No, no, *no*. Not that."

"Why not?" Julie shook it. "Might be creeps out there in Montana, too."

"Because I'm pretty sure taking *that* on a plane will be asking for trouble." For someone with no eyes, Hat was doing a great job of eyeing the spray bottle. "I'm fairly sure that counts as a low-grade explosive."

Julie's phone buzzed just as she was zipping up the bag. It was a text from Taylor.

I'm outside.

Be right down, Julie typed.

She hooked the bag over her shoulder and donned Hat, then clattered down the wooden steps. Lillie had left the back door open again. Julie made sure Pookie and the cat were inside before sticking her head through it.

"Okay, Lillie, I'm leaving," she called. "My colleague's here to pick me up."

Lillie blinked up at her. "All right, dear. See you tonight."

Julie's stomach clenched. "Um, I'm going to be away

overnight, Lillie. I'll see you tomorrow night, okay? Probably quite late. I'll call you, though."

"Oh, yes, of course." Lillie got up and doddered over to pat Julie's cheek. "You be safe now."

"Of course." Julie pulled Lillie into a quick hug. "Call if you need anything."

Lillie returned the embrace with enthusiasm. "Sure, dear."

Julie hit the button for the garage door and it rolled open, revealing a pure white Aston Martin that shimmered in the sun.

Taylor leaned against the driver's side door, resplendent in designer jeans and a tight white T-shirt that traced the lines of his shoulders and chest. He gave Julie a grin from under his Ray-Bans and waved.

"Oh, *my*." Lillie pressed a hand to her chest. "*I'd* have an emergency if I had to work with a hottie like *that* every day."

"Lillie!" Julie giggled. "Bye now."

"Bye, honey. Say hello to Mr. Sexy over there for me. Is he single?"

Julie pretended not to hear that last part.

CHAPTER ELEVEN

"The department couldn't stretch to business class?" Julie grumbled, shifting in the narrow seat. "I thought the captain loved us."

Taylor had folded himself roughly in half to fit in the seat beside hers. "Where did you get *that* idea?"

Hat had cast his privacy bubble spell. It was barely visible as a faint rippling in the air, like heat, but the big man sitting in the seat beside Taylor seemed oblivious. He was scrolling through his phone. Luckily, the bubble had also cut off the sound of the crying baby three rows ahead.

"Do you want the window seat?" Julie glanced out of the window beside her. Right now, it only offered a view of the runway and the bustling airport.

"Oh, no, definitely not. You've only ever flown to *DC*." Taylor shook his head. "I'm not depriving you of your first ever view of the West."

Julie laughed. "Be all squashed, then."

The plane jolted as it began to taxi. Julie grabbed the armrest. The privacy bubble *also* blocked out the sound of the announcements, and she frantically fumbled for her seat belt.

"You okay there?" Taylor raised an eyebrow.

The plane was gathering speed. Julie glanced out of the window just briefly and then decided to screw her eyes shut instead. "Yep," she groaned.

"Taking off is the worst part. You'll be okay once we're in the air."

"Uh-huh," Julie grunted.

"Want a barf bag?" Taylor held one up.

"Don't talk about barfing," Julie moaned. She took a deep breath to settle her stomach. "Let's talk about centaurs instead. You said the other day that they're usually horse ranchers when they live in the human world?"

"Yes," Hat chimed in. "Most centaurs used to live in the human world back when you lot got around by horse."

Julie opened her eyes and risked a glance out of the window, then stared at the back of the seat in front of her instead. "Makes sense."

"Nowadays, most centaurs live in Avalon," Hat went on. "But a few still exist who tend horses like their ancestors did."

Julie called up her training on centaurs. *Centaurs can communicate telepathically with horses.* "I'm guessing that their skills were a lot more important a few hundred years ago."

"Well, yeah, to humans." Taylor folded his arms, trying to make himself fit in the little space. "They're still a vital part of the paranormal world. Not as powerful as the royal families, of course. But individual groups of paranormals like centaurs make up a significant portion of our world."

The plane steadied when it reached cruising height. Julie peered out of the window at the blanket of clouds and felt herself relax a little. "So, they're mostly warriors and ranchers. They'd be the brawn of the operation, right?"

Hat scoffed. "Oh, no. Centaurs are renowned for being scholars and readers, too."

"Interesting," Julie mused. "Sounds like they're the whole package. Kaplan is seriously going to like this."

Taylor nodded. "They're good folks to have on your side in a pinch. If you manage to avoid offending them, you make a friend for life."

Julie raised her eyebrows. "What if you don't avoid offending them?"

"Well... Let's just say you get a nice hoof-shaped scar to remember your stupidity by," Taylor told her in all seriousness.

Julie grimaced. "Okay, no offending the centaur. Noted."

She looked out of the window again, and Taylor patted her shoulder. "Feeling okay now?"

Julie leaned closer to get a better view and grinned. They were already leaving New York City behind, and it was strange to see the city looking so small and so far away. "I'm feeling more than okay. This life is pretty amazing."

"Good." Hat cuddled down against her head. "You'll learn to enjoy flying."

"I think I'm already learning." Julie sighed. "I'm so grateful for this job and all the new horizons it's given me. I just wish..."

"Wish what?" Taylor prompted.

She leaned her head against the window. "I wish there was more I could do about the Yeti thing, you know. I know I only met Leafeyes and Palladius once, but it's so screwed up what happened to them. Do you think they had families?"

"Best not to think about that," Hat told her. "Focus on what you've got to do to help. Recruit this centaur."

Julie nodded and settled back in her seat. For now, that would have to do.

Julie had never seen so much open space before. She leaned out of the rolled-down passenger window, gaping at the endless plains. Golden grass speckled with brush contrasted with misty mountains that marched against the impossibly blue sky.

"There you go, fly catching again." Taylor chuckled behind the wheel of the Jeep they'd rented at the airport.

Julie sagged back into her seat. "It's endless. I guess I knew Montana was big, but my mind hadn't grasped what that meant until we got here. How far from here does Cironius live?"

"Another half-hour drive." Taylor glanced at her. "I was hoping you'd sleep a little longer, since you were so wired during the flights."

"I napped all the way out of Great Falls. If I sleep more now, I'll never sleep tonight." Julie shrugged. "Do you know where we're staying yet?"

"Centaurs often make excellent hosts," Hat chipped in.

Taylor shrugged. "Yeah, we should be fine, but I checked the availability of motels in Great Falls just in case."

He turned off the freeway and onto a single-lane road that gradually narrowed and became bumpier until the asphalt gave way to gravel. The Jeep bucked over the rocks and potholes.

Julie clutched the handle over the window. "Glad we rented this thing instead of that flashy BMW you were eyeing, Taylor."

"I have a weakness for fast cars, okay?" Taylor grunted as he navigated a huge pothole. "But yeah, this was the right choice."

"A portal would have negated the whole rigmarole this trip has been," Hat grumbled.

Taylor hit a huge ditch, and Hat shot off Julie's head and skidded down the dashboard. She grabbed him before he could hit the floor and secured him on her lap. "Well, why didn't you open one for us, then?"

"Open a portal?" Taylor shook his head. "Only the OPMA and other agencies connected with the Eternal Throne have that ability, and it's extremely expensive. There's no way we can deploy a portal for a recruiting mission."

"Hey, I didn't mind the flights. This has been pretty fun." Julie pointed out the rusted metal gate ahead. "Is this it?"

Taylor slowed to a halt. In front of them, the gravel road had narrowed to a track. Miles of post-and-rail fencing stretched across the plain. On their left and right, the ranch was guarded by mountains. A swath of ponderosa pines surrounded the back of the fenced pasture, and Julie could just about make out a wooden ranch house cupped among the trees. The pastures were peppered with herds of horses grazing in the sunshine, their tails swishing at flies.

"It's so peaceful," Taylor remarked.

"Yeah." Julie placed Hat on the dashboard and opened the door. "I'll get the gate."

She had just laid a hand on the latch when the sound of hooves came from the tall grass behind her, and she heard a deadly, metallic sound. The cocking of a shotgun.

"Turn around real slow," a deep voice drawled, "and let me see your hands, human."

Julie did exactly as she was told. It was not the kind of voice that left room for disobedience. She found herself looking into the two black holes of oblivion at the end of a double-barreled shotgun. At the other end, a weathered face with deep brown eyes squinted through the sights.

"What are you doing here?" Cironius Achilleos growled, his straight, coffee-colored hair stirring in the wind.

"I'm from the OPMA," Julie stated firmly. At least, that was her intention. It came out as more of a squeak.

Cironius raised his head, but he didn't lower the shotgun. "Okay. Lemme see some ID."

Julie kept one hand up and reached into her pocket with the other, producing her ID. She held it up and the centaur lowered the weapon and stepped back, his hooves crunching on the dirt.

"All right, then." He nodded and tugged at the brim of his tall, black Stetson. "Sorry about that. We've been dealin' with some bad apples around here. About time you lot showed up."

Julie glanced at Taylor, who was watching wide-eyed from the car.

"Uh...well, we're glad to be here," she managed lamely.

Cironius jerked his chin toward the house. His equine half was a gorgeous russet that shone glossily beneath his rippling muscle. Julie guessed the same must be true of his human half, which was wrapped in a pale blue shirt. Holstering the shotgun by his shoulder, he turned away from her. "Come on in."

Julie wobbled her way back into the Jeep as Cironius swung the gate open. "Thanks for the backup, guys," she hissed.

Hat snorted. "I knew he wouldn't shoot you."

Taylor smiled unconvincingly. "Yeah, me too."

"Sure you did." Julie watched as Cironius' powerful hindquarters propelled him along the track at a canter. With every stride, iron shoes flashed on his hind hooves. The Jeep followed close behind. "It had *nothing whatsoever* to do with the fact that he could kick you into oblivion, right?"

"Right," Taylor agreed unconvincingly.

Hat obligingly became a leather Stetson that fit perfectly on Julie's head. The ranch house was a sprawling, single-story building with a wraparound porch. It had a broad barn door instead of a front door.

As Taylor and Julie got out of the Jeep, Cironius emerged from the front door with a tray in one hand and two chairs in the other. The porch was utterly devoid of chairs otherwise, although there was a beautiful old pine table. Cironius set the tray down and planted the two chairs side-by-side next to it.

"Have a seat, folks," he rumbled, but he rested a hind foot and remained standing.

Like horses, centaurs have a stay apparatus in their limbs, allowing them to use almost no muscular strength to keep themselves standing up, *Julie's orb training told her. Some centaurs may also sleep standing up.*

Taylor took a seat. "Thank you."

Julie followed suit. Cironius poured them each a brimming glass from a jug of sweet iced tea and gestured to a bowl of what looked like oat cakes. "Help yourselves."

"Thanks." Julie took one and nibbled at the edge of it. It was sort of dry, but pleasantly sweet.

"I'm glad to see you." Cironius swished his tail at a fly. "It's been months since I sent that request to the OPMA."

Julie glanced at Taylor, who looked as nonplussed as she felt. *What request?*

Hat snickered. *You'll find out.*

What are you up to? Julie demanded. When he didn't respond, she turned to Cironius. "Which request was that, sir?"

Cironius raised elegant eyebrows. "The reason you're here, surely? To help me with my wolf trouble."

Julie and Taylor exchanged puzzled glances.

"I'm sorry." Taylor apologized, setting down his glass. "We're recruiters. We're here to offer you the opportunity to join the OPMA yourself."

"Me, in the OPMA?" Cironius gave a deep chuckle that had the edge of a whinny in it. "Leave my ranch and horses? No, son, I'm afraid not. It's nice of you to ask, but no."

"We offer an excellent salary and benefits package," Julie told him. "With the political climate being what it is, we're in serious need of solid warriors like you."

Cironius' face creased in a smile. "I don't think you understand, ma'am. Achilleos centaurs have been ranchin' this land for hundreds of years." He made a sweeping gesture with one burly arm. "Once, we supplied horses to the nation. Now, I rescue mustangs. These horses have a forever home with me. If I left, no one would look after them." He shrugged. "Politics are always changin', but horses always need to be fed. For hundreds of years, my family has done that."

Julie smiled. "I was wondering why you didn't sound Greek, with a name like Cironius Achilleos."

Cironius laughed. "Greek? My family's been in Montana for generations." He shook his head. "So no, ma'am, I'm sorry, but I can't join the OPMA. My place is here."

Julie stifled a pang of disappointment, but she could understand his perspective as she gazed at the fields of grazing horses. She didn't think she'd want to leave a place like this, either.

Don't think you're getting out of telling me why you keep sending us on snipe hunts, Hat, she added in silence.

Hat said nothing.

"Well, folks, I'm awful sorry you came all this way for nothin'." Cironius drained his glass at a gulp. "You're welcome to stay the night. I'm afraid I ain't the best host right now, though."

"Wolf trouble?" Julie guessed.

"Yup." Cironius nodded. "Well, they ain't wolves, exactly. A pack of rogue werewolves done got themselves exiled from the town a few miles away. The rest of the pack had enough of them rabble-rousing and attractin' attention from the humans." He touched his hat to Julie. "Present company excepted, of course."

Julie smiled. It was a refreshing change from "no offense."

Taylor frowned. "Have they been hunting your horses?"

"Not huntin', exactly. Just spookin' them. Makin' them run for the sake of it." Cironius frowned. "Horses have an amazing ability to hurt themselves, 'specially when they're spooked. I've been fixin' up hurt legs and mendin' fences for months. What worries me the most is we're on the edge of foalin' season. Nine times outta ten, a spooked horse'll run. But the tenth time, it'll be a mare with a foal, and she'll kill you as soon as look at ya. If I don't teach those young Weres a lesson, one of these mares will, and it won't end well."

Julie glanced at the horse standing by the fence nearby. It

lifted its head and opened its mouth wide in a yawn, revealing blunt but enormous yellowish teeth. She didn't want to think what it would feel like to have those clamp down on a limb.

"But don't you two worry yourselves about that tonight." Cironius stomped a huge hoof. "You won't be in any danger. I'll patrol as usual and let off a few shots if I see them, scare them off. The OPMA will eventually send someone to arrest them, I'm sure."

"They're..." Taylor sighed. "Really shorthanded."

"Well, we're here already. I bet there's something we can do to help." Julie looked at Taylor. "Even if that's not why we came out here in the first place, we can still be useful, right?"

Hat snickered and Julie straightened him on her head a little more forcefully than usual.

Taylor shrugged. "Sure. We'll do what we can."

Cironius folded his arms, a smile creeping over his craggy features. "I don't know what a pair of recruiters can do, but I'll take any help I can get right now."

Julie grinned. "I think you'll be surprised what we can do."

Cironius nodded. "Well then, I'm real grateful to ya. I'll show you to your rooms. Patrol starts at moonrise. Until then, feel free to explore the ranch or get some rest." He chuckled darkly. "It's gonna be a long night."

CHAPTER TWELVE

Cironius' home had stone floors and rubber mats instead of chairs next to all of the tables and in front of the TV. "Easier on the hooves," he explained as he showed Julie and Taylor to their rooms.

Julie was a little surprised to find that her room had a thick, woven rug instead of a rubber mat, and a double bed pushed up against a wide window overlooking the ranch. She tossed her duffel bag onto the bed and stared out of the window for a few moments.

"Time to take a nap?" Hat suggested.

Julie pulled him off her head and fixed him with a severe look. "Did you send us out here to help Cironius with his wolf trouble?"

Hat's brim curled smugly. "I guess you'll find out, won't you?"

"Cryptic magic mentor asshole," Julie grumbled, returning him to her head. "No, I'm not going to nap. I'm far too wired for that. Let's explore the ranch."

"Have you been around horses much?" Hat asked as Julie headed back down the wide hallway and out of the huge front door.

Julie shrugged. "I petted a carriage horse in Central Park once. I've never actually been on one. But I went through the horsey stage like kids do, and I read every horse book I could find, so I know a few things."

She spotted a barn on the left of the house and headed for it. With the weather so nice, the horses were outside. They watched her curiously over the fence as she trudged across the grass.

"A few things?" Hat prompted. "Like what?"

Julie stopped when the sound of trotting hooves announced the arrival of a horse at the fence. The big animal stretched out its nose, sniffing at her, and she reached out to rub it firmly between the eyes.

"Enough to know that this is a buckskin mare," Julie told him, referring to the horse's deep butterscotch coat and black limbs, mane, and tail.

The mare huffed in her face, her breath sweet and grassy. Her belly hung low with pregnancy.

"We're going to stop those Weres chasing you around, okay, girl?" Julie murmured.

The mare snorted again and lowered her head to nibble the grass.

Cironius spoke unexpectedly from the shadowy doorway of the barn. "She likes you."

Julie looked up with a startled laugh. "Next you'll tell me that she doesn't normally like strangers."

Cironius ambled forward, smiling. "Oh, no. If Ambush thinks you might ever, *ever* have had carrots in your possession, she'll be all over you."

Julie laughed. "I'll take note of that."

"She's the lead mare. The boss of the herd." Cironius leaned his muscular forearms on the fence and fondly watched Ambush graze. "She's the one I'm worried about. She'll tear a Were to pieces, wolf or man, if she thinks her family is under threat."

Julie reached out and gently ran her fingertips over the mare's smooth hide. Ambush twitched under her touch. She smiled and turned to Cironius. "Do you mind if I raid the barn for a few things? Ropes, tack, that sort of stuff?"

Cironius raised an eyebrow. "There's plenty of both in the barn. I've taught my fair share of humans and paras to ride here."

Julie grinned. "Okay."

"What do you have in mind, Miss Meadows?" Cironius asked.

Julie shrugged. "I don't know yet, but I'm sure it'll be good."

Cironius laughed. "Okay, then. I'm gonna be out checkin' the fences for the next little while. Help yourself to whatever you need if it's gonna help me with those Weres."

He trotted off, and Julie made for the barn. The interior smelled pleasantly of alfalfa and straw. Ten large stalls faced each other over a clean-swept aisle. Julie pushed open a side door and stepped into the tack room.

The room was well-organized, the walls hung with headstalls, saddles, breastplates, and long, stiff lariats with tight nooses on the end.

She closed her eyes and dug into her subconscious, looking for information on adolescent werewolves. The orb training obliged. *At the adolescent stage, werewolves are known for making questionable decisions.*

"You and me both," Julie grunted, taking a few lariats down from their pegs.

Werewolves are pack creatures who thrive on close connections and the sense of purpose that comes from serving the best interests of the pack. Adolescence is a challenging time for all Weres, but especially those whose animal and human natures are at odds. When human adolescents become surplus to the family's requirements and are allowed to grow idle, they will often turn to inappropriate behaviors to stimulate their agile minds

This is particularly difficult for werewolves. The solution most packs choose is to separate the adolescents from the main pack. However, these splinter packs remain within pack territory and are reabsorbed into the group once the challenging phase has passed. Werewolves are known for being among the fiercest, most loyal, and most useful troops in battle due to their natural inclination to work together and make sacrifices for the good of the pack.

"Troops?" Julie almost dropped the headstall she was holding as the seed of an idea took root. It was gone almost as soon as it had arrived, Julie's focus on making what she needed from the equipment she'd found.

Hat snickered again.

When Julie returned to the house, laden with bits of tack, rolled-up ropes and her notepad covered in scribbles, a deliciously spicy aroma was floating out of the big door. Her mouth watered in anticipation.

"What *is* that?" she whispered to Hat, reaching the porch.

Hat laughed. "I hope you like vegetarian food."

It didn't smell like anything Julie had eaten during her vegetarian stage when she was twelve.

Before she could ask more questions, Taylor came out of the house. He raised an eyebrow at her laden arms. "What are you up to?"

"More than you, by the looks of it," Julie retorted with a laugh. "Bed head looks good on you."

Taylor grinned sheepishly, smoothing down his ruffled hair. "I don't sleep well on flights, okay? So, seriously, what is all this?"

Cironius appeared in the doorway, watching with interest.

"I was looking at what my orb training showed me about adolescent werewolves, and I realized I had to get creative with a solution," Julie explained. "My fighting skills are still novice-level."

"Generous, but okay," Taylor muttered.

"Hey!" Hat protested.

Julie narrowed her eyes at him. "*Anyway*. What we want to do is teach the Weres to leave the horses alone, right?"

Cironius nodded. "But we don't want to hurt them. They're just dumbass kids, is all."

"Exactly." Julie grinned, her plan coming together. "You know how Kaplan allowed me to believe that mind wiping was the same as death, Taylor?"

Taylor grimaced at the chuckle from Cironius. "Yeah, I'm never going to forget that."

"Well, we're not going to hurt these Weres, but *they* don't have to know that." Julie outlined the rest of her plan to them.

When she finished, Cironius' laugh rumbled from deep inside his belly. He clutched his human ribs, while his equine ribs fluttered visibly with laughter. "My people are smart, Miss Meadows, but we ain't sneaky neither. Your quick thinkin' sure is impressive."

Taylor smiled, leaning against the doorway. "Oh, you ain't seen nothing yet, Cironius."

"I'll admit, I ain't been gettin' much sleep. I've grown so close to the problem I can't hardly think straight anymore. I never woulda come up with somethin' like this." Cironius beamed. "Scarin' the Weres away from the horses hasn't been real effective. But this? This is gonna work."

"I hope so." Julie spread her hands over the equipment piled on the table. "Can you guys help me to set this up?"

"Sure. I'm just gonna turn down the stove real quick. Grub will be ready when we get back." Cironius clopped into the kitchen.

"Yeah!" Taylor grabbed a few ropes and strung them over his shoulders. "I can't wait to get my hands dirty."

"I hope you can keep up, city elf," Julie teased.

"He won't have to." Cironius stepped back out of the house. "We'll ride there."

"Ride?" Julie swallowed. "I don't know if we can."

Taylor scoffed. "For your information, I ride very well. I *am* a prince, you know."

"You'll be quite safe, Miss Meadows." Cironius winked. "The mount I have in mind for you ain't trampled any riders yet."

Julie kept her arms wrapped tightly around Cironius' waist, trying not to giggle too loudly as he cantered along a ten-foot gap between the woods and the fence line, heading for the eastern edge of the ranch.

"Easy on the heels there, miss." Cironius' voice rumbled through his chest. "You're diggin' them right into my ribs."

Julie loosened the death grip of her legs. "Sorry."

"I'm just impressed she hasn't fallen off yet," Taylor yelled over the wind that whipped through his hair. He was riding a gray gelding with enviable grace. The animal's saddlebags were laden with the ropes and tack.

Cironius slowed to a walk as they approached a small, rundown barn inside the nearby pasture.

"Is this the place?" Taylor asked.

"I think so." Cironius pointed to the south. "The town's over on the other side of the mountains. The Weres live in the mountains, near as I can tell. The boys are pretty much livin' wild, I think."

"Well, they *do* have a wolf form." Julie gave up on getting rid of the horsehair. "So they come onto your property through these woods?"

"Yeah. Not always from this side, though. I patrol all the woods at night, but as soon as my back's turned they sneak around behind me and come through the woods somewhere else." Cironius grunted in frustration. "Then they jump through the fence and charge the horses. Barking and snapping at their heels gets the whole herd runnin'."

"I guess they're unlikely to come from anywhere other than the woods," Julie murmured. "They'll want to use the cover."

Cironius nodded. "Exactly. If they come straight over the plains, the horses see them coming and bolt before they can reach them. No fun in that, is there? So this is as good a place as any to set up."

Julie grinned. "Controlled chaos. That's what we're going to create."

"Seems like nothing but chaos to me," Taylor muttered, but he was bouncing with excitement as he tugged the ropes out of the saddlebags.

Setting up took longer than Julie had expected. The light was fading by the time they'd finished. Cironius slapped his hands clean and extended one to Julie. "Hop on up, miss. Time for dinner."

Ah, yes. A delicious vegetarian dinner. Julie's stomach growled as she took Cironius' hand and scrambled up onto his back. She could only hope that tofu wasn't on the menu.

Tofu was not on the menu.

Julie stared at the spread laid out on the porch table when she came out of the house, freshly showered and wearing black jeans and a hoodie. The smells of cinnamon, chili peppers, herbs, and cream rose from the table, which groaned with food. There was a huge bowl of thick soup with chunks of fresh vegetables floating in it, a mountain of mashed potatoes with a rich butter-garlic smell rising from them, and a vibrant salad made with sweet potatoes, kale, and black beans.

Julie's mouth watered. "Whoa."

"All fresh, organic, and local." Cironius spread his arms, standing at the head of the table. "What I don't grow myself, I barter for. All this good grub was grown either here or on my neighbors' farms."

"That's pretty cool." Julie sank into her chair. "It looks and smells incredible. Thanks."

Cironius laughed, a heavy rumble in his chest. "Well, I got plenty to celebrate." He hefted a huge glass of a ruby red wine that sparkled alluringly in the porch's fairy lights. "I have company, help, and plenty to go around. Let's feast!"

"Amen to that!" Taylor crowed with enthusiasm.

Julie's first bite of the vegetable soup transported her to a distant plane where everything was fresh, pollution had never existed, and humans had never tainted the earth. Well, humans and paranormals, she amended. Taylor caused as many carbon emissions as any human.

You're ruining your own mental image, Hat chuckled.

Julie dug into the soup. *You're just jealous because you can't taste this.*

The feast had just been rounded off with an amazingly sweet and fresh fruit salad when the first shafts of moonlight, the full moon hanging fat and low in the sky, pierced the porch.

As if on cue, Julie heard the cries of wolves in the distance.

Julie had never heard wolves in real life before, but some primal instinct in her immediately recognized them. The hairs on the back of her neck prickled. She sat up straight. "Is that them?"

"Yes," Cironius rumbled. He set down his wine and stamped a front foot beneath the table, shaking his head so that his mane poured down his back. "They're here."

"Okay." Julie pushed her chair back, glad they'd had time to finish the meal before the Weres arrived. "Let's do this. Everyone okay with the plan?"

"Absolutely." Taylor pulled a black beanie over his head. "Let's go kick some werewolf ass!"

They strode out from the porch, and Taylor jogged into the barn to saddle the gray gelding. Cironius descended gracefully to one knee and Julie scrambled onto his back, not at all gracefully.

Cironius' face was drawn and distant. He was talking to the herd.

"All right," he growled. "I've sent them into the open in a bunch. Ambush sure ain't happy about it." He rose to his feet and Julie clung to him to keep from falling off. "We gotta do this tonight. She's ready to trample the next wolf she sees."

Taylor reappeared with the gelding and swung easily into the saddle. "To the east?"

Cironius nodded and set off at a brisk canter. There were no shenanigans this time, but Julie still had to hang on tightly as they galloped along the lane between the pasture fence and the trees, hooves beating a steady rhythm on the earth.

Julie spotted the rundown barn across the fence from where they'd set the trap. Cironius slowed to a walk.

"Are they here?" Julie whispered.

She looked across the moonlit pasture. Ambush was standing at the head of a herd of restless horses, milling, snorting, and stamping their hooves loudly. When one of them tried to push past her toward Cironius, Ambush pinned her ears and snapped a warning, and the horse hurriedly rejoined the herd.

"No. Not yet," Cironius murmured.

Julie grimaced. "Ambush looks *pissed*."

Taylor's horse danced under him, rolling his eyes to show the whites.

Cironius stroked the butt of his shotgun resting in the holster by his equine shoulder. "Soon. Soon."

A distant clamor of howling rose from the western side of the ranch, the piercing voices rising into the air.

"No! What are they doing over there?" Julie hissed.

Cironius swung around, almost jolting her off his back. "It's a diversion. What do you wanna do now, miss?"

Julie bit her lip. "Okay... We're going to have to make it look like they've fooled us. Otherwise, they won't risk coming here. We've got to assume they've seen us."

Cironius nodded. "Buckle up."

Julie bit back a yelp as the centaur surged along the lane at a racing gallop. Taylor leaned low over his horse's neck, urging him forward, and the two matched strides for a few breathless seconds. Julie noticed that Taylor was pale and grim.

What's up with him? she wondered.

No idea. Seems really quiet, doesn't he? Hat observed. *Isn't that a nice change?*

Helpful as always, Hat, Julie retorted.

"Stop. *Stop!*" Taylor called as he sat back in his saddle and pulled on the reins.

His horse struck out with all four legs and slid to a halt, leaving long black scars in the earth. Cironius jolted to a stop so sharply that Julie slammed hard into his back. He turned around, front hooves lifting from the earth in a half-rear.

"What is it?" the centaur thundered.

Taylor raised a hand to his head.

"Taylor?" Julie hissed. "What's wrong? Are you okay?"

"I... Yes. I'm more than okay." Taylor raised his head, a strange, wild light in his eyes. "I'm hearing...*everything.*"

They stared at him, bemused.

Taylor hesitated, searching for an explanation. "It's weird. I know Aether Elves have heightened senses. I figured my senses had always been super until now."

Didn't seem super to me, snorted Hat.

"Being out in nature has sharpened them." Taylor swallowed. "I can smell and hear everything. Things moving in the woods. The traffic on the freeway. Insects in the undergrowth. *Everything.*"

Julie blinked. The freeway was miles away. "Whoa."

"More importantly, I can hear six wolves." He pointed at the eastern woods. "They're heading for the herd."

Cironius nodded sharply. "Okay. Should we go back?"

"Not all of us." Julie slipped off his back and almost landed squarely on her ass. She grabbed at his holster to stay upright. "You go on, Cironius, in case they go after the herd. But let them howl the all-clear to the others. Otherwise, they won't come close enough."

Taylor nodded. "They're hanging back, by the sound of it."

"We'll hide in the barn," Julie decided. "Then we'll make sure none of them get through."

"I don't think any of them will," Cironius hazarded, chuckling. "See you real soon, I guess."

He wheeled on his hindlegs, leaning into a plunging gallop that took him out of sight within a few seconds.

"Come on then, Miss Mastermind." Taylor held out a hand. "Up you get."

Julie groaned. "One day I'd like to ride my own horse."

"Today's not that day, though." Taylor beckoned. "Come on."

Julie grabbed his hand, which was soft and well-manicured, and kicked, scrambled and dragged her way onto the horse behind the saddle. She clutched the back of the saddle, panting.

"You *really* need to learn to ride," Taylor chuckled.

Julie resisted the urge to slap him around the back of the head. "Shut up and ride, bro."

"Not like this," Taylor told her. "You'll have to hang on to me, or you'll fall on your face."

Julie scoffed. "I'm good. Thanks."

"Suit yourself." Taylor tapped the horse with his heels, and the animal shot forward.

With a yelp of panic, Julie threw her arms around Taylor. She spoke to distract herself from the ripple of his muscles as they rode back to the barn. "So, super senses, huh?"

Taylor slowed the horse as they approached the barn. "I guess elves were intended to be out in nature."

Julie grinned. "It's pretty cool."

"Shhh." Taylor stopped the horse. "I'm not the only one with super senses, although these Weres' adrenaline seems to be running so high they haven't noticed us. Let's get to the barn."

Julie scrambled off the horse. Taylor dismounted fluidly and tied the gelding to the fence. They squeezed between the posts and slipped into the barn. Crouching in the fragrant straw, Julie peered through a knot-hole in the wood. She could see nothing but the fence, the grassy lane, and the dark tangle of pine trees.

Boo! Hat barked.

Julie jumped, almost falling. *Hat, you asshole!*

Hat snickered.

Another howl rose from across the property. Julie's head whipped around, although she knew she wouldn't be able to see the Weres. There was a thunder of hooves in response from the herd.

They galloped in tight circles, slamming into each other, kicking up their heels and snorting. But Cironius was in communication with Ambush. The mare kept them in line with quick snaps of her teeth, even though Julie could see her big muscles quivering with rage.

"There!" Taylor gasped. "They're coming!"

A few seconds later, Julie didn't need super senses to hear the rush of panting breath and the snapping of twigs as the pack of six wolves charged out of the woods. She held her breath, her heart pounding in her chest as the howls and snarls of excitement rose from the darkness. Every instinct she had was telling her to run—

Then, a high-pitched yelp, followed by more panicked yips that turned into muffled cursing.

"Got them!" Julie crowed.

Taylor grinned, holding up a hand. "All six of them."

Julie high-fived him enthusiastically. "Let's go and see."

"Whoa, cowgirl." Taylor laughed. "I'd prefer we do that when our centaur armed with a shotgun gets here."

I've contacted him. He's coming, Hat offered.

"Wow, being useful for once?" Julie teased.

It didn't take long for Cironius to return, his brown flanks streaked with white, foaming sweat. He brandished his shotgun, grinning widely. "C'mon, kids! Let's go and see what we caught."

Julie and Taylor scrambled through the fence and followed Cironius into the tree line. Moonlight gleamed on the centaur's haunches as they ran.

Cironius threw back his head and let out a deep guffaw when they reached the clearing where they'd been working earlier.

Six young Weres, five of them in human form, were dangling from the traps Julie had built earlier out of lariats, headstalls, multiple sets of reins, and a bunch of old halters. The largest of the boys hung upside-down from both ankles, his shock of blond hair almost touching the ground.

He strained to reach the ropes tying his legs, yelling, "I told you something was up, Chester! Why wouldn't you listen?"

"Well, *you're* the one who keeps saying you're the pack leader, Isaiah!" a shorter Were crammed into a net with three others snapped.

The fifth Were was biting angrily at the rope that held him to a tree but since he was using human teeth, he wasn't making much progress. He paused to level a glare at the luckless Isaiah. "Yeah, some pack leader *you* are."

"Shut up!" Isaiah shrieked, making another futile attempt to loosen the rope around his ankles.

The sixth Were was a little gray wolf caught in a net too small to allow him to shift back into a human. He whimpered furiously, clawing at the air.

Taylor grinned at Cironius. "The harvest sure produced some weird fruits this season, huh?"

Hat and Cironius both burst out laughing.

Fruits... Julie's earlier thought solidified in her mind. *They are also known for being among the fiercest, most loyal, and most useful troops in battle.*

She had been considering that this hadn't been too bad for a fruitless recruiting mission. But maybe it didn't have to be fruitless at all.

"Hat," she whispered, "I have a better idea."

CHAPTER THIRTEEN

The Weres hadn't heard Cironius and Hat laughing. They were far too wrapped up in yelling at each other. Julie wondered if her plan was too ambitious. The Weres seemed so immature, even though most of them had to be around her age of nineteen.

Her eyes rested on Isaiah. The blond Were was straining to break free, his shoulder muscles bunching powerfully under his tight shirt. He looked like someone she wanted on hand in a fight.

She tugged at Hat's brim to get his attention. *Can you tell Taylor and Cironius telepathically?*

Hat straightened to attention. *Okay. What's your idea?*

Julie grinned. *A little game of good cop, bad cop. Tell them to just go with it. I think I know why you sent me out here in the first place.*

Hat's voice held a trace of smugness. *I'm sure you do.*

Taylor nodded minutely at Julie to show he was on board. Julie touched Cironius' equine shoulder. "I think it's time we got their attention."

"Sure thing." The centaur raised his shotgun and cocked it. The metallic sound echoed through the clearing, and the six werewolves instantly fell silent.

"Okay, boys," he rumbled. "I think it's time you learned your lesson about chasin' people's horses."

The boys said nothing. Their round eyes were fixed firmly on the double barrels of the shotgun.

"Now, now, Cironius." Julie stepped forward and reached over her head to lay a hand on the centaur's forearm. "I have a better idea in mind."

"This idea works just fine." Cironius pointed the shotgun at Isaiah's head. With a yelp, the young Were raised both hands.

"Don't shoot!" he whimpered. "Don't shoot!"

"Give me a good reason not to, son." Cironius sighted down the twin barrels. "You've caused plenty of trouble on my ranch."

"Well, there *is* an alternative to turning them into floor rugs, you know." Julie smiled at the Weres. "I'm not sure if they'd like to hear about it."

"We would!" Chester cried as he squirmed against the net. "Please, ma'am, tell us!"

The other Weres joined him in the clamor, and Julie nodded at Taylor.

Taylor held up his OPMA ID. "My name is Taylor Woodskin, and this is Julie Meadows," he told the Weres. "We're from the Official Para-Military Agency, and we want to offer you a whole new life. A life where you can get all the travel and adventure you've ever dreamed of. Enlisting will get you a home, a future where you can make a difference, and, in a way, a new pack."

"As well as an attractive pay and benefits package," Julie added. "Oh, and we'll take you a long, *long* way away from angry centaurs with shotguns."

"Seems you boys should take that option," Cironius snarled.

The Weres were silent for a few long seconds. Even the one in wolf form had stopped whimpering and was observing Julie with sharp yellow eyes.

She realized that a mixture of adrenaline and testosterone seemed to be clogging their brains. "Let me clarify. We're offering you the chance to become soldiers in OPMA. Trust me, it's a much better option than living wild in the woods and chasing Cironius' horses. Wouldn't you rather be chasing down criminals and enemies of the Eternal Throne?"

Isaiah glanced at the other young Weres, judging their reactions to the offer. They were all looking at him with wide eyes.

Chester spoke up first. "That sounds... Pretty great, actually."

The Were who was bound to the tree strained to look at Julie. "We would get paid? Like, *money?*"

"Oh, yes. It's a good salary, too," Taylor confirmed. "No more eating raw deer and sleeping in dens for you."

"I like the idea," Isaiah hedged, "but I'm not going unless you're all going, too." He smiled at the others, suddenly looking older and less idiotic. "We do this together, right? We do *everything* together."

"We do this together!" the other Weres chorused.

Aww, Hat snarked. *Positively heartwarming.*

Shhhh! Julie hissed. *Wasn't this your idea from the start?*

Hat permitted himself another cryptic snicker.

"So what do you say, boys?" Julie asked. "Are you in?"

Isaiah smiled at her, nodding from his upside-down position. "We're in. So, will you cut us down now?"

"Not so fast, son." Cironius lowered the shotgun but he still held it with practiced comfort. "There's a few things you gotta make right first."

The Weres stirred, whimpering.

"I've got a whole bunch of downed fences as a result of your balderdash. Not to mention lost horseshoes in all of the pastures. Y'all're gonna fix those fences and find the shoes." Cironius stomped a hind foot. "I'm sure your old pack would appreciate you makin' amends, too."

"You'll have to talk to them." Taylor nodded. "Your alpha will need to sign your forms to join the OPMA."

"Nooooo," Chester groaned. "He's going to be *so* mad."

One of the other Weres in the net shook his head. "He won't do it. I bet you he won't."

Isaiah sighed. "Look, I know he was pretty pissed with us when we last saw him, but I think he'd let us go. You guys, we did some pretty stupid stuff. There's no denying it."

There was some sheepish mumbling from the other Weres.

"I think Ezekiel will be glad that we're not his problem anymore," Isaiah agreed. "He'll sign the papers."

"I agree, son." Cironius grinned. "Zeke and I go way back. He'll be all too glad to have trouble taken off his hands."

Julie beamed. "So, if your alpha signs for you, are you ready to ship out to New York City when you've fixed up the ranch?"

Chester let out a low whistle. "We've never been that far from home."

Isaiah held up both hands. "We'd jump at the chance, miss. Well, not literally. We're still dangling from trees."

"Let's cut them down, Cironius." Julie planted her hands on her hips and grinned at the centaur. "I think we've accomplished our mission here."

Ezekiel Woods shoved a sheaf of papers into Julie's hands. It had surprised her to learn that Cironius had a printer. He'd sheepishly admitted that he wrote books and preferred editing with a literal red pen.

The papers were still hot off the printer, but each of them bore a flourishing signature from the pack alpha.

"Is that all, miss?" The tall Were tucked his pen back into the pocket of his jacket.

"Yes, thank you." Julie paused. "Seriously, thank you. I think this is going to be as good for them as it will be for OPMA."

Julie, Taylor and Ezekiel were standing on the porch. From where they stood, they had a front row seat to Cironius barking orders at the six clumsy young Weres as they tried to repair a fence in one of the pastures while the horses grazed contentedly around them.

"I think so, too. I've been worried about them taking so long to straighten out." Ezekiel turned back to Julie and held out a smooth hand with fingers that ended in blunt black claws. "Thank you."

Julie nodded. "Thank *you* for coming out so early in the morning."

"Anything to get those boys off my hands." Ezekiel chuckled. "Besides, I've got meetings in town that I need to get to."

Julie and Taylor shook his hand, and the werewolf tucked himself into the front seat of a pickup truck and drove away.

Julie raised an eyebrow at Taylor. "You didn't tell me that the alpha of the pack was the mayor of the town."

"Alphas of local Were packs are often involved in local politics," Hat supplied.

Julie laughed, patting his crown where he sat on her head. "Thanks, Hat. Hey, thanks for this little 'snipe hunt.'"

Hat's brim curled smugly. "Anytime."

Taylor checked his watch. "We'd better get going or we'll miss our flight."

Julie had barely bothered to unpack. She grabbed her backpack from the porch table and hooked it over her shoulder. "I can't wait to see Kaplan's face when we tell him that we signed him *six* new recruits with nine days to spare on our deadline."

Fishing the Jeep's keys out of his pocket, Taylor chuckled. "He might even smile. Wouldn't that be something?"

A tattoo of hoofbeats accompanied Cironius cantering across the pasture. He jumped the fence with effortless grace and trotted to a halt by the porch. "On your way already?"

"I'm afraid so." Julie held out a hand. "I'll miss this place, though. You have a beautiful home."

Cironius clasped her hand in both of his, completely

engulfing it in his massive grip. "You two have done me a real good deed. I can never thank you enough, but you've got my number. You know who to call if there's ever anything I can do to repay you."

He shook Taylor's hand, and then they were in the Jeep and bumping along the track to the gate. When Julie got out to open the gate, Cironius was still standing in front of the porch, imposing and majestic. He raised a huge hand in farewell, and Julie grabbed Hat off her head, still in his Stetson form, and flourished him.

"Hey!" Hat scolded as she got back into the Jeep. "Stop waving me about like a common hat."

"You're the one who chose to be a hat in the first place," Julie reminded him as she made him comfortable on the backseat.

Taylor steered the Jeep onto the gravel road. "Well, that was a very productive night in Montana, don't you think?"

"*Extremely* productive." Julie sat back, stretching out her legs. "I look forward to getting home to my five thousand dollar bonus. Don't you?"

"Oh, yeah." Taylor grinned. "Especially since the royal accountant won't be able to see it."

Julie looked over at him as he slipped on his sunglasses against the morning glare.

"You know, your plan was pretty brilliant," the elf told her. "It was an inspired brainwave to recruit those Weres once you'd caught them."

"Thanks." Julie tipped back her head and relaxed. "Not too shabby yourself, Mr. Super Senses."

Taylor laughed. "I doubt they'll work the same in the city, but they definitely came in handy." He paused. "Hey, Julie?"

"Yeah?"

Taylor's fingers flexed on the wheel, and he was silent for a second. "Working with you is... Well, it's an honor."

"Awww, you're so sweet," Julie teased to cover the warmth that welled in her chest. "Such a softie."

Taylor switched gears. "Oh, shut up, human."

"You shut up, elf."

Laughter filled the Jeep as it headed for the airport, leaving Cironius' beautiful ranch far behind.

"Meadows! Woodskin!"

Kaplan's voice thundered through the communal office as Julie and Taylor stepped out of the elevator, still scruffy and bleary-eyed from the flight. They exchanged a grimace.

Well, this is going to be fun, Hat commented.

Julie scoffed. "Come on. How could he be anything *but* impressed?"

Still, there was a fluttering sensation in her stomach as they hurried to Kaplan's office without stopping to put down their bags. When they stepped into his office, the powerful man was standing with his back to them, surveying the campus.

Julie could only hope that this was a good sign.

"Sit," Kaplan rumbled.

She obeyed. Taylor perched on the edge of his armchair. Julie noticed that six recruitment forms were scattered across Kaplan's desk. Hat had sent the paperwork over before their flight took off that morning.

The burly captain turned around slowly and gestured over the papers with one hand. "What is this?"

"Recruitment forms, sir." Julie smirked. "For six werewolves. Strapping young men. They'll be a credit to OPMA."

Kaplan sank into his office chair and fixed them both with a long stare. Then, he shook his head, and a laugh—an actual *laugh*, with joy in it—rumbled up from the pit of his stomach.

"So it *is* true! You did recruit six paras in a single day." Kaplan leaned forward, the wide smile on his face looking out of place as if his muscles had forgotten how to make the expression. "You know, you two astound me."

Taylor's jaw dropped. "Astound you, sir? In a good way?"

Kaplan folded his arms, his face relaxing as his smile widened. "In an excellent way, Woodskin. You two are hands down the best recruiters I've ever had."

Julie narrowed her eyes. *Well, aren't we being suspiciously nice today?*

Hat sighed. *Take the win, Meadows.*

"In fact, I think it's time your success was acknowledged by the whole department." Kaplan leaned back in his chair and interlaced his fingers behind his head. "This is cause for celebration."

Taylor perked up. "Sir, if I may—"

"You most certainly may not, Woodskin." Kaplan leveled his gaze at the elf. "Whatever your suggestion is, I have a better one."

"S-sir?" Taylor stammered.

Kaplan's smile curled almost to his ears. "You two will prepare a presentation for the other recruiters on how you've shot up to the top of your department in numbers."

Taylor's face fell. Julie had known better than to expect anything other than more work. "Actually, I have a better idea."

"A better idea?" Kaplan's eyes narrowed. "Are you interrupting me, Meadows?"

"Sorry, sir. I was talking to Ellie—Elspeth Feathertouch, when it came to me." Julie met Kaplan's eyes. "She was talking about how happy she was that she'd joined OPMA. I thought we could have her give a testimonial about it and use that to create a recruitment video."

Kaplan raised an eyebrow. "You want to create recorded proof that the paranormal military exists?"

Julie slumped in her chair. "Well, when you put it like that..."

Taylor shook his head with a regretful smile. "It'd be in direct contravention to the rules laid down by the Eternity Throne to keep humans from finding out about us."

"Oh. I guess I missed that." Julie sighed. "Sorry. I got carried away by the idea."

Kaplan spoke more gently than usual. "It's not a bad idea, Meadows. If it wasn't for the rules, I'd say it'd be worth a shot."

"What if we made the wording sort of ambiguous, not mentioning the PMA directly, and only sent this kind of material to Avalon?" Julie suggested. "I mean, I'm sure your trolls could make sure it didn't get leaked."

"Let's hope so," Kaplan muttered. "I'll think about it, though." He raised an eyebrow. "Any more brilliant ideas?"

"Actually, yes." Julie grinned. They'd discussed this on the flight. "We could do an in-house survey to learn more about recruiters' motivations."

"That's a good idea, sir. Respectfully." Taylor cleared his throat. "The IT trolls could throw something together."

Kaplan raised the other eyebrow, too. "*Motivations*? Need I remind you of that five thousand dollar bonus you insisted on, Meadows?"

"It's a motivation for *me*, sir, but what about someone like Taylor?" Julie gestured to her partner. "Our salary is pretty good. A lot of recruiters might not need the extra cash. What else could we use to inspire them to go the extra mile? We need to give recruiters as well as recruits a sense of purpose."

Kaplan snorted. "What, actually deliver on what we promised them?"

"Strangely enough, sir, people tend to go the extra mile when they feel like their bosses are doing the same." Julie held up her hands. "Don't eat me."

Kaplan sighed. "I've lost my taste for human flesh. Go on."

Julie couldn't decide whether or not he was kidding about the human flesh thing. Regardless, she plowed on with the pitch she'd rehearsed on the plane. "Lackluster management is going to create a lackluster department. You want star performers, treat them that way."

Kaplan's jaw dropped. Taylor's face was ashen with shock, but he had to raise a hand and rub his upper lip furiously to stifle the laughter that Julie could hear bubbling in the back of his throat.

Kaplan regained control and raised his chin, fixing Julie with a hard glare. "Some would say that duty to the throne should be incentive enough."

Julie shrugged. "What about the throne's duty to those who serve it?"

Well, well, well. Feisty today, aren't we? Hat snarked.

Kaplan redirected his glare at Taylor. "Woodskin, what do you have to say about this?"

Taylor held up his hands as though to defend himself, then dropped them back into his lap. "Our results speak for themselves, sir."

"You, too?" Kaplan let out another brief bark of laughter. "Well, you two amaze me, but I can't argue with that."

"Sir, there's one thing that we've found most successful, and that's finding paranormals who don't fit in with their lives and offering them a change without any false promises." Taylor shrugged. "It worked on Ellie, and it worked on the Weres."

"We think that recruiters should focus on this, sir," Julie added. "It gives recruiters a sense of purpose to know they've improved someone's life. I think it should be part of the recruitment videos and recruiter incentives."

Taylor nodded. "The IRSA should incorporate this into its recruitment algorithm."

"All right, all right." Kaplan held up a hand. "It's worked for you two so far. Fine. But before I can think about incorporating any of your suggestions, you need to prove this."

Julie swallowed. "Prove it, sir?"

"Bring me a high-value recruit who fits that description." Kaplan grinned. "Then we'll talk."

Julie crossed her arms. "Challenge accepted, sir."

Kaplan chuckled. "Oh, I thought it would be. Now go home. You have work to do tomorrow."

CHAPTER FOURTEEN

Julie stepped out of the Uber, stifling a yawn. Lillie's house was the most welcome sight in the world with the lights on and the curtains drawn against the twilight.

"Thank you," she called to the driver as she slammed the door.

The little hatchback drove away as Julie fished in her pocket for her keys. *I can't wait to see Lillie and Genevieve.*

I can't wait to snuggle up on my comfortable chair for a rest. Hat wriggled on her head, back in his fedora form. *It's been a long and awkward two days.*

I hear you. The flights were fun, but I don't miss those seats. I loved the ranch, but I'm ready for my own bed. Julie stretched for a second as she hit the button for the garage door. *It feels good to be home.*

Genevieve was waiting in the garage, her pewter flanks shining. Julie gave her a little pat as she walked past. The rumble of the garage door prompted a few barks from Pookie, but the back door was closed. Julie opened it, frowning because it was, as usual, unlocked, and peered inside.

Lillie was stretched out and snoring loudly on the sofa. The cat lay in a happy curl on her stomach, her hand still resting on his back where she'd fallen asleep petting him.

Pookie danced around Julie's feet, her tail wagging madly as she stepped into the house and pulled a blanket off the back of the sofa to cover Lillie and the cat. The old lady barely stirred.

A soft bark from Pookie caught her attention. The little dog was standing by her food bowl. It was empty, as was her water.

"Oh, Lillie," Julie murmured. She tiptoed into the kitchen and refilled the animals' food and water bowls. *Lillie never used to forget to feed her pets*, she told Hat. *I don't know what's up with her.*

Maybe she's senile like me, Hat sniffed.

Julie snorted inwardly as she left Lillie's house and clumped up the stairs to her apartment. *You're still so bitter about that.*

You would be bitter too if you'd been stuck in the warehouse for as long as I was, Hat grumbled.

Julie stepped into her apartment, feeling a wave of relief wash over her. "No place like home." She put Hat down on the counter and opened the freezer to fish for the coffee grounds.

Hat hopped from the counter to the kitchen table. "It's admittedly the least auspicious home I've ever lived in, but I like it."

Julie laughed. "Well, thanks for that, Hat." She tipped the grounds into the coffee machine and opened her fridge. Her heart thudded painfully as she looked into its total emptiness. No milk, no vegetables, no leftovers—

Hat's voice made her jump when he spoke up from behind her. "You took the perishables down to Lillie, remember?"

"Oh, yeah. I forgot." Julie's shoulders relaxed and she closed the fridge. "It's nothing an online grocery order won't fix, but for a moment there it felt like the way it used to be before I got drafted into OPMA."

"*Fake* drafted," Hat reminded her. He paused. "Did you really run out of food?"

"All the time." Julie shrugged. "Lillie gave me packets of ramen when she saw I was desperate. It's one of the reasons why I want to help her. Anyway, I'm not going back down there and waking her up now."

"Takeout, then?" Hat suggested.

"Definitely." Julie scooped up Genevieve's keys. "I feel like a drive in my own car after being cooped up on public transport and in the office all day."

"Yes!" Hat jumped onto her hand, and she lifted him onto her head. "Let's go!"

Julie laughed. "I thought you hated my driving."

Hat chuckled sheepishly. "Well, maybe I missed Genevieve too, you know."

Julie started to wonder if a magical hat could fall in love with a classic car and decided not to think about it. The familiar purr of Genevieve's engine filled her ears as she backed the Mustang out of the garage and headed for the nearest KFC drive-thru, craving spicy fried chicken. Cironius' food had been amazing, but Julie was ready for something greasy and bad for her health.

She pulled to a halt at a red light and a police cruiser that had been parked in an empty lot nearby pulled out and rolled up behind her. She glanced in the mirror, but the cop didn't turn on his lights.

"I'm not even doing anything," Julie grumbled, taking her time to drive off when the light turned green. "Genevieve, what do they know about you that I don't?"

The cop in the mirror had a bushy gray mustache. Julie shook her head as she turned toward the KFC and the cruiser followed her all the way to the drive-thru before peeling off and driving away.

"I wonder what Lillie used to get up to, back in the day?" Hat pondered.

"I don't think I want to know." Julie shook her head. "Have you noticed it's only the older cops who follow Genevieve around? I bet she's shown them a thing or two, haven't you, girl?" She patted the steering wheel.

"I bet she's got some great stories," Hat observed.

"I'll have to ask her about it when we go for that road trip."

Julie pulled up in front of the order mic and rolled down the window.

She placed her order and drove through to the next window, which was staffed by a young man. He had his back to her, packing her order into a paper bag. Julie steeled herself for the usual unwanted stares. She slipped a hand down to the center console and took a grip on her pepper spray just in case.

The young man turned around, holding up her bag, and his eyes widened in appreciation. But instead of resting on Julie, they slipped straight past her and ran down the smooth lines of Genevieve's bodywork.

"Whoa!" the young man gasped, shoving the paper bag through the window. "Is this the 429 or the 351?"

Julie took the bag, relaxing. "She's the 429."

His mouth made a little "O" of amazement. "I've never seen one in real life before. I'll bet she purrs like a kitty."

Julie touched the accelerator and Genevieve gave a throaty roar that reverberated through the cramped drive-thru. The guy cheered, and Julie drove off laughing. "I love how guys stare at Genevieve instead of me."

"It's one way to deflect unwanted ogling," Hat agreed.

Julie rolled to a halt by the same red light. This time, the police cruiser was absent. She stifled a yawn, stretching her shoulders as she waited for the light to turn green. Around her, old apartment buildings, some of them abandoned, towered against the night sky. Streetlamps cast black shadows in the narrow alleyways dividing them.

Glancing in the mirror, Julie realized that there weren't any other cars at this light. She shifted in her seat, glancing down the alley to her left. An eerie prickle ran over her skin, and she took in a sharp breath.

"What is it?" Hat turned to face her.

"A weird feeling. A weird but...familiar feeling." Julie peered into the alley again and spied a crumpled silhouette just beyond the slant of light from the nearest streetlamp. *Probably just a pile of garbage bags*, she told herself. "It's the same feeling I had on Saturday night in the parking lot."

The light turned green and Julie was about to get out of there at high speed when the garbage bag heap stirred and rose. She bit back a yelp. The stooped silhouette had the unmistakable prickle of hair on its shoulders.

It was a Yeti.

The Yeti sloped off, heading deeper into the alley. Julie gunned the engine and turned Genevieve sharply into a gap between two of the buildings that was barely wide enough to accommodate the Mustang.

"What are you doing?" Hat squawked.

"Going to find out what that Yeti's up to." Julie unclipped her seat belt and cracked the door. She could only just squeeze out, but she managed.

"What? No!" Hat jumped onto the driver's seat. "Julie, what are you thinking?"

"I'm just going to check it out," she reassured him. "This might be our chance to find out what the Yetis are doing."

"Are you crazy? You're a recruiter, not an agent. Get back in the car!" Hat thundered.

Julie shook her head. "Chill, Hat. I'm not going to *fight* the Yeti. I'm just gonna follow it from a safe distance. I'll call it in if I see anything suspicious."

"Well, at least take me with you, then," Hat protested.

"You've got to look after Genevieve. Nothing can happen to her. I don't want to think about what it'd do to Lillie, and this isn't the safest area." Julie closed the door.

Julia Meadows! Get back here! Hat yelled into her mind.

Julie had already tucked her pepper spray into her pocket. She ran across the street, narrowly dodging a creepy-looking sedan. She reached the alley where she'd seen the Yeti and flattened her back against the wall before peering cautiously around the corner.

It was pitch dark, but her eyes had had a moment to adjust. She saw dumpsters, trash, empty space…and gigantic footprints in the mud, leading away from where she stood.

Julie tugged out her phone as she slipped into the alley. She tapped on Taylor's name and sent a text.

Spotted a Yeti. Following it to see what it's doing.

Immediately, Taylor texted back.

DON'T GO IN ALONE!!!!!!!!

"As if I'm gonna listen to you," Julie muttered to herself. She stuffed her phone in her pocket and trotted along the alley, sticking to the sides to avoid scuffing the existing footprints. *No wonder they're called Bigfoot,* she thought.

Her phone chimed again. It was Taylor, of course.

I'm on my way. Don't do anything stupid!

You're doing something stupid, aren't you?

Send me your location! I'm on my way!

Julie!!!!

It felt good to know Taylor was coming to back her up. Julie sent him a live location link so he could track her movements, then made sure her phone was on vibrate before she tucked it away again.

Julie slowed at the end of the alley and peered out cautiously. She caught a glimpse of the huge, hairy Yeti darting down a side street. Breaking into a run, she sprinted across the street and ducked behind a parked car, then peered cautiously over the trunk.

The Yeti was lumbering down another alley, its coat bathed yellowish in the light of a flickering streetlamp. Julie waited until its back was turned before darting from behind the car to the cover of a nearby dumpster. Sticking as close as she dared, she continued to follow the Yeti down alleys and side streets, using whatever cover she could. Her hand was sweating on her pepper spray, but the kick of excitement in her chest kept her hurrying after her quarry.

Julie's phone buzzed insistently a few times. Ignoring it, she followed the Yeti as it headed deeper into Brooklyn. The apartment buildings gave way to warehouses, then factories. The salt tang of water grew stronger. She glanced up at a street sign as she edged to the end of an alley. She was on 43rd, and the roar of Gowanus Expressway was at her back.

Peering out of the alley, she spotted the Yeti sticking to the shadows as it loped up the street with hulking grace. She was about to follow it when her phone buzzed again. She plucked it out.

I'm almost there. Just stand still and wait for me!

"As if, Taylor," Julie mumbled. She looked for the Yeti, then froze in her tracks, glancing up and down the street. It was gone. It must have gone down a side street when she was looking at her phone.

Cursing inwardly, Julie dashed across the street and took cover behind the dumpster at the mouth of an alley. Peering out from behind it, she glanced down the alley. It looked pretty empty, but was that a Yeti footprint in the dirt about halfway down?

Julie slipped out from behind the dumpster and jogged over to the footprint, crouching down. No. It was just a puddle. She straightened up, wiping a sweaty palm on her jeans, and a hand closed around her free elbow.

Adrenaline surged through Julie's body, hot-wiring the muscle memory that hours in the gym had taught her. She whipped around, twisting her elbow from the strong grip, and dodged easily when another hand snatched at her. Raising her pepper spray, she squeezed the trigger, and a potent homemade combination of cayenne pepper, alcohol, and oil rose into the air in a thick cloud.

"*Shit*! That burns!" Malcolm Nox howled, leaping out of the noxious cloud.

Julie dropped the pepper spray bottle like it was red hot, stumbling back as she spat and shook her hands madly, trying to get the stuff off her skin. When she'd chosen an air freshener bottle to hold her pepper spray, she hadn't considered the fact that most of the spray would end up on her. Her hands were on fire.

Some had ended up on her face, too. She dragged a sleeve across her eyes to wipe aside the tears. "Malcolm, you *asshole*!" she barked at the young vampire.

Malcolm was doubled up a few yards away, rubbing frantically at his eyes. "You didn't need to pepper spray me. Well, *us*."

"What did you expect, grabbing a woman out of nowhere?" Julie planted her hands on her hips, blinking watery eyes. "You're lucky I didn't kick your balls up into your throat."

"Don't you need to be able to see what you're doing for that?" Malcolm spat in the dirt and wiped his mouth with a sleeve. "And for spraying people, for that matter."

Julie scoffed. "Still managed to hit you."

Malcolm poked the bottle with a toe. "What kind of potion is that, anyway?"

"It's just pepper spray," Julie told him.

Malcolm raised his eyebrows. "Felt like garlic to me."

Julie snickered. "Maybe I *should* carry some garlic, in case I'm grabbed by vampires in a dark alleyway."

"Ha!" Malcolm grinned. "As if you'd do such a thing."

The purr of an engine announced the arrival of an Audi RS. Its paintwork was so deeply black that it seemed to swallow the streetlights, and its tinted windows added to the effect of seeming like it was composed entirely of shadows.

Julie dived for her pepper spray as the car purred to a halt. But when the driver's door crashed open, it was Taylor who tumbled out.

"Julie!" He slammed the door and jogged up to her, his eyes widening when he saw her reddened face. "What happened?" Whipping around, he spotted Malcolm and stepped between them.

"Nothing, Taylor. Chill." Julie laughed. "Malcolm surprised me and I pepper sprayed the shit out of us both."

"What are you doing here?" Taylor demanded, wheeling on Malcolm.

"Calm down, dude." Malcolm held up his hands, smiling to defuse the situation. "I was tracking that Yeti again. You know, the one who mugged me."

Julie turned to the vampire. "Is that him? The one that was going up this street?"

"I think so." Malcolm nodded. "I've been tracking him all the way from Staten Island."

"I spotted him in Bay Ridge and followed him here," Julie told him.

Taylor folded his arms. "All on your own. You can be glad Malcolm was the only thing that found you. Where's the Yeti now?"

"I lost track of it." Julie pouted. "Your text distracted me."

"Well, I'm sorry for trying to protect you," Taylor grumbled. "Where's Hat?"

"Guarding Genevieve. She's parked in Bay Ridge." Julie ran a hand over her bare head. "Can you still track that Yeti, Malcolm?"

"Obviously." Malcolm snorted. "I can smell him from here. I know his scent almost better than my own."

Julie cocked her head to one side. "Why are you so bent on tracking him down, anyway? OPMA is working hard to catch all of the Yetis and find out what's behind the weird way they're acting."

Malcolm lowered his gaze, scuffing a toe in the dirt. "I'm…just tired of my Sire treating me like a stupid teenager, I guess. I'm almost fifty, after all. I'm almost of age. He could start giving me some responsibility… Some respect."

Julie studied him for a moment before speaking. "That's why you're getting married?"

Malcolm shrugged. "I need to show him that I'm ready for more responsibility. Hopefully the handfasting will do that, and if it doesn't, well, if I take care of the mugger myself, maybe this will finally show Sire that I'm ready for a seat at the adults' table."

Julie glanced at Taylor, wondering if her partner could empathize with Malcolm's predicament.

The elf gave a tiny shrug. "I mean, I get where you're coming from, Malcolm."

"Yeah, even though I'm not convinced going after a gang of dangerous criminals on your own is the best way to show your dad that you're responsible," Julie added.

Malcolm threw up his hands. "I feel like I've tried everything else. Nothing seems to please him."

Taylor gave the vampire a little mock punch in the upper arm. "Hey, I get it. Trust me."

Julie thought of her mom and felt a pang of guilt. She needed to give her a call. At least she'd texted her to let her know she was safely back from Montana, and sent her a few photos—not including any werewolves or centaurs—from the trip. Aloe vera juice was better than constant disapproval, she guessed.

"Well, anyway, we could use some vampire super senses to help us find the Yeti again." Julie turned to Taylor. "How's your hearing?"

"Screwed." Taylor grimaced. "Seems like it only really works out in the wild. But what's this about finding Yetis?"

"I told you, we just want to see what they're doing." Julie glanced down the alley again. "It would help to know where they've gone."

Taylor shifted his weight. "I think we should call it in."

"No!" Malcolm protested hotly. "Please. At least let me show you where they are. I've been watching this Yeti for a long time, and he keeps going into the same factory. I think there might be more of them in there."

Taylor pulled out his phone. "Malcolm, it's not that I don't have sympathy, but this is dangerous."

"I'm a vampire, remember?" Malcolm grinned, showing the tips of his fangs. "Come on, Taylor. We're just going to see where they are. Then we can call it in."

"They'll take forever to get here, anyway," Julie pointed out. "We need to keep tabs on the Yeti and make sure it doesn't slip away, or we'd just be sending them on a wild goose chase."

Taylor sighed. "Okay." He slid his phone back into his pocket. "Let's check out that factory of yours."

Malcom led Julie and Taylor to the corner of the street. From their vantage point behind a parked van, they assessed the large, blockish building. While some of the other factories in this part of Bush Terminal were rumbling and clattering with activity, this one was dark and silent.

"It's abandoned," Malcolm told them. "I've never seen human activity here, and I've been tracking the Yeti here for a few days now."

"Are you sure this time that it's the one who mugged you?" Julie double checked.

Malcolm huffed. "Yes, I am, for your information."

Taylor studied the building with a considering frown. "How are we going to get in without the Yetis finding out we're here?"

"The Yetis use that side door." Malcolm pointed at the entrance. "I thought we could go through the window with the broken pane near the loading bay. We could lift the board out and slip inside."

Julie was about to reply when the squeal of tires screeched through the night. All three of them whipped around to see the headlights barreling directly toward them. The brakes screamed, and the car swerved violently, one front wheel bumping painfully up the curb.

The driver's door banged open and an irate vampire leaped onto the sidewalk. Cassidy's long black hair was windblown around her face and her red eyes throbbed with an intensity Julie had never seen before.

Slamming the door of the bright red Porsche Carrera, she strode straight to Malcolm, her eyes flashing dangerously at Julie. "What are you *doing* here?" she demanded, her nasal New York accent twanging loudly even to native ears like Julie's. "And what are you doing with *her?*"

Malcolm held out his hands. "Please, Cass. Keep your voice down!"

"Answer my question, Malcolm!" Cassidy yelled.

Julie stepped forward, keeping her tone calm. "It's not what you think, Cassidy. We were—"

Cassidy rounded on Julie and lunged at her with a wordless shriek and her hands outstretched. Her perfectly manicured French tips had transformed into a set of deadly claws, sharp and white and clean as a cat's.

Julie stumbled back with a yelp despite herself as Cassidy swiped at her face, her claws cutting the air inches from her skin.

Malcolm flung his arms around Cassidy and hauled her back. "Cassidy! Will you stop?" he growled. "We're tracking the Yeti. That's *all*!"

Cassidy fought to pull away, panting furiously. Her fangs protruded from beneath her upper lip as she snapped them in Julie's direction. "Oh, so you'd track a dangerous enemy with *her*, not me?"

"Snap out of it, Cassidy!" Malcolm seized Cassidy's shoulders and turned her to face him, giving her a gentle shake. "She just happened to be here. It's not like it was planned."

"Oh, you think that's a good excuse, do you?" Cassidy bellowed.

Taylor put a hand on Julie's shoulder and stepped between her and the vampires. "Are you okay?"

"I'm fine." Julie grimaced toward the factory. "But those Yetis are going to know we're here in a matter of seconds if those two don't quit arguing."

Taylor sniffed. "Yeah, VampBitch's timing is as bad as ever."

"Taylor!" Julie couldn't hold back a disbelieving laugh. "Malcolm is right here."

"She's still a bitch," Taylor grumbled. "I think we need to call this in before the Yetis get away, even if we don't have definitive proof that they're in there."

"Either that, or we should get popcorn." Julie sighed as the two vampires continued to argue at the tops of their voices. "Okay. Call it in. We're going to draw far too much attention if they don't work it out quickly."

"How could you be running around with a *human*?" Cassidy was sobbing, huge fake tears running down her cheeks. "How could you do that to me?"

"Cassidy! Don't be speciesist," Malcolm hissed.

"Yeah, I don't think working it out is going to happen." Taylor pulled out his phone and took a step aside, making a call.

Cassidy's shoulders sagged. "Speciesist is a strong word, Malcolm. How could you say that to me?"

"Well, Cass, you're acting that way." Malcolm's grip gentled on her shoulders. "Come on. This isn't you. You know that I love you. Why would I trade you in for *anyone* else, regardless of their species?" His voice lowered, growing warm and deep, and he rubbed his thumbs along her shoulders.

The tears came a little more slowly, though Cassidy was still shooting Julie venomous looks. "Come home with me, Malcolm. Please."

"I can't. You know I have to do this." Malcolm switched his grip to her hands. "Please, go home, love."

Cassidy's lower lip trembled again. "I want to help."

Malcolm squeezed her hands. "You can help by going home where you're safe, okay? I can't concentrate knowing that you're in danger."

Cassidy looked at Julie again. "But *she* can help you?"

"That's because she's not my fiancée." Malcolm pulled her in for a forehead kiss. Cassidy resisted, her face still twisted with anger. "Please, baby," he pleaded. "I'm begging you."

"Fine." Cassidy pulled away from Malcolm abruptly. "Do what you want."

She shoved past him and strode back to her car, then threw herself behind the wheel and drove off in a cloud of smoke from the tires.

Julie gritted her teeth at the screech of rubber.

"Sorry about that." Malcolm grimaced, turning to her. "She's a little…intense sometimes."

Julie raised an eyebrow. "Sometimes?"

"Intense?" Taylor added after ending his call. "That's being kind. I'm surprised you convinced her to leave."

Malcolm scowled at Taylor. "Hey, that *is* my fiancée you're talking about."

Taylor dropped his phone into his pocket. "OPMA agents and

soldiers are enroute. Maybe the Yetis will still be here when they get here."

Malcolm turned back to the building. "Okay, so are we going to try the loading bay window?"

"Wait a minute." Taylor held up his hands. "Aren't we going to wait for backup?"

Malcolm sighed. "I need to do this. You two can wait here, but I'm going in. If I wait for the authorities to get here, I'll be pushed out and my plan to show Sire what I'm made of will be dust in the wind."

Julie took a step toward Malcolm. "You can't go in alone. I'm going with you."

"Julie, this is madness," Taylor hissed.

"You can't stop me. I'm not letting Malcolm do this alone." Julie grinned. "What harm could it do to scout ahead before the agents get here?"

Taylor groaned, but when Malcolm and Julie started down the street toward the factory, he followed close behind them.

CHAPTER FIFTEEN

Lifting the board away from the broken windowpane proved easy once Julie was balanced on Taylor's shoulders. Carefully avoiding the broken glass, she gripped the windowsill and pulled herself headfirst into the dark interior of the factory.

She landed almost soundlessly on top of a plastic-wrapped bale of fabric. Regaining her footing, she crouched beside the bale while her eyes adjusted to the darkness. The open space was dusty and silent. Pallets of inventory, long racks, and enormous steamers filled the space around the floor.

"Julie!" Taylor hissed. "Are you okay? I told you we shouldn't have sent her in first!"

Malcolm chuckled. "She's fine, Taylor. Don't worry about her. She can handle herself."

Julie called up to the window. "Malcolm's right, you know. I *am* fine, and I *can* handle myself."

"Well, get out of the way so that I can get through the window, smartass," Taylor grumbled.

He came in after her, rolling gracefully off the bale and landing on his feet on the dusty floor. Malcolm followed.

"I'm not sure they're even in here," Julie whispered. "It's abandoned, like you said."

"It's all dusty." Taylor ran a finger along the plastic. "Like no one's been here in a long time."

Julie nodded. "I think this was a clothing factory."

"But all of the equipment and inventory is still here." Malcolm frowned. "Isn't it weird that none of this stuff has been sold if the company went under?"

"You'd think the factory would have been repurposed by now," Taylor agreed.

"Not only that. There's no sign of squatters, in a city with fifty thousand homeless." Julie looked around, rubbing away the goosebumps that broke out on her arms at the strangle, tingling sensation on her skin. "It's so quiet. *Too* quiet."

"Good point." Malcolm crouched, sniffing at the air.

Julie wished she'd picked up her pepper spray bottle. "Are you sure this is where the Yeti went?"

"Definitely." Malcolm nodded. "I can smell Yeti."

"Me too." Taylor turned left and right, glancing into every corner.

"Okay." Julie shrugged. "All I smell is moldering clothes and general abandonment, but I guess we should take a look around."

Malcolm straightened. "Good idea. I'll go this way, and you two go that way?"

Julie shook her head, hard. "Uh-uh. We stick together. This isn't Scooby Doo."

Taylor took a step closer to her. "I'm with Julie on this one."

Malcolm shrugged. "I guess backing each other up isn't a stupid idea. The Yeti scent seems stronger this way."

Taylor gestured. "Lead the way."

The vampire crept forward with Julie and Taylor sticking close behind. It didn't take long before he stopped and pointed at the floor. "Look."

Julie leaned closer. In the faint light coming from the streetlights outside, she could just make out huge, barefoot tracks in the dust.

"Yetis!" she whispered.

"They look like they're going through that door." Malcolm started forward. "Come on!"

"I don't—" Taylor began, but his protest was cut short by Julie jogging after the vampire. He suppressed a muffled curse as he followed.

The door was half open. Malcolm cautiously pushed it wider, but the room beyond was empty. "Looks like a maintenance area," he whispered.

Julie nodded. Bright yellow buckets, industrial-sized mops and brooms, and huge barrels of disinfectant stood everywhere. There was a huge furnace in the corner. The dull gleam of cast iron told them it had been there since the factory was built. On the other side of the room, they spotted a narrow door leading into deep shadow, and a series of grimy concrete steps heading down into the musty darkness.

"He went that way," Malcolm whispered.

They approached the door slowly. When they got closer, Julie could read the sign on the door. *Sewer System Entrance.*

"Gross!" She stepped back, keeping her voice to a hiss. "Are they down *there*?"

Taylor wrinkled his nose. "Sure smells that way."

"Smells a lot of other ways, too." Malcolm groaned. "Well, I guess we'd better go after them."

"That's disgusting. I signed up for Yeti fighting, not for swimming around in a sewer," Julie grumbled.

Taylor raised an eyebrow at her. "Fighting? I thought you were only planning to scout ahead." He enclosed the last two words in air quotes.

"Shhh. You'll give us away," Malcolm hissed. He cautiously began to descend the steps into the sewer.

Taylor gestured to Julie. "After you."

"Well, aren't you a gentleman," Julie muttered. She pushed past him and took a few slow steps down the stairs. A pale light suddenly illuminated a circle of space when Malcolm held up his phone flashlight.

"Thanks," Julie whispered, reaching him. Taylor was right behind her.

"No need to whisper, I think." Malcolm held up his phone and shone it around. "The Yeti's been gone for several minutes already, by the smell of it. He went that way." He pointed down a sewer tunnel.

Julie wrinkled her nose, groping for her phone. "A lot of other things have been gone from this earth for several *months* already, by the smell of *them*."

"Oh, no. That's not decaying flesh. That's just human excrement." Taylor held up his phone and turned on its flashlight.

Julie scoffed. "Wow, thanks. Helpful." She went to switch on her phone flashlight and spotted some very empty-looking bars in the corner of her screen. "Hey, do you guys have any signal?"

Taylor glanced at his phone. "No, nothing."

"Me neither." Malcolm grinned, his fangs gleaming eerily in the low lighting. "Now Sire won't be able to find me even if the captain tattles on me again."

"Yeah, but Kaplan won't be able to find us, either," Julie pointed out. "I'd better let him know where we are just in case."

"We'd better turn back," Taylor grouched, but he didn't protest when Julie jogged up the steps and fired off a quick text to the captain.

Going into the sewer system at this address. Yeti smell a few minutes old.

Julie saw he read the text almost immediately, but she hurried to rejoin Taylor and Malcolm downstairs before she got a reply.

Holding up her phone, she looked around the tunnel. It was dark and slimy, with fungus clinging to the walls. There was a chipped concrete platform down either side and gray water slopped unhealthily in the middle. Julie heard squeaking and scrabbling from the other side of the tunnel. When she whipped her phone in that direction, she saw nothing, but she had the uncomfortable impression that something small had just darted out of the light.

"Where's that running water coming from?" Taylor whispered.

Julie pointed her flashlight at the rusty pipes that were set at regular intervals in the sides of the platforms. "Inlet pipes."

"Inlet for what?" Malcolm muttered. "Actually, no, don't answer that, Julie. I just *know* that you know." He squared his shoulders. "Come on. The Yeti went this way."

He squelched forth, and Julie hurried after him, keeping her phone's flashlight on. She could still hear the occasional squeal of rodents in the darkness. *Rats don't bother you*, she told herself. *Relax*. Still, the hair on the back of her neck stood on end.

"They never tell you how bad it smells down here in the movies," Julie observed.

Malcolm had a hand over his mouth and nose. "Try having vampire senses."

"You know, I think I'll pass on that." Julie paused by a grimy wall and dug a pen out of her pocket. Using the tip of it, she scratched an arrow into the grime, adding the point to indicate the direction they were going.

Taylor peered at the arrow. "What are you doing?"

"Marking which way we went, in case agents come down here after us," Julie explained.

Malcolm hadn't slowed down. "Then we'd better reach the Yetis before they do."

"Really bent on this revenge thing, huh?" Taylor mumbled.

Malcolm paused, reaching a fork in the tunnel. Two identical tunnels ran off in either direction. Even with his hand over his nose, Julie could hear the vampire sniffing.

"This way." He gestured to the right tunnel with his phone. "It's more than just the single Yeti's scent right now. It's a buildup of scent, like this path has been used a lot over time by a bunch of different Yetis."

"How close are we?" Julie whispered.

Malcolm shrugged. "With the sewer smell, I'm amazed I can follow their trail at all. There are too many layers of scent. I don't know where he is."

Taylor gripped his phone tighter. "So he could be right around the next corner."

Malcolm nodded. "I guess we just have to go slowly."

They advanced as quietly as they could. Julie's phone helpfully informed her that its battery was starting to run low. She ignored it. Every time she swept the weak beam in a new direction, there was a scrabbling of tiny paws and she caught a few glimpses of hairless, naked tails sliding along the concrete.

Several more forks in the tunnels eventually led them to the first real evidence Julie had seen of Yeti activity. The tunnel had once ended in an iron gate. Now, the gate lay propped against the tunnel wall, corroded by time. There were great chunks of bare brick exposed where its hinges had once been sunk deep into the walls. The hinges were still attached to the gate, crusted with concrete and bits of broken brick. Something huge had ripped it clean out of the wall.

Julie plucked a tuft of fur from a sharp edge on the gate. It was mingled black and brown. She half expected it to feel wiry, but it was unspeakably soft. She might as well be touching a snow leopard. "Look at this."

"Yeti fur," Malcolm confirmed her suspicions. "They're close. Very close."

Julie swallowed. "We're a long way from the exit. We've been walking for, what, an hour?"

Taylor glanced at his phone. "Twenty minutes."

It felt like so much longer. Malcolm raised a finger to his lips, and they crept through the gateway and into a larger junction chamber.

Julie's heart gave a painful thud in the back of her throat, and she shone her phone frantically in every direction as squeaking rats skittered into the shadows. Six tunnels branched off from the chamber, including the one they'd just stepped out of. All of them looked empty...except for a faint glow emanating from the tunnel on the opposite side of the chamber.

She slid a hand over her back pocket, wishing she had her pepper spray. Or something deadlier than that. Thinking of the shotgun under Lillie's sofa, Julie remembered the times that Dad had told her that every woman should carry a handgun.

"I should have gone for that firearms certification Dad wanted me to do," she whispered to Taylor.

The elf sighed. "'Scouting ahead' isn't as easy as you thought, right?"

Julie punched him in the arm. "Give it a rest, Taylor."

"Shhh, both of you!" Malcolm whispered. "Come on."

He headed for the glowing tunnel, and now even Julie could pick up the scent of Yeti. It was a musky, oily smell, not exactly unpleasant and not quite animal, either, but strong. There was no water in this tunnel, and they crept along the middle. Julie's boots crunched a few times, and squelched at others. She resolutely kept her eyes up to avoid seeing whatever it was she was stepping in.

Taylor had to hunch his shoulders to fit underneath the roof of the tunnel.

In a matter of yards, the glow was brighter. Julie had thought it was a fire or something at first, but the glow was bluish and the temperature seemed to be dropping the farther they went. She shivered, running a hand over her goosebump-covered arms, and not just because of the increasing cold.

The glow was eerie. Was it some kind of magical fluorescence? She wanted to ask, but the silence in the tunnel was almost absolute except for their footsteps.

Julie was staring so intently at the glow that she almost crashed into Malcolm when he stopped. "What?" she hissed.

"Shhh!" Malcolm gestured to a branch in the tunnel up ahead. As before, the tunnel to the right held the bluish glow, but this time it widened after the fork. He peered intently down the tunnel for a few seconds before heading for the glow.

Taylor's hand on her shoulder stopped Julie from following. "Are you sure about this?" he whispered in her ear.

She brushed aside a ticklish piece of hair stirred by his breath. "We can't let him go alone, and we're not going to stop him."

Taylor lowered his hand. "I guess you're right."

They started forward when a gargling roar filled the tunnel with haunting and intense echoes, its pitch fluctuating wildly.

Julie grabbed Taylor's arm. "You never told me Wookies were real!"

Before he had a chance to reply, three Yetis burst out of the darkness.

CHAPTER SIXTEEN

Julie had just about enough time to spit a string of curses before the Yeti was upon her. She caught a vague impression of glowing eyes, yellowed tusks, and massive, outstretched hands in the semi-darkness. She dodged, hard, like Taylor had taught her. Then she kicked the Yeti in the nuts with all of her might, like nineteen years of being female had taught her.

To Julie's relief, the Yeti let out a guttural roar and fell to its knees.

Malcolm and the second Yeti rolled past in a blur of shrieking and clawing. She looked around wildly for Taylor, who was grappling hand-to-hand with the third Yeti.

His knuckles were white where he gripped the creature by its wrists. The Yeti lowered its head and roared in Taylor's face, ruffling his hair, then forced its weight down on him. Taylor's knees buckled, but he dropped and rolled out of the way as the Yeti pushed, forcing its momentum to bring it crashing to the floor on its face. The Yeti sprawled out and lay still, stunned by the impact.

Taylor whipped around to face her. "Julie, look out!"

Julie ducked just in time as another Yeti lunged at her. Taylor charged and tackled it by the waist, his shoulder slamming into its ribs as two more Yetis came out of nowhere.

Malcolm had one pinned to the floor with a boot on its back as he swiped at one of the new attackers, his sharp claws singing through the air. The other went for Julie, clenching its hands into fists as it let out a roar that flapped its loose lips.

"Come at me, asshole!" Julie raised her hands to her face, her feet settling into a fighting stance. "Come and get some!"

"Julie, no!"

Taylor's yell sounded distant as the Yeti charged her. Julie dipped to the side to avoid its first blow, then lashed out and landed a jab and a punch on its ribs. It whirled to face her, its giant arm flying toward her face.

Julie grabbed its forearm with both hands and cursed again as its massive strength lifted her off her feet. Kicking madly, her boots landed punily against its belly. The Yeti roared again, reaching for her with its free hand. Still clinging to its other arm with both hands, she chomped down hard on its thumb when its hairy fingers clawed at her face.

The Yeti let out a moaning cry and shook her off. Julie landed on her feet and crouched, ready to dodge a blow, but Taylor grabbed the Yeti from behind. He threw an arm around its neck in a chokehold and squeezed to cut off its air supply. The Yeti thrashed, but in a matter of seconds it had crumpled to the floor.

A Yeti screamed behind Julie. She whipped around as one of them fell with Malcolm's claw marks raked across its face. Malcolm stepped back toward her, fangs flashing as the sound of more footsteps thundered from around the corner.

"How many more of them *are* there?" Taylor stepped in front of Julie, his hands raised. The graze across his cheek slowly oozed blood.

"I don't know." Malcolm sniffed, dragging a sleeve over his upper lip to staunch his bleeding nose. "But it sounds like a lot."

Taylor bent down and picked up a broken brick from the

floor of the tunnel. "We're outnumbered. Julie, you should go back and call Kaplan."

Julie shook her head and raised her hands to her face, the way Taylor had shown her. "Kaplan knows where we are. I'm not leaving you guys to fight them alone."

Taylor gave her a despairing look over his shoulder as another tide of Yetis charged them, all tusks and gigantic fists. He lobbed the brick into the forehead of one, knocking it back. Julie unleashed a defiant yell as she raised her fists and braced herself for the impact of another.

Before it slammed into her, Taylor grabbed the Yeti's arm and twisted it behind its back. He sent the Yeti smashing face first into the wall with a shove. Malcolm was flitting among the other Yetis, his claws and fangs drawing squeals of pain from their attackers.

Taylor charged at the wall of Yetis waiting at the bend in the tunnel with a roar. He knocked aside the hands of one and grabbed it by the throat. Another yowled and closed its giant hands over his shoulder.

"Let him go!" Julie screamed, running up to the Yeti and kicking it in the shins. It slammed a massive hand into her chest and knocked her back.

Taylor planted an elbow in its ribs, bringing it howling to his knees. It swiped at his ankles and he narrowly managed to dodge, still choking out another opponent. Julie grabbed the half brick that he'd thrown earlier and smacked it into the back of the Yeti's skull, and it fell face first to the floor.

Malcolm and another Yeti tumbled past them in a flurry of blows. Julie dealt the tumbling Yeti a swift kick to the ribs as it rolled past. It roared and clawed at her, giving Malcolm an opportunity to sink his fangs into its shoulder.

The Yeti scrambled to its feet and fled, clutching its shoulder and wailing.

Malcolm spat Yeti fur out of his mouth. "Ugh!"

"Taste rank, don't they?" Julie sympathized. "Come on. Let's see where it went!" She glanced back at Malcolm to make sure he was following her.

"Julie, look out!" Taylor screamed.

She reacted a split second too late. The charging Yeti was upon her. She threw out her arms to shield herself as the Yeti barreled into her, throwing her sideways. She impacted the wall of the tunnel, the back of her head bouncing against the bare brick, and she slid to the floor with spots swarming in her vision.

Her ears were filled with a high-pitched ringing, so she only distantly heard Taylor's roar. He flashed across her blurry vision and collided shoulder first with the Yeti.

The Yeti was huge and furious and kept its balance. It gouged him with its claws, cutting deep into his back. Dark stains spread over the back of Taylor's jacket, but he kept going until he'd rammed the Yeti against the wall.

They exchanged a flurry of blows, Taylor's fist smashing against its jaw. The Yeti knocked his hands aside and lunged at him again. Julie expected the Yeti to grab Taylor around the throat, but instead of going for the kill, it slammed both hands into his shoulders and sent him staggering backward.

Julie frowned. The small movement sent pangs of pain through her splitting head. Her thoughts were coming too slowly. Taylor and Malcolm drifted in and out of focus as they continued to struggle with the Yetis.

Why didn't that Yeti grab Taylor by the throat?

For that matter, why had none of the Yetis used their deadly tusks in this fight?

Malcolm flashed across her vision as Taylor grappled with the Yeti. His claws raked across the Yeti's ribs, then he whirled and rushed at another that was crouched in the tunnel with its big fists curled in defense.

The Yeti yowled, the sound tinny and distant to Julie's ringing ears, and swiped at him with a hand. However, when Malcolm sank his teeth into the Yeti's fleshy palm, it didn't take the opportunity to bite back.

Defense.

Julie blinked at the bend in the tunnel, willing her double vision to clear. The blue glow was more intense here, and she could see something swirling in it. The Yetis weren't trying to kill them, she realized. They were trying to stop them from getting around that bend and seeing whatever it was that was giving off the blue light.

The light sparkled on little flecks of something white that blew around as if driven by wind. It looked like...*snow?*

It can't be snow, Julie. She shook her head sharply, trying to clear it as she struggled to get back to her feet. The floor pitched underneath her and she crumpled again with nausea lurching in her stomach.

Taylor backed up toward her, holding up his fists as three more Yetis came clumping around the bend in the tunnel and rushed at him. Malcolm was tussling with a fourth, stumbling over the stunned bodies of the defeated with sweat trickling down his pale face as he slashed at them with his claws. Taylor landed a punch on the cheek of one Yeti and a roundhouse kick in the belly of another, but the third knocked his foot out of the way, sending him stumbling off balance.

"Taylor!" Julie yelled when it seized him by the front of his jacket and hoisted him into the air.

Taylor tucked his head in, narrowly avoiding his skull hitting the top of the tunnel. His bloodied back smacked against the brick and he let out a grunt of pain. The Yeti flung him to the ground beside Julie with a terrible, bone-rattling thump. His eyes rolled back in his head, and he lay still.

Julie dragged herself to her knees and spat blood, bunching her hands into fists that trembled in front of her face. "If you want to get him, you'll have to go through me, you giant asshole!"

The Yeti threw back its head and roared, the muscles flexing in its hairy chest. Julie braced herself for the attack. Then, the flying figure of another Yeti was flung into its chest, knocking them both to the ground as yet another wave of Yetis came rushing down the tunnel toward them.

"Impressive!" Julie yelled to Malcolm. "Didn't know you could throw a full-grown Yeti."

"Neither did I." Malcolm stepped in front of her, placing himself between her and Taylor and the approaching Yetis. He was shaking visibly, and blood ran from a cut on his cheek.

Taylor let out a groan and sat up abruptly, wincing. His wild, disoriented gaze settled on the tunnel.

Julie grabbed his arm. "Taylor, are you okay?"

He shoved her aside and tried to get to his feet, his eyes fixed on the charging Yetis.

"We can't win this fight," Malcolm muttered, gritting his teeth and raising his claws. "We can't."

Taylor had made it to his feet, but he was swaying and there was blood soaking through his jacket. Julie forced herself to get up from her knees. The floor bucked under her, but the Yetis were rushing at Malcolm and there were so many of them.

A fresh roar shook the tunnel, but it was nothing like the gargling Wookie cry of a Yeti. This roar was loud and pure and raw and animal, with harsh, breathy notes that reverberated primal anger.

The pounding of heavy footsteps was accompanied by a massive blur of gold striped with black that hurtled past Malcolm and launched itself into the Yetis. The Yetis were scattered like bowling pins.

Despite Julie's blurred vision, she was able to make out that their rescuer was feline and almost as big as the Yetis. Its giant claws flashed out, opening bloody lines on every Yeti they touched.

The Yetis' bellows of anger turned into screeches and yelps of pain. One of them lunged at the golden creature, throwing its arms around the animal's neck. The feline sank its claws into the Yeti's back and flung it aside, then pounced on another. The Yeti's scream cut into a wailing gargle as the creature's jaws closed around its neck.

The rest of the Yetis had had enough. They scrambled down the tunnel, yipping and screeching, and were gone.

The feline creature stood panting in front of Malcolm, and Julie blinked away the last of her double vision. It was... It was a *tiger*. A male tiger, all lithe feline grace and brutal power.

His tail lashed against his flanks, and his claws were extended, ice-white and razor sharp as they scored deep marks into the floor of the tunnel. The growl that emanated from the tiger's chest was so low and deep that it shook Julie's bones.

The tiger was bathed in the bluish glow for a few seconds before it suddenly winked out, leaving them with only the light of their phones, which lay scattered over the tunnel floor. Julie groped for the nearest one and held it up. The tiger was facing them, watching them, and his eyes were burning amber.

Burning amber, and somehow, familiar...

Malcolm's knees buckled. He slumped to the floor, raising a trembling hand to the cut on his cheek. Looking down, almost uncomprehendingly, at the blood on his fingers, he returned his gaze to the towering tiger that stood just a few inches away from him.

He took a deep breath. Julie felt around on the floor for that handy half brick.

Then Malcolm spoke. "Thanks for the save, Uncle Jack."

Taylor wriggled his fingers at his phone, hoping he wasn't too badly injured for his magic to work. It floated into his hand and he held it up. In the weak light of both phone flashlights, the gigantic tiger sat down on his haunches and curled his tail around his paws like a house cat.

He must be a Bengal tiger, Julie noted dully, *judging by the amount of white on his belly and the insides of his legs.*

"You're an idiot to have gotten yourself into this situation in the first place, Malcolm." The deep, rumbling voice came from the tiger.

Julie stared at him, her throbbing brain refusing to cooperate. That voice! She knew it from somewhere.

The clatter of footsteps came from deeper inside the tunnel. "This way!" an unfamiliar voice shouted.

"The medics will take you to the surface," the tiger continued. He fixed his eyes on Julie. "Meadows, Woodskin, are you hurt?"

Taylor crouched beside Julie. "Are you okay?"

"I'm fine. Just got my bell rung." Julie tapped the side of her head and took Taylor's arm, allowing him to hoist her to her feet. "I'm okay. Wait, did you just call me Meadows?" she asked the tiger.

He yawned, exposing teeth as long as Julie's index finger, and gave her a familiar burning stare. "What else do you expect?"

Julie felt her jaw drop. *"Captain?"*

The tiger's outline shimmered, his body morphed. The next moment, a familiar enormous figure in a red OPMA uniform was standing in front of them with his arms crossed and a scowl of annoyance on his face.

"What did I tell you about restricting your activities to recruitment?" Kaplan snarled.

"You're a Weretiger?" Julie grinned. "That's pretty awesome. Can you roar when you're in human form?"

Kaplan emitted a huffing sigh as agents in blue uniform came running in carrying flashlights and weapons and wary expressions.

"That way," he growled, pointing down the tunnel. "Go after them, and try not to destroy the crime scene while you're at it."

The agents stampeded past, followed a few seconds later by three medics in purple uniforms wearing combat boots and weighed down by bags of equipment.

"These three need your attention." Kaplan gestured at Julie, Malcolm and Taylor. "I'll make sure those Yetis don't come back."

Without another word, he turned to face the direction the Yetis had come from and stood motionless in a guard stance. Julie briefly wondered whether he was carrying a weapon before concluding that he *was* a weapon.

Taylor nudged her toward the nearest medic. "She's hurt the worst."

"Don't listen to him." Julie let go of his arm and somehow managed not to fall over. "He's bleeding. Malcolm, too."

"Luckily there are three of us." The nearest medic, an elegant elf with straight black hair and piercingly green eyes, winked at Julie. "We've got you."

A dwarf with a glorious black beard was examining Taylor. "We've got lacerations and venous bleeding over here, boss."

"Better get them to the surface quickly," the elf looking Malcolm over told the second dwarf, whose well-groomed silvery hair made him look more like a prince than a medic. "Can your patient walk, Dirk?"

The silver-haired dwarf nodded. "Just about."

"All P3, then. Walking wounded." The elf patted Julie on the arm. "Means you're not going to die today."

"That's...reassuring." Julie offered.

"There's a manhole about twenty yards that way." The bearded dwarf pointed to the place where the tunnel forked and shuddered visibly. "Let's get them up to the surface and out of this *disgusting* tunnel."

"Good thinking." The elf took Julie gently by the arm. "Come on. Let's get you patched up. Lucky for you, I did a few tours on human ambulances, so I probably won't kill you by accident."

"Gee, thanks," Julie muttered.

They headed down the tunnel, Malcolm leaning heavily on the silver-haired dwarf's broad shoulders. Julie looked back at him. "By the way—*Uncle* Jack?"

Taylor snickered.

A faint flush crept into Malcolm's pale cheeks. "Uh, yeah. He's my godfather."

When they rounded the corner, there was a dead end just a few yards away. The bearded dwarf made a brief motion toward the manhole cover, and it levitated obediently out of its place. Glorious, fresh air whistled into the tunnel, and Julie felt as though she was taking her first breath in ages as they moved toward the light.

Kaplan waited until that crazy-ass human and the two princely stooges had been safely taken away before he started down the tunnel, following his agents. As he moved, he slipped fluidly into his tiger form, trotting down the tunnel on silent paws.

His nose twitched when he rounded the corner and the tunnel reached an abrupt dead end. There was an open manhole above letting in a cold, electric beam from a nearby streetlight. The light wasn't the only thing that was cold.

Despite the warm June air drifting in from the street above, the tunnel was covered in snow drifts.

Kaplan's insulated paws barely felt the bite of the cold as he prowled across the snow to the bottom of the ladder that led up to the manhole. When he looked up, a burly dwarf with ochre skin, was crouched at the opening with his gun in his hands.

"Agent Johannsen," Kaplan growled.

The agent looked down at him. "Manhole was open when we got here, sir. The others are in pursuit."

Kaplan nodded, but he didn't think that the Yetis had escaped unseen up this ladder, through the narrow manhole and out into the streets of Brooklyn in a matter of seconds. He pawed gently at the snow. It was real, all right. Not the tacky stuff that

Warlocks could conjure out of thin air. No, this was proper snow, snow that had blown in from a distant mountaintop.

His lip curled in annoyance as he sniffed at the air. It wasn't a pleasant thing to do. This was a sewer, after all. A sewer that had recently contained several bleeding, sweating Yetis.

Some of whom had recently shit themselves, Kaplan noted with some pleasure. But there was another smell, fresher and sharper than the others, one that made his claws flex with annoyance.

The smell of a recently closed magic portal.

CHAPTER SEVENTEEN

The black-haired elf kept a hand on Julie's arm to steady her as they stepped through the magic portal. It made a weird ticklish sensation on Julie's skin, just as the one back in Avalon had done.

When she stepped out of the portal, she realized that they were standing on the lawn outside the OPMA HQ building. The two dwarves exited the portal with Malcolm and Taylor, and the elf chuckled with satisfaction as she touched the silver star of life symbol on her chest. The portal disappeared with a faint sizzling noise.

"Pretty cool, huh?" The elf grinned at Julie. "Better than an ambulance, anyway."

"*Much* better than those flying ones we had one year." The silver-haired dwarf shuddered. "Those didn't last long. Not after that one Werecat OD'd on catnip and jumped naked out of the doors at the first whiff of antidote."

"Naked in his human form," the bearded dwarf clarified.

The elf led Julie up to the doors of a side wing of the PMA. A glowing neon sign in red letters over the sliding glass doors proclaimed it to be the emergency room.

"Ever been to the para-ER?" the elf asked.

Julie shook her head, then winced and raised her hand to her throbbing skull.

The elf patted her on the shoulder. "Dr. Olena's on duty tonight. You're in luck. She runs the ER, and she's the best there is."

The ER was quiet, with low, soothing lighting and a meticulously clean tiled floor. Julie obediently followed the elf to the desk inside the doors, where a well-built orc in purple scrubs was squinting through half-moon glasses as he typed at the computer.

"Got three P3s for you, TJ," the elf announced.

The orc gave them a smoldering glare. "Well, you're in luck. Quiet tonight. No wait." He waved an arm. "Take them through, but leave their IDs with me."

The elf led Julie past the desk to a hospital bed and drew the curtains around it. "Here comes Dr. Olena." She gave Julie a last smile. "See you around, I'll bet. You look like the type who's always in trouble."

"Hey!" Julie protested feebly.

The medic disappeared, then the curtains were brushed aside and an elegant elf in a long white lab coat stepped through them. She was tall and achingly beautiful, with silver hair so long that it brushed against the hem of her calf-length coat. Her almond-shaped eyes were pale blue, contrasting beautifully with her skin, which was the color of warm desert sand.

Sylthana Elf, Julie's training slurred. She fished for more information, but it wasn't forthcoming. Thinking too hard made her head hurt.

"Good evening." The Sylthana Elf's smile made elegant little dimples in both cheeks. "You must be my first ever human patient."

"Reassuring," Julie quipped.

"It's okay. I've treated plenty of Weres in their human form. It can't be all that different." The Sylthana Elf winked. "I'm Dr. Olena. You're Julia Meadows, right?"

"Everyone calls me Julie." She sagged back against her pillows, which were deliciously soft.

"Okay, Julie. I hear from the medic that you were in a fight with a suspected head injury?"

Julie winced. "Yeah."

"Okay. Can you tell me what day it is, and where you are?"

"Depends if it's past midnight or not. Either Thursday or Friday, and I'm in the para-ER."

"Good." Dr. Olena slipped a blood pressure cuff around Julie's arm and a monitor onto her fingertip. "Do you mind if I open the curtains? I'd like to keep an eye on you while I check on your friends."

"Sure."

Dr. Olena slid the curtains aside. Taylor was sitting on the bed beside Julie's, shirtless and hunched forward, gripping the edge of his bed with both hands. His teeth were gritted as a Woodland Fae nurse in purple scrubs hovered her hands gently over his back. Julie saw a faint purple glow emanating from behind him.

"You okay, Taylor?" Julie asked.

The elf nodded without speaking.

"Magical healing can be a little painful." Dr. Olena looked over the nurse's shoulder. "It's coming together just fine, Your Highness. You'll be fit as a fiddle in a few minutes."

"Uh-huh," Taylor grunted, sweating profusely.

Beside him, Malcolm was contentedly sipping from a plastic cup with a straw in it. The fluid in the straw, Julie noticed, was crimson.

"Hey, is that human?" she called over at him.

Malcolm rolled his eyes. "I save a human's life, and this is what I get for it," he told Dr. Olena. "Stereotypes."

"Well, it *is* human." Dr. Olena glanced at the screen showing Malcolm's monitors. "Donated, though. And it's working."

Dr. Olena came back over to Julie and peered into her eyes

with a little flashlight, then asked a nurse for a bedside X-ray and held the sheets of film up against the light, frowning.

"What about me, doc?" Julie asked weakly. "Where's my magic fix?"

"I'm afraid I don't have one for you." Dr. Olena set down the X-rays. "You have a concussion, and I could fix that in a minute." She held out a hand and purple light played over her fingers. "But because you're human, I'd rather you healed the old-fashioned way, with rest and time. Magic might do you more harm than good."

"Seriously?" Julie sighed. "Taylor and Malcolm get to be fixed up in minutes, but I'm stuck with a headache?"

"I can give you some Tylenol, but that's about it." Dr. Olena spread her hands, grimacing. "Sorry."

One of the nurses had brought Julie a couple of pills to swallow with a cup of water when the glass doors slid open and one enormous and angry Weretiger in human form brushed straight past the orc at the reception desk and came striding into the ER.

Kaplan's bushy eyebrows were almost touching as his gaze swept over Julie, Taylor, and Malcolm. "I see these idiots haven't managed to get themselves killed, Dr. Olena."

"No, sir. They'll all be okay." Dr. Olena boldly reached up and gave Kaplan's massive bicep a reassuring pat.

Kaplan's eyebrows kissed in the middle of his craggy forehead. "Are they ready to be discharged?"

"Yes, sir. Prince Taylor and Mr. Nox are fully healed. Miss Meadows can't be healed with magic, but her concussion will heal well at home with rest." Dr. Olena turned to Julie. "Avoid screens or reading for a day or so, and get yourself checked out at a human ER if you have any decreased level of consciousness. You shouldn't be alone, either, so someone needs to keep an eye on you. Oh, and remember that I still need you to come in for a mandated physical sometime."

This was the first Julie had heard about a mandated physical.

"The physical can wait," Kaplan growled before Julie could protest.

"Thanks, doc." Julie swung her legs off the bed, waited for the room to stop spinning, and stood up. Taylor was magically beside her, taking her elbow and steadying her. She didn't slap his hand away this time.

"Good." Kaplan glared at Julie, his eyebrows practically having a full-on makeout session. "The three of you. My office. *Now*."

"Sir, Meadows is not well." Taylor's hand tightened on Julie's elbow.

Kaplan flashed his teeth. "I said *now*, Woodskin."

Julie was grateful that there was an elevator straight from the ER to the third floor. It felt strange to enter the familiar floor from the elevator on the other side of the room than usual. She tried not to lean on Taylor too much as they walked across the communal office and into Kaplan's office.

When the captain thumped the door open and strode inside, a tall, elegant figure unfolded himself from one of the armchairs. Malcolm stopped dead in the doorway. It was Julius Nox.

Julius' eyes flashed over his son, the corners of his mouth turning sharply downward.

"Sit down before you fall down and make a spectacle of yourself, Meadows," Kaplan barked, throwing himself into his office chair behind the desk.

Julie sagged into the other armchair. Julius resumed his seat, and Taylor and Malcolm stood awkwardly in front of the desk. Taylor's hands were folded behind his back, and Malcolm fidgeted, his eyes looking everywhere except his father.

Kaplan leaned forward, his fingers interlaced on the desk. "I have to say, I think that you three might just be the three stupidest people who have ever stood in this office, and that's saying something."

"Sir, it was my fault." Malcolm raised his chin. "Taylor wanted to turn back. I was the one who kept going, and they didn't want to leave me alone."

"Oh, they didn't, did they?" Kaplan snapped, his eyes flashing to Julie. "Tell me, why would you follow a friend into terrible danger instead of trying to stop him, Meadows?"

Julie's head felt like an orc was hitting it repeatedly with a sledgehammer. She resisted the urge to fold her arms on the desk and prop her forehead on them. "I don't know, sir."

Kaplan's eyes widened a fraction. "Oh, that's it? No snark? No witty comebacks?"

Julie swallowed the wave of nausea that came with the pain. "No, sir."

Taylor glanced at her, then turned back to Kaplan. "You're right, sir. We should have tried to dissuade him. It's not all his fault."

"It certainly isn't!" Kaplan thundered. "You're a recruiter, Woodskin. A *recruiter*! Do you understand that? Your fighting skills might make you a hotshot in the gym, but you can't take on a pack of Yetis with only a powerless human and an adolescent vampire for help!"

Taylor hung his head. "Yes, sir." He paused. "Did you call my parents, sir?"

"That's none of your business, Woodskin." Kaplan folded his huge arms. "What you three did tonight was foolish beyond expression. You put your lives at risk instead of waiting for people who are trained for these kinds of situations. I never want to see anything like this from any of you ever again, do you understand?"

"Yes, sir," Taylor mumbled.

Julius had said nothing, but his eyes never left Malcolm. The aura of disappointment he radiated was palpable. Taylor's face was gray with shame.

"As for *you*, Meadows," Kaplan snarled, "you don't know enough about this world to plunge headfirst into danger every time you see it. Stop it. Am I making myself clear?"

"Yes, sir." All Julie wanted was to go home, get Hat and Genevieve, and sleep for a week or so.

"Very well." Kaplan sat back, pinching the bridge of his nose, and Julie noticed the lines of exhaustion on his face. "Dismissed."

It felt unfair to have to get up again, but Julie hoisted herself to her feet and stumbled out of the office. Julius swept past with Malcolm's arm clenched in one hand, and neither vampire said anything.

Taylor took Julie's arm and steadied her. "Shall we take a taxi back to where we left our cars?"

Julie nodded, then winced and thought better of it. "Okay."

The taxi ride seemed to take hours. Julie curled up on her seat, her throbbing head cupped in one hand. Taylor only asked her every six seconds or so whether she was feeling sleepy or not.

"Of course I'm sleepy," she snapped at last. "It's like one in the morning and I didn't even get to eat my KFC."

"Fair enough." Taylor laughed. "That sounds a bit more like the Julie I know."

"Oh, shut up." Julie sat up as the taxi came to a halt. "Hey, your car's still here!"

"That's a relief." Taylor paid the driver after they climbed out of the taxi.

The black Audi had a parking ticket under the windscreen wiper. He plucked it off and tossed it onto the seat. "Which street did you say you left Genevieve in again?"

Julie told him. "Hat's gonna be *pissed*."

Taylor chuckled as they drove off. "You can say that again."

Hat was more than pissed. Hat was throwing himself repeatedly against the driver's window when Julie arrived. Relieved that Genevieve was safe and sound, Julie unlocked the door, and Hat immediately flew into her chest.

"Stupid, stupid, *stupid* little human!" he yelled. "You said you were just going to *check it out*, but then you were gone for hours. There was a bunch of OPMA communications activity nearby, and then you were just *gone*! What kind of a partner are you, huh? What kind of a friend would lock me up in the car for..."

Hat stopped when Julie didn't argue back. "Are you okay?"

"Mindspeak, Hat," Julie reminded him weakly. She set Hat down on the roof and leaned against the car. "You're lucky the street's so quiet."

Are you okay? Hat asked in her mind, much more quietly.

"I'm fine. A concussion." Another wave of nausea ran over Julie and she leaned more heavily against Genevieve's roof.

Taylor stepped forward. "Hey, I'm not sure you should drive."

The buzzing in Julie's ears had returned. She took a few deep breaths, riding it out, and swallowed the nausea. "I'm okay." She straightened up and smiled brightly at Taylor. "I'll be fine once I—"

The world tilted and Julie's legs gave out. She had a sensation of falling, and cracked concrete and tangled weeds rushing toward her face. Strong hands closed around her arms, and her vision turned black for a few dizzy seconds before she realized that she was leaning against Taylor, her head lolling on his shoulder. She tried to straighten up, but he kept an arm around her shoulders.

"Julie?" Taylor's voice came distantly through the ringing in her ears. "Julie!"

"Ugh...I'm okay," Julie slurred.

"No, you're not okay." Taylor's voice was shaking as he supported her over to the passenger side of Genevieve.

Julie's legs felt like noodles. She wanted to protest, but she was too dizzy to do anything except lean heavily against Taylor as he opened the door. She allowed herself to be stuffed into the passenger seat.

"Gonna puke," she moaned.

"It's okay. I've got you." Taylor leaned over her to buckle her seat belt. She batted him away, doing it herself. He smelled like the earth after rain, she realized foggily.

Leaning back against her seat, she took a few deep breaths, her vision slowly clearing. "Not gonna puke anymore." She sat up a little straighter. "I'm okay now."

"No, you're not." Taylor leaned on Genevieve's roof, his brow wrinkled. "I'm taking you to the nearest human hospital."

Julie waved a hand. "No. Please. I don't want to go."

"You should get checked out," Taylor insisted.

Hat wriggled over the center console and into her lap like a needy kitten. "You're hurt," he whispered.

"Dr. Olena said I just need rest and someone to keep an eye on me." Julie closed her eyes. "Lillie can do that. Please, Taylor. Just take me home."

Taylor sighed. "Okay... If you're sure."

"I am," Julie told him. "Home. Please."

Taylor closed the passenger door and Julie felt Genevieve rock slightly as he slipped into the driver's seat, having to slide it back considerably to fold his legs into it.

Julie opened her eyes. "What about your car?"

"I've just texted the butler. He'll send someone to come and get it." Taylor started Genevieve, and the familiar purr of the engine filled the air. "I can see why you like this old car so much."

"Old car!" Julie spluttered. "*Old car!*"

"Don't excite her, you stupid elf," Hat snapped. "She needs rest."

"Okay, okay, I take it back." Taylor smiled as he backed Genevieve out of the alley, but his eyes were still wide.

Julie managed to raise a finger, hoping she was pointing at the real one of the two Taylors swimming in her vision. "You put one scratch on Genevieve..."

"Don't worry." Taylor laughed. "I'll be careful."

"Okay." Julie relaxed into her seat, closing her eyes.

"Hey, no." Taylor put a hand on her knee, jiggling it slightly. "No falling asleep."

Julie pried her eyes open and listened to Taylor prattle aimlessly for the entire ride home. Hat sat on her lap, trembling and completely silent.

When Julie opened the car door, she was greeted immediately by the sound of a cocking shotgun and the apparition of Lillie in her bathrobe and curlers standing in the back doorway with the gun aimed at the center of Taylor's chest.

The elf immediately threw his hands in the air, even though the barrel of the shotgun was making wobbly figure eights as Lillie struggled to hold its weight.

"Lillie! Lillie, it's okay." Julie scrambled out of the car and almost pitched face first onto the garage floor. Taylor grasped her shoulders, gently steadying her, and Hat fell on the ground with a heavy thump. Julie scooped him up, clutching him in both hands.

"One wrong move, mister, and I'll blow you into next week!" Lillie hollered.

"Lillie, no!" Julie squawked.

Lillie squinted at Julie, keeping the gun aimed vaguely in the direction of Taylor. "He do this to you, honey?"

"What? No! No." Julie shook her head and the resultant pang of sharp pain squeezed an involuntary whimper from between her teeth. "He's helping me," she ground out.

Lillie lowered the gun and stowed it behind the door, then

bustled across the garage floor, grasping Julie's free arm. "Oh, sweetie, what happened?"

"We..." Julie hesitated. It felt like her thoughts weren't quite working right. She couldn't come up with any explanation that didn't include Yetis.

"Julie noticed a man snooping around who looked like the same guy who mugged a friend of hers a few weeks ago," Taylor supplied. "She texted me what was going on and followed him. It ended in a fight. Julie was knocked out. She's been checked out at the ER, and she has a concussion."

"Followed him!" Lillie shook her head. "What are you, crazy?"

"A little, maybe," Julie whispered.

Lillie glared at Taylor. "Why didn't you stop her?"

Taylor lowered his gaze. "I should have."

Julie cut in. "He tried. I didn't let him. Lillie, please, I need to sit down."

The old lady jumped. "Of course. Of course. Bring her inside."

"I can go to my apartment," Julie protested as Taylor guided her into Lillie's house.

Lillie scoffed, shoving sofa cushions and the cat out of the way. "There's no way, honey. You're staying right here where I can keep an eye on you."

Taylor lowered Julie onto the sofa. He grabbed a blanket from the arm of the sofa and draped it over her before placing Hat gently on the coffee table. "How's your head?"

"It's fine. I wish you'd all go away and let me sleep," Julie grumbled. The sofa felt deliciously soft after the bumpy ride home in Genevieve.

"The doctor said someone should watch her and make sure that she didn't lose consciousness." Taylor stepped back, looking at Lillie. "She said it was okay to let her sleep as long as someone was watching her."

"Don't worry, son." Lillie patted his elbow, which was about as high as she could reach. "I'll be right here with her. Sorry for almost shooting your face off."

Taylor grinned. "I'd expect nothing less from the owner of a magnificent beast like Genevieve."

Lillie's cheeks turned pleasantly pink. "Oh, you like her?"

"She's a classic, isn't she?" Taylor gave Lillie the keys. "One of the best there is."

Julie narrowed her eyes at him just so that he'd know that she knew that he was unashamedly sucking up to Lillie. Taylor smirked back.

"Well, aren't you quite the catch?" Lillie chuckled, giving Taylor's chest a prod with an arthritic finger. "Oooh, and rather firm, too."

Julie groaned. "Lillie!"

"Do you need anything?" Taylor pulled out his phone. "Can I do anything for you?"

"You can let me sleep." Julie pulled a sofa cushion under her head.

"We'll be fine, dear." Lillie bustled around Julie, tucking in the blanket and rearranging the cushions. She brushed some of Julie's hair out of her face. "Are you hungry, dear? Thirsty?"

"Just tired," Julie mumbled, and before Lillie could finish asking her if she wanted to watch some TV or take a shower, she was asleep.

CHAPTER EIGHTEEN

"Turmeric has powerful anti-inflammatory properties. I'm just saying, we should give it a try."

"She's exhausted, poor dear. Been asleep like this for hours. I been waking her now and then to check on her." A soft hand fluttered on Julie's shoulder. "I woke her half an hour ago. Let's give her some time to sleep some more."

Something cold was pressed against Julie's forehead. There was a pounding pain in her temples, but at least she didn't feel like she was going to puke at any moment. Still, maybe she was hallucinating. Surely her mom wasn't *here*, in Lillie's house.

"Well, then I'm going to rub some of this on her acupressure points. It'll make her feel better when she wakes up."

Julie moaned. She wasn't hallucinating. That was definitely her mom. She pulled off her ice pack and forced her eyes open. Morning sunlight was pouring into the cluttered living room. The cat lay curled up and purring on Julie's thighs, Lillie was perched on the edge of the couch beside her, and Rosa stood over her, clutching a bottle of arnica oil.

"Mom, I swear, if you touch my acupressure points I'll acupressure you in the face," Julie groaned.

"Julia, honey!" Rosa set down the arnica oil and bent to give her a peck on the cheek. "How are you doing? Up to some juice?" She held up a glass with a dreadfully familiar greenish liquid swirling around in it. "It'll make you feel better."

Julie moaned, running a hand over her aching face. "If you try feeding me aloe vera juice, I swear I'll aim the throw-up at you, Mom."

Lillie got up. "How about some sweet tea instead?"

"Here. Put the ice pack back on." Rosa grabbed it and thrust it into Julie's hands. "It'll do you good."

"Okay, okay." Julie obediently applied the pack to her head again, wincing. "When did you get here?"

"Lillie called me right away and I came on the first train this morning." Rosa pinched Julie's cheek. "I just had to make sure my sweet baby was okay."

Julie squeezed out a smile. "Thanks, Mom."

"Do you want some more pillows?" Rosa fussed. "We thought of moving you up to your room, but you seemed so comfortable here."

"I'm okay here," Julie told her.

"You hungry? I can fix you something. Or get you something. A Happy Meal, even." The offer of McDonald's showed just how worried Rosa was.

"Mom!" Julie tried not to laugh because it made her head hurt. "I'm not six years old. Thank you, but please give it a rest."

Lillie came tottering in from the kitchen, carrying a tray of glasses and a pitcher of unsweetened tea. "Well, you're starting to sound a little more like yourself, dear." She set the tray down on the coffee table and glanced at the other side of the room. "I'm sure glad she had you around to protect her, Taylor."

Julie felt her cheeks reddening. She hadn't seen the elf sitting awkwardly in a tatty armchair next to the TV. Taylor was practically motionless, his hands folded in his lap. "Taylor! You're still here?"

Taylor smiled warmly. "Like Lillie said, we woke you every hour through the night to make sure you were okay. I wanted to help." He was pale, but not in the grayish tone he had when he was embarrassed.

Julie saw lines etched around his eyes and mouth, and black circles under his eyes. "That was really kind of you, thank you." She sat up, realizing with some surprise that she could do so quite easily. "Do you need a ride home?"

"Oh, no. I'll just call someone." Taylor straightened, looking like he wanted to say something. He smiled again. "I'm glad you're okay."

"Thanks for getting me home last night." Julie rearranged her blanket around her knees, leaving the cat happily in place. "Sorry for collapsing on you."

"Hey, what are partners for?" Taylor got to his feet. "I'd better get home, though. I'll see you later, Julie." He cleared his throat. "When you're ready to go back to work."

Julie scoffed. "Ready? I was born ready,"

Taylor rolled his eyes at her. "Bye, Lillie. Bye, Mrs. Hernandez." He waved at the two older women, both of whom practically swooned, and headed out.

"Here's your tea, dear." Lillie thrust the glass into Julie's hands. "I'm going to find you something for breakfast." She pottered back into the kitchen.

"Julia, darling." Rosa fixed her with a Look, the one with a capital L. "Are you completely out of your mind?"

"What?" Julie frowned. "Did I do something weird last night? My memory's a bit foggy."

"Yes, you did, honey!" Rosa threw up her hands, her curls bouncing on her shoulders. "You practically ignored that sweet, worried, caring, and, may I say, *absolutely smoking hot* young man—"

"Mom!" Julie's cheeks warmed.

Rosa shrugged. "I'm married, not blind, sweetie. I know a

looker when I see one. That young man could be a supermodel if he wanted."

Julie tried not to imagine Taylor in the modeling agency they'd recruited Ellie from. She somehow managed to keep the grin off her face. "Taylor and I are just friends."

"That's just my point, honey." Rosa tipped some ice into her tea and sipped it. "You need to do something about that before he loses interest."

Julie chuckled. "Interest?" She imagined all the Fae and elven girls that Taylor had falling at his feet. He was a prince, after all.

"Exactly. You may have his attention now, but if you play hard to get for too long, he's going to go looking elsewhere." Rosa wagged a finger. "It's not often that you come across a man who's the full package, you know. Handsome, rich, *and* caring? Julie, you must be insane not to be all over him."

Julie cringed. "It's not like that with Taylor."

Rosa arched an eyebrow. "You know, honey, if you bat for the other team, it's okay. But if not, you should jump on him!"

Julie busied herself with a long sip of her tea, hoping her mom would drop the subject.

Rosa, of course, did not. "He hasn't left your side all night. All night! I noticed the cut of that sexy little suit, too. He's well-off. Marry him, and you'll be set for life."

Julie sighed. "I'm not getting into anything with Taylor even if I was attracted to him, which I'm not. We have to work together, there's a no-dating policy, and I like my job."

"Ha!" Rosa mumbled the next few words into her tea. "The job that's landed you on your landlady's sofa with a concussion."

Julie lowered her teacup. "What was that?"

"I'm just saying, honey. What kind of job has you walking the streets at night? Not a respectable one, that's for sure. You'd be better off swinging on a pole. At least you'd have security guards there."

Julie groaned. "Last night had nothing to do with my job,

Mom." Technically true, as Kaplan had so thoroughly pointed out last night. At least, Julie thought he had. Her memory was a little fuzzy there. "Besides, the pole was never an option. My job is plenty respectable, thank you."

Rosa shrugged. "If you say so, baby."

"I do say so," Julie told her firmly.

"Well, in that case, I'm glad you have a hunk like Taylor looking out for you." Rosa sipped her tea. "You could have gotten really hurt if he wasn't around, you know. You have to stop making such silly decisions."

Julie wasn't in any state to argue with her mom's old-fashioned views. "I was helping a friend, if you must know."

"A friend? A *friend*?" Mom raised her eyebrows. "The one who got mugged? Sweetie, in what universe was it a good idea to try to handle something like this on your own? You should have called the police."

Julie shrugged. "Yeah, well, hindsight is 20/20, I guess."

"I don't think you should hang out with that friend of yours. He sounds like trouble, he really does." Rosa dropped some more ice into her tea. "Why don't you spend more time with Taylor?"

"*Mommmm!*" Julie sank back into the sofa. "Drop it. I'm going to Malcolm's hand— Malcolm's wedding soon."

"Wedding!" Mom snorted. "Pity the poor girl *he's* ending up with."

Julie grimaced. "Believe me, she doesn't need anyone's pity."

"Oh, a little jealous, are we?" Rosa grinned. "Is this Malcolm rich and handsome too? Because in that case, maybe you'd be a steadying influence."

"Malcolm's rich, handsome, and *a friend*," Julie emphasized. "Seriously, Mom. I don't need a man in my life right now."

"Maybe not right now, honey, but you do know that ninety percent of your eggs will be dead by the time you're thirty, right?"

Julie leaned her head back against the sofa and groaned. "Kill me now."

"You say that now, but it's never too soon to start planning these things." Rosa gestured in the direction of Julie's abdomen. "I know you're still young, but you're going to want kids someday, and that's always a consideration when you're looking at men."

"You're making it sound like I'm going shopping for men like they're cars or something," Julie protested.

"It's not all that different, honey." Rosa shrugged. "You've got to think about what's practical for you. Just think of the beautiful babies you'd have with Taylor!"

"Mom!" Julie put down her glass and covered her ears with both hands. "Gross!"

Rosa sniffed. "You'd think you'd be over the boys-are-gross stage."

"I'm in the everything-you-say-about-men-is-gross stage," Julie moaned.

Lillie returned, blessedly, like an angel of mercy and patted Julie's shoulder. "I've got some scones in the oven for you, dear."

"Do you feel up to that juice yet?" Rosa asked brightly.

Julie lowered her hands. "Not in the next fifty years or so, Mom."

"You'll feel so much better once you've had some." Rosa sighed, shaking her head. "I know you don't believe me, but it has so many benefits. It'll settle your stomach, for one thing."

Julie didn't want to ask if she'd puked last night. Not now that she knew Taylor had been around for the whole thing. At least she was still wearing her rumpled clothes from yesterday, so no one had tried to undress her.

On the other hand, she smelled like she'd had a long flight, spent an afternoon at work, crawled around in a sewer, survived a fight with large stinky monsters, and then slept in them, which was pretty much what had happened.

Lillie glanced sideways at Julie, then turned and smiled at Rosa. "So, Rosa, tell me more about this aloe vera juice. Does it help for digestion?"

Rosa perked up immediately. "It has amazing benefits! It contains large amounts of—"

"I'm gonna take a shower," Julie announced.

She fled the house as Rosa launched into a monologue, grabbing Hat from the coffee table. She paused at the doorway just long enough to mouth "Thank you," to Lillie, who gave her a discreet thumbs-up.

Freshly showered, Julie felt like an entirely new person. She pulled on her bathrobe and padded into her apartment, still toweling her hair. Her shower had fogged up the windows and she paused to open the one just above her head, allowing in a cool early-summer breeze.

She couldn't get enough fresh air after last night in the sewers.

"Quarter past eight," she announced to Hat. "I might even make it to work on time."

Hat was on the kitchen counter in the form of a somber black top hat for some reason. "I doubt it."

"What's got your panties in a wad?" Julie asked.

"Nothing." Hat shuffled around, putting his back to her. "You've got a text."

"Aww, c'mon, Hat. You're not still mad, are you?" Julie picked up her phone from the kitchen counter and winced. She had a text from Kaplan.

MEADOWS. NO WORK TODAY. MEDICAL LEAVE UNTIL CONCUSSION CLEARED. OLENA SAYS SEVERAL DAYS. CHECK BACK ON MON. KAPLAN.

"Why does he text like an old guy?" Julie wondered aloud. She huffed, taking her phone over to her comfy chair. She sagged down into it with a sigh. "That sucks. What am I supposed to do with myself all day?"

Hat grunted. "Read?"

Julie glanced at the half-read book waiting for her on her nightstand. That could work. She hefted it into her lap, but her phone buzzed as she was about to open it.

You ok?? Sorry about last night.

It was Malcolm. Julie opened the chat and shot back a text.

I'm fine! How about you? Your dad seemed pretty mad.

Malcolm responded instantly.

What else is new?

Julie smirked to herself and sent him a bunch of laughing emojis. She scrolled through her phone and pulled up Taylor's chat.

You home safe?

It seemed Taylor was in a texting mood, too. He answered right away.

On my way to work. How's your head?

Julie smiled, texting back.

Much better now. Sorry about my mom. She's weird.

I like her, Taylor responded.

Julie sent a few laughing emojis.

I don't even like her so you don't have to pretend.

No, seriously, she's cool. A little weird but cool. Taylor sent a frowning face. **Why are you awake? You should be in bed.**

I'm fine, Mom. Julie sent a few chicken emojis.

Taylor responded with an eyeroll emoji.

I hope you're on leave.

Yeah. Thought you might get a day off, too, Julie responded.

No rest for the wicked. Taylor added a shrugging emoji.

Julie sighed, wishing she could be on her way to work, too. Still, her splitting head told her that that was a bad idea.

You'll keep me up to speed on what's going on, won't you? Let me know if they caught the Yetis?

Sure. Doubt it though. Anyway, I'm here now. Have a nice day. Try not to die, ok?

Julie rolled her eyes and sent him the middle finger emoji. He responded with a gif of a goat eating an ice cream, for whatever reason.

She scoffed at him and tossed her phone aside. The ice cream had made her realize that she was finally more hungry than nauseated. When last had she eaten, anyway? On the plane? She put her book aside and wandered over to the kitchen.

Hat was still sitting on the counter, being conspicuously

silent. Julie grabbed an apple from the bowl beside him and cut it into wedges. "Hey, what's with the top hat look?"

"Oh, nothing." Hat sighed, his crown drooping.

Julie laughed. "Drama queen."

She carried the plate of apple wedges back over to her chair, curled up in it, and picked up the book. It was a good one, but she was only halfway down the page when the steady pounding in her head returned. She paused, rubbing her temples with two fingers.

Hat shuffled around to face her. "Head hurting?"

Julie shrugged and turned the page. "It's nothing major."

"Ha! Yes, I suppose, in comparison with what might have happened."

Julie looked up. "What's that supposed to mean?"

Hat scoffed. "As if you'd listen to me even if I said anything."

"Hat!" Julie set down the book. "Come on, buddy. Are you really still mad?"

"Mad? Mad?" Hat bounced onto the kitchen table and skidded to the edge of it. For someone without any eyes, he was great at glaring. "Oh, no, I'm not *mad*. Hurt, worried, downcast, disrespected, disappointed—"

"Okay, okay." Julie pushed aside the plate and got up. Apple wedges were not going to cut it for this conversation. "In my defense, I didn't know last night was going to turn out the way it did. I just wanted to see what was going on."

"It's that Nox boy." Hat's brim flattened against the table. "He's nothing but trouble."

"Malcolm's under a lot of pressure and trying to prove himself to his dad." Julie fished a box of cookies out from the cabinet and stuffed one into her mouth. She was famished.

"And *you* are a sensible young woman who should have known better!" Hat shot back.

Julie chewed her cookie slowly before answering. "I've already gotten this from Mom, you know. Like I told you, I couldn't have left Genevieve alone."

"Genevieve is a *car*. You are a *person*. I shouldn't have been left behind when you were heading off into danger!" Hat's English accent intensified the more he yelled.

Julie helped herself to another cookie. "Is this about you being worried about me, or you being offended because I didn't think I needed a magical artifact to spy on a Yeti?"

Hat was silent.

"Come on, Hat," Julie cajoled. "You're not a weapon. I wasn't going to take you into a dangerous situation when I thought you might be better off in the car."

"Oh, so now I'm a weakling, am I?" Hat snapped.

"I didn't say that. I love you, but I don't take orders from you." Julie leaned against the counter.

Hat spluttered. "I have the wisdom of millennia! I'm one of the most magical artifacts in the *world*!"

"Yeah, well, I'm a woman and I know what I want to do, and I can make my own mistakes." Julie folded her arms. "I'm an independent person and I don't need a crusty old hat to tell me what to do."

"A crusty old—" Hat squirmed, unable to contain his fury. "I was afraid for you!"

"I know." Julie went over to him and ran a hand over his crown. He wriggled out from under her touch and waddled on his brim to the other side of the table. "I'm sorry for scaring you."

"The world is so big, and you're just a girl," Hat grumbled.

"Just a girl?" Julie huffed, stepping back from the table. "Excuse *me*, I'm a woman, for one thing, and for another, what's *'just a girl'* supposed to mean?"

"You're taking this the wrong way." Hat spun to face her. "In my day, knights rode side by side with ladies. They didn't let ladies go crashing into sewers to fight Yetis for no reason."

"I had a very good reason," Julie pointed out. "And for your information, those ladies didn't need knights any more than I do. They could've taken care of themselves too, if they'd been given the chance. Quit being such a patriarchal asshole. Do I look like a damsel in distress to you?"

Hat was silent for a few seconds. "No," he mumbled.

"Come on, Hat. I don't want to fight." Julie sat by Hat at the kitchen table and held out a hand. "I don't want you to think I don't care about you or respect you, but I'm not going to let you tell me what to do, either."

"I know." Hat sighed. "I just worry about you."

"I appreciate your concern." Julie wriggled her fingers at him. "But I'm still my own person."

"I suppose you're free to do what you like." Hat wriggled across the table with bad grace and plopped down in her hand.

"Yes, I am. I very much am." Julie laughed. "Now I'd like to curl up in my chair with my magical artifact friend and read, only my head hurts too much."

"I can help with that, at least." Hat sniffed. "If I'm allowed to help you."

Julie raised an eyebrow. "Hat!"

"Okay, okay." Hat made a small *poof* sound and became a colorful pink-and-purple beanie. "Put me on."

Julie smiled and pulled him over her ears. She glanced at her reflection in the shiny surface of the fridge. "Very cheerful."

"Hold on. I'm only getting started." Hat hummed for a moment, concentrating, and a delicious coolness spread through him where he touched her throbbing head.

Julie groaned with appreciation, leaning back in her chair.

"Better?" Hat asked.

"Much better." Julie patted him lightly. "Thank you."

"I suppose..." Hat paused as Julie returned to her chair and pulled her book back into her lap. "I suppose we could agree to disagree on some things."

Julie smiled, cracking her book open. "I suppose we could."

CHAPTER NINETEEN

Even with Hat's cooling properties, Julie's head still throbbed too hard to read. She put the book down and stretched out on her bed with her eyes closed, longing for sleep. A gentle snooze had just taken hold of her when her apartment door banged open.

"Just stopping in to say goodbye, Julia!"

Julie groaned and pulled her pillow over her head.

Rosa didn't decrease her volume one decibel as she strode over to the bed and patted Julie on the shoulder. "Aw, sorry, honey. Did I wake you?"

"Not really." Julie relented, lowering the pillow. "Sorry for disappearing on you. I guess I just needed some peace and quiet."

"Of course, honey." Rosa bent down and kissed her noisily on the cheek. "You think about what I said about that handsome young Taylor fellow, won't you? And make sure you drink your juice. I brought it up for you." She swirled the glass in her hand and put it on Julie's nightstand.

"Sure looks like you did," Julie mumbled.

"What was that, honey?"

"I said, thanks, Mom." Julie managed a smile. "And thanks for coming."

"Of course, baby." Rosa looked around the apartment. "Are you going to straighten this place out a little when you feel better? Those curtains and that rug are a bit...loud."

"Mom!" Julie groaned.

"Okay, okay, I'm leaving." Rosa patted her shoulder again. "I'll text you. Just call me if you need anything. *Anything.*" Her gaze paused on the tray of aloe vera juice bottles, still dusty and plastic-wrapped, and her shoulders dropped a little. "Stay out of trouble, honey."

"I will."

Rosa headed across the apartment, her heels clicking loudly. When she reached the door, Julie sat up. "Mom?"

Rosa paused in the doorway. "Yes, honey?"

Julie managed a smile. "Love you."

"Love you too, Julia." Rosa blew her a kiss and was gone.

Before Julie could re-attempt her nap, she heard shaky footsteps coming up the stairs, and Lillie wobbled in carrying a basket of fresh, steaming scones. She set the basket down on the kitchen table. "I brought you something to eat, dear."

"Thanks so much, Lillie." Julie got up, tempted by the aroma coming from the basket. "They smell amazing."

Lillie's weathered face creased into a smile. "I'm glad you like it, sweetie. I'll leave you in peace now."

"No, wait." Julie felt a pang of guilt. She hadn't even started planning that road trip she'd promised Lillie on the weekend already. "Why don't we sit and eat together?"

Lillie's eyes crinkled in pleasure. "If you're sure, dear."

"Of course I'm sure." Julie readjusted Hat on her head so that his soothing, cooling surface pressed against the particularly sore spot on the back of her skull. "I've got butter and jelly in the fridge."

They sat together at the table, and chatted while they ate. The scones tasted as good as they looked. Julie wolfed them down, wondering when last she'd sat at a table and had a real meal. At Cironius' house? It seemed like a million years ago.

She met Lillie's eyes across the table, relieved to see the brightness in them. Maybe the little memory slips had just been standard old person stuff? Maybe it was all over now.

Julie selected another scone and cut it open. "Hey, Lillie, I've been meaning to ask you something."

Lillie smiled at her. "What's that, then?"

"It's about Genevieve." Julie buttered her scone. "I notice that the older cops seem to be watching me wherever I go. Like they're following her."

Lillie gave a raucous chuckle. "Oh, I'm not surprised, honey."

Julie grinned. "Yeah, but why?"

"Genevieve must have something of a reputation among the cops around here." Lillie's eyes sparkled behind her thick glasses. "Not a single street racer in Bay Ridge could keep up with her in her day. I don't think they could keep up with her now, either. Not with me behind the wheel." She flexed her gnarled old fingers hungrily.

Julie giggled. "So you used to dice people at red lights?"

Lillie's grin was wicked. "Of course I did, honey. What else do you do with a Mustang Mach 1?"

Julie laughed. "I bet Genevieve could tell some pretty amazing stories if she could talk."

"She sure could." Lillie cackled. "Did I tell you about the time my sister and I were in a car chase?"

"No?" Julie hesitated. Lillie never talked about her late twin.

"Well, it's quite a story." Lillie sat back in her chair. "Lucy and I had had a long day. Just one of those days, you know. Work, husbands and kids driving us crazy... Of course, that was before Tim died and before she divorced Alfred—and good riddance to him, too."

Lillie's lips curled in a smile. "We needed to clear our heads, so we told the men we were going to get groceries and she swung by the house to pick me up in Genevieve."

Julie leaned forward. "So Genevieve belonged to Lucy, at first?"

"Oh, Genevieve always belonged to both of us, but she was at Lucy's at the time." Lillie grinned, memories lighting her from within. "I hopped in with Lucy and off we went. Not to the grocery store, though. We headed for the interstate. That was always where Genevieve could really let rip."

Julie giggled. She'd never had the guts to test the big engine beyond sixty.

"Well, one thing led to another. There wasn't a whole lot of traffic on a Saturday afternoon back then, you understand. Lucy stepped on it," Lillie told her. "The needle twitched up and up. Sixty. Eighty. A hundred. I had my hand out the window, yelling with the speed of it all, and Genevieve wasn't even trying yet."

Julie could imagine a younger Lillie, one whose face was less lined with grief, casting all her worries to the wind as the Mustang ate up the distance and her sister whooped behind the wheel.

"Of course, it wasn't long before we got some unwanted attention." Lillie's eyes were distant as the past played out on her mind. "The cops who watch you today were rookies back then, but they already knew to keep an eye out for Genevieve. I heard the siren and I said to Lucy, 'Well, shit, we're gonna have a big fine on our hands. How fast you going?' And Lucy said, 'Fast enough it'll be more than a fine, if they can catch us.' So I said, 'Well, better not let them catch us, then.'"

Julie laughed. "Lillie!"

"What? We didn't want to spend the night in a cell." Lillie emphasized her point by waving her scone. "So Lucy says to me, 'Lil, what do you take me for? Gennie can outrun any old cruiser with her hands tied behind her back.' And she steps on it."

Julie gasped. "How fast did you go?"

"Oh, we lost the cops around one-thirty, but we kept going for a little while just to be safe." Lillie grinned. "They say Gennie's top speed is about one-fifty-two. I'm telling you, with Lucy behind the wheel, there was nothing that 'Stang wouldn't do."

Her eyes grew misty, and she looked down at the table. "Of course, we got a fine in the mail anyway, but it was worth it." A sigh escaped her. "Everything was worth it with Lucy by my side."

Silence fell over them like a shroud. Julie selected another scone and buttered it, not knowing what to say. It was a few seconds before Lillie sat up, brightening again. "Did I tell you about the time we *did* get caught and the cop offered to let us go if I flashed him?"

"What? Did you?" Julie gasped, appalled.

"Of course not, but he *did* let us go," Lillie told her. "It was a Saturday morning, midsummer, we had a bunch of kids in the car, and we were on our way out to Coney Island for the day..."

Malcolm pulled the right trigger. A burst of blood erupted from the zombie's chest, and it spun for a moment with the force of the bullet's impact before crumpling to the ground, its limbs bent at odd angles, eyes staring glassily at nothing.

"Yeah, baby!" ItzMeZee189 yelled in Malcolm's ears.

Malcolm didn't respond as his avatar on the massive screen in his suite crouched beside the dead zombie and patted it down for ammunition. His fingers moved automatically on the controller as the unit of gamers jogged through the abandoned building, looking for more zombies.

"Still got any grenades left, Jay?" ItzMeZee panted.

JK1997 groaned. "Nope, I'm out."

"It'd help if you'd quit throwing them in the middle of empty spaces instead of at the zombies," GothChick50 teased.

"Dude, it was intense back there, okay?" JK1997 shot back.

"Let it go."

"Cool it, bro," ItzMeZee drawled. "Hey, Ed, you gonna back me up here?"

"Huh?" Malcolm hadn't been listening. The tag over his avatar's head read DefinitelyNotEdward1897.

"C'mon, bro. Where's your head today?" GothChick50 asked. "You've been totally distracted."

"Sorry." Malcolm sat up and glanced out of the window at the pitch darkness beyond. Or it would have been pitch darkness to a human. The vampire could see every needle on the spruce tree outside, every detail of the moonlight playing on the wall.

The wall. He felt as though it was strangling him. He flexed his fingers on the controller, feeling a dark hunger rise within him. Closing his eyes, he took a deep breath, imagining that he could smell that rank Yeti stench, feel the tearing of flesh on his fangs.

For the hundredth time tonight, he saw Julie being thrown against the wall. He saw her go limp and slide to the ground. The memory made his guts twist. He was grateful that Cassidy hadn't been there.

If it had been Cassidy...

"Ed? Ed?"

ItzMeZee's voice jerked him from the memory. Malcolm opened his eyes and realized that his avatar was jogging persistently into a wall, getting nowhere. He knew how it felt.

He'd been so close, and the Yeti had slipped through his fingers.

"Yo, Ed," JK1997 barked. "Get with it, buddy."

Malcolm looked at the controller in his hands and realized that his fingernails had grown into claws, digging deep into the plastic.

"I've got to go." His words came out strangled. "Sorry."

"But you just got here!" ItzMeZee protested.

Malcolm ignored him. He put down the controller and

switched off the screen with a brisk gesture of one hand, then got up and went over to the window. He could just see the lonely figure of Sire in the greenhouse, tending those precious plants of his.

"I'll show you," Malcolm murmured. "I'll show you."

He couldn't leave through the door. Perkins would undoubtedly betray him to Sire. Malcolm pushed the window open, gripped the sill in both hands, and pulled himself out onto the wall. The creepers and ornamental lighting made it child's play to scramble to the ground.

When his shoes hit the dirt, Malcolm hesitated, glancing back toward the greenhouse. Maybe Sire was right. Maybe Uncle Jack would be better off handling this.

All the same, Malcolm turned and jogged across the lawn, ducked behind the roses, skirted around the swimming pool and pulled himself up onto the wall. Hesitating for an instant, he raised his head and sniffed the air, smelling distant Yeti scent.

It was a good night for hunting.

Julie crawled into bed and pulled the sheets up to her chin, relishing the softness of her pillow as she rolled onto her side. A couple of Tylenol and a hot shower had worked their magic on her aching head, and she eyed the book on the nightstand with a prickle of anticipation.

Hat hopped up onto the nightstand beside it, almost knocking over her coffee mug. "Feeling better?"

"Much better." Julie smiled. "Lillie was a welcome distraction."

Hat laughed. "Do you believe all of her stories?"

"Some of them are a little crazy, but…" Julie grinned. "I know Lillie, and yeah, I believe them. But now I'm ready for a little peace and quiet. It was nice having her here for the day, though."

"Do you know what happened to Lucy?" Hat asked.

Julie picked up the book and slid it open. "I don't want to ask. I think that's the reason Lillie is so depressed, because she doesn't have Lucy anymore."

"She has you now," Hat pointed out.

Julie shrugged. "I guess that's something." She yawned, her eye catching the last line she'd read, and the book drew her gently into a different world.

Her neck was growing stiff from the pressure of the pillow and her wrists were aching from holding up the massive book when the little bell by the door jangled.

Julie sat up, stifling a yawn, and put the book aside. "What time is it?"

"Quarter to nine," Hat supplied. "If you want to have that early night, you'd better get rid of your unwanted visitor."

"She's not unwanted, you ass." Julie swiped playfully at Hat's crown and slipped out of bed before grabbing her bathrobe and the pair of fluffy unicorn slippers she'd bought as a special treat to herself. "Lillie, come on up!"

The stairs creaked, and Julie started the coffee machine, feeling a pang of guilt. She should have checked that Lillie had eaten something for dinner.

There was a discreet knock at the door, and Julie frowned. Why would Lillie knock if Julie had already invited her in? She felt a sudden thump just behind her breastbone. If it wasn't Lillie, who could it be at this hour?

She glanced around for her pepper spray, cursing silently when she remembered that she'd lost it in the alley. Then sense returned and she figured that burglars wouldn't ring the doorbell.

Julie padded across to the door in her unicorn slippers and opened it wide.

Julius Nox stood on her doorstep, his Armani suit tracing the slender outline of his figure. His fangs flashed in a polite smile. "Good evening, Miss Meadows. May I come in?"

AUTHOR NOTES RENÉE JAGGÉR

DECEMBER 7, 2022

Thank you for reading through to the back of book two in the new series.

I'm not in Arizona. Again. I'm in Washington, DC, visiting friends and eating too much good food. So far, the favorite is between the Indian food down the street and the Vietnamese tamarind soup across town. Honorable mention to the kimchi dumplings from two blocks away.

My little town in Arizona has good food, but it's in no way diverse or gourmet. Mind you, I don't define gourmet by high prices or beauty but by deliciousness. That's why the tamarind soup with shrimp is right up there with samosas and baingan bartha and aloo paratha. The crab cakes were good but not comparable to the soup. I can get crab cakes in the Southwest, no matter if they are frozen.

I have hung out with friends since I've been here and have seen lots of museums and national monuments. One favorite was the international spy museum, where I saw the Enigma decoding machine from Bletchley Park and also learned that the French executed Mata Hari. Well, I learned many things, some of which will appear in future books, but those two stand out. The t-shirts in the museum's shop also assert that pigeons are government drones and don't really exist, but I'm not sure I believe that ;-)

I am playing hooky from museums today and getting some work done. It's cloudy and sometimes rainy, and tea and work just sounded better. Well, when your work is like mine! Tomorrow, I will jet off to see more friends in another city before going back home on Sunday. I love being an author! I can work from anywhere and do…

The next book is already with the publisher, but I will be writing the one after that from Scotland again. Have to get more material for the series coming after this one! Yes, there are more cloudy skies and rain in my future, but the tea and fresh scones are great, and the company too.

Jo always appreciates it when I go away since my mother is much more indulgent with her than I am, and she likes visiting Storm. Mom feeds them fresh human-grade dog food and gives her beef bones to boot! Jo is sure she runs the world, and the way she is indulged, she might get me to believe it too.

As always, thank you to my proofreaders! They make my books the best they can be. I hope you enjoyed the continuation of Julie's journey! Her world will keep changing, as will she.

Until we speak again, I hope your skies are sunny and your days are filled with happiness and good books!

Renée

BOOKS FROM RENÉE

Para-Military Recruiter
(with Michael Anderle)
Drafted (Book 1)
Recruiter (Book 2)
Accepted (Book 3)

Reincarnation of the Morrigan
Birth of a Goddess (Book One)
The Way of Wisdom (Book Two)
Angelic Death (Book Three)
A Cold War (Book 4)
A Battle Tune (Book 5)
Broken Ice (Book 6)
A Torn Veil (Book 7)
Sins of the Past (Book 8)
The Wild Hunt Comes (*coming soon*)

The WereWitch Series
Bad Attitude (Book One)
A Bit Aggressive (Book Two)

Too Much Magic (Book Three)
Were War (Book Four)
Were Rages (Book Five)
God Ender (Book Six)
God Trials (Book Seven)
The Troll Solution (Book Eight)
Winner Takes All (Book Nine)

Callie Hart Series
Thin Ice (Book One)
Cold Blood (Book Two)
Feelings Run Deep (Book Three)

BOOKS BY MICHAEL ANDERLE

Sign up for the LMBPN email list to be notified of new releases and special deals!

https://lmbpn.com/email/

For a complete list of books by Michael Anderle, please visit:

www.lmbpn.com/ma-books/

CONNECT WITH THE AUTHORS

Connect with Renée

Facebook: https://www.facebook.com/reneejaggerauthor

Website: https://reneejagger.com/

Connect with Michael Anderle

Website: http://lmbpn.com

Email List: http://lmbpn.com/email/

https://www.facebook.com/LMBPNPublishing

https://twitter.com/MichaelAnderle

https://www.instagram.com/lmbpn_publishing/

https://www.bookbub.com/authors/michael-anderle

Printed in the USA
CPSIA information can be obtained
at www.ICGtesting.com
LVHW090012040624
782127LV00004B/689

9 798885 419659